SECRETS IN THE WOODS

ALEXANDRIA CLARKE

Copyright 2019 All rights reserved worldwide. No part of this document may be reproduced or transmitted in any form, by any means without prior written permission, except for brief excerpts in reviews or analysis.

❀ Created with Vellum

1

---

*G*etting stabbed hurt.

The skinny girl—just past her thirteenth birthday—assumed as much when she'd seen the rival student flick open the switch knife and swoop in toward her. Assuming and feeling were two different things. She wasn't quick enough to dodge the first attack entirely. The knife missed the middle of her torso, where the other girl had placed her aim, and sank instead into the fleshy skin of her stomach. The blade tore free, ripping an ungodly hole in the teenager's side. She clapped her palm to the wound and gritted her teeth as the attacker dodged away.

Middle school students closed in, forming a tight circle around the two girls. The outdoor courtyard, a place to relax or snack during study hall, was bereft of teachers. The hot afternoon sun slanted over the classroom buildings, right into the skinny girl's eyes. Three more days of school—if she'd made it three more days without causing trouble, she would have been out of there for the summer.

Everyone at school hated her. She was quiet and weird and never spoke to anyone. The teachers stopped calling on her because they knew she wouldn't answer, but her grades were impeccable, and she was rarely seen without a book. The other kids called her stuck-up, a brat, or worse. They didn't know her, where she'd come from, or how she ended up at *their* school, where the pecking order was not to be challenged. Despite her silence in class, she could think of several instances in which she should have kept her mouth shut.

Sixty seconds ago, one such instance had occurred. Billie Miller had, once again, gotten under her skin. Her biting reply was enough for Billie to pull that knife out of her hoodie pouch. The girl blanched. She'd taken the bait, and it was exactly what Billie wanted.

Billie's teeth bared in a grin. She was huge for an eighth grader, over five feet tall with plenty of mass to share. The skinny girl was no match, but at least she had speed and grace on her side. As Billie darted in, slashing with the knife, the girl quickly sidestepped the weapon. Billie lost her balance, and the girl helped Billie's head meet a brick wall with a rough shove. The crowd of students jeered and tightened around Billie and the smaller girl, their arena rapidly shrinking.

Billie did not take kindly to her potential concussion. She wiped the girl's blood from the handle of the knife and adjusted her grip. She lunged again. This time, the skinny girl didn't get as lucky. She ricocheted off a larger boy behind her, who shoved her back into the ring. Billie's knife landed on the girl's forearm, and she slashed through the skin—once, twice, three times. Blood spurted across the concrete. The girl's head swam.

Gasping, the girl made a fast, desperate grab for the knife. To everyone's surprise, the weapon switched hands. The girl set her feet, glaring at her opponent. The crowd roared. Billie stumbled but regained her balance. Not to be outdone, she raised her meaty fist, ready to pummel the younger girl.

The girl braced herself. At the last second, she tilted her head away, lessening the blow from Billie's fist. It still rocked her brain like a car crash, but the damage wouldn't last. Billie, all her weight pressing forward, was close. The girl, without a single beat of hesitation, thrust the knife under Billie's arm and up.

A long, silent moment followed. The crowd quieted. Billie's eyes went wide. The girl stood her ground. Billie staggered backward, clutching her torso. Blood, thick as red paint, poured down Billie's jeans and drenched her white sneakers. Someone screamed. At last, a teacher noticed the brawl.

The crowd split like a firework. No one wanted to be caught near the fight. The girl tried to run too, but her head pounded and her side hurt, and it was impossible to run in a straight line. The teacher—a bald man with a wiry mustache who taught history to the sixth graders—seized the girl by her injured arm. She yelled, but he had no regard for her pain.

"What did you do?" he shouted, shaking her roughly. "What did you do?"

Across the courtyard, Billie Miller lay still, blood pooling around her. Her eyes gazed unseeingly toward the sun.

The girl trembled, the knife still in her hand.

Sixteen Years Later

"Nat, do you mind wiping down treatment room two? Erin's patient was sweating like a pig, and my guy's going to be here any minute."

Something buzzed in my ear. Was someone talking?

"Nat?"

A bug?

"Natasha!"

I whirled my desk chair around and jerked my focus away from my computer. Trevor, one of the physical therapists I worked with, stared at me with an expectant expression.

"Welcome back to planet Earth," he teased lightheartedly. "How are the aliens?"

"Sorry, Trevor." I shook my head to clear it. "I was looking something up."

He leaned over my desk, the one I shared with the other assistants at the outpatient rehabilitation facility, and examined the open tabs. "Ooh, movement therapy. That's fun. Are you thinking about going back to school?"

A certain bitterness flooded my tongue. Trevor was a decent guy, but he had a bad habit of never listening when I spoke. After all, I was just an assistant.

"I already have a degree," I reminded him. "But jobs are thin on the ground."

"I'm sure that's not true," he said. "A bunch of rehab places are hiring dance therapists. It's the fanciest new trend." His eyes drifted toward the ceiling, and I had a feeling he would've completed the roll had I not informed him of my degree moments earlier. "I guess it's a good way to get patients moving, but I don't see what the fuss is. We do all the same stuff here."

It was best not to argue with him. I pinched my lips together and forced myself to smile. "Yeah, it's probably getting popular for no reason at all. I can't imagine it's effective for treating physical, cognitive, and emotional irregularities."

Trevor's smile slipped, like he couldn't figure out whether I was being sarcastic or not. He cleared his throat. "Right. Anyway, about the treatment room? I don't mean to rush you, but my patient will be here soon. I really don't want to breathe in B.O. for the whole hour."

I grabbed a tub of antibacterial wipes from underneath my desk and saluted Trevor with them. "I'm on it."

"Thanks, Nat. Oh, and the boss wants to see you."

I paused in the doorway. "For what?"

Trevor shrugged. "No idea. Guess you'll find out."

As I wiped down the treatment room, chairs, and any equipment that bore signs of sweat, I wondered what the boss wanted with me. I wracked my brain, trying to remember if I'd made trouble in the last few days. To be honest, there wasn't much trouble to get into at the rehab center. All I did was clean rooms, run laundry, and help the therapists with whatever they needed. I had no patients of my own to worry about or any real responsibilities other than keeping the rehab center clean and efficient.

"Here we are! In you go, Jeff."

Trevor's voice interrupted my reverie as he led his patient into the treatment room. I binned the used antibacterial wipes and smiled widely as Jeff—an older man with scapular issues—shuffled by me.

"Looking good, Jeff," I said.

"You flatter me, Natasha," he grunted, waving off my compliment with a stiff arm. "When's that dance class taking off? I want to get my jive on!"

I chuckled and tucked the wipes under my arm. "Not sure I'll ever get to host it."

"That's a shame." Jeff lowered himself into a chair with a groan and gazed at me with a fondness he never afforded to Trevor. "I would've liked to sweep you off your feet."

I clapped my hand to my heart. "You hopeless romantic."

"What can I say? I gotta stay young!"

I swatted Jeff's knee playfully. "Have a good session, Jeff. I'll see you after."

"Don't forget," Trevor muttered as I passed him. "Michael—"

"—wants to see me," I finished for him. "I know."

THE DOOR to Michael's office was always closed. He liked the mystery it spread through the rehab center. We never knew if he was in his office or roaming the halls, hoping to catch his employees in a rare act of laziness. He was a small man with extraordinarily large hands, and you wouldn't know he was balding until he unintentionally revealed the shiny circle bereft of hair on the topmost part of his head by leaning over paperwork on his desk.

Today, Michael stood at the large window that looked out on the grounds behind the rehab center, his massive hands clasped behind his back. The moment between my knock on the door and him turning to face me lingered longer than it should have.

"You wanted to see me?" I said, forcing him away from the window. "Is something wrong?"

Michael sat behind his desk. His chair was pumped to its highest position. Though it made him look taller to the untrained eye, I imagined only his toes touched the floor, hidden by the furniture.

"How you doin', Nat?" The forced casualty in his tone made my nose itch. He caught sight of my wrinkled expression and cleared his throat. "Everything okay out there?"

"To my knowledge," I replied shortly. "Everything okay in here?"

Michael's long fingers spread like spiders across the shiny desk top. He pushed his leather-backed chair to and fro, unable to keep still. "Everything's fine. In fact, everything's great. We found someone to fill the certified aide position."

My heart dropped like a stone in a pond. "Oh?"

He cleared his throat again. "Yes, she really impressed me in the interview, and she's got quite the resume. Graduated from—"

"I don't need to hear her credentials, Michael," I said. "Just get on with firing me."

He caught my eye, and I found legitimate remorse there. "Natasha, you're a great employee. You've been wonderful to have. You get on with the staff so well, and you always do what's asked of you. If I could keep you and the new aide, I would, but I'm afraid we don't have the budget."

I shoved my hands into the pockets of my scrubs. "It's cool, Michael. I knew it was a matter of time."

"She'll be starting immediately," Michael went on. "I can pay you for another two weeks while you look for a new job. If you need a letter of recommendation, don't hesitate to ask. Anyone will be lucky to have you."

I reached over his desk to shake his hand, regretting it as soon as our palms touched. His was cold and clammy. "I appreciate that. Thanks for everything. I'm heading home, unless you need anything else?"

He opened his mouth as if to ask me for one last favor then thought better of it. "No, I'll have Trevor take care of it. Thanks, Nat. And good luck out there!"

A WEEK AGO, someone at my shitty apartment complex had popped the lock on my car and ripped the radio out of the dashboard. It was the newest and most expensive part of my car; the rest of it was from the early 2000s and begging for an upgrade. With no radio, the ride home was quiet except for the hum of the tires against the pavement and that obnoxious rattle in the back seat, the source of which I'd never identified.

I pulled my crappy car up to my crappy apartment and trudged into my crappy unit. I looked around at the bare beige walls. They bore spackle marks and small holes from where the previous tenants had hung pictures or shelves. A yellow stain blossomed on the ceiling above the kitchen from when a pipe burst on the third floor. I did have a balcony, but it looked right into the windows of the apartment complex next door. More than once, I'd forgotten to pull the shades and gotten out of the shower to see a crowd of college boys ogling me from the adjacent building.

The only thing I liked about the apartment complex was the stray tuxedo kitten that sauntered up the stairs one day and meowed impatiently in front of my door until I let him in. I called him Jean Paul because the marks around his eyes reminded me of the philosopher's weird round glasses and because he spent most hours lounging on the back of my armchair, pondering his existence.

"You're getting fat, JP."

He hopped off the armchair, stretched his front paws in front of him, and meandered over to me. I leaned down to pet him as he butted his head against my legs.

"I've got bad news," I told him. "You're going to have to get over your aversion to the bargain bin cat food. I just lost my job."

Jean Paul gave an anguished meow and rolled over to show me his extended belly. I knew better than to pet it. He had strict rules about consent, and his claws were sharp.

"Sorry, buddy."

With a sigh, I dropped my car keys and work bag by the door, kicked off my shoes, and stripped off my scrubs. I hated bringing the smell of the rehab center home with me. Best to keep it all as close to the exit as possible. Half-dressed, I took an open can of the expensive cat food from the fridge and dumped what was left of it into Jean Paul's bowl. He wolfed it down.

"I'd advise you to savor it, but you won't." I tossed the empty can into the trash, warmed up a bowl of leftover adobo, and ate it over the kitchen counter. Jean Paul finished his meal, licked his lips, and began washing himself. "You missed a spot. No, by your ear. Your other ear—you got it."

I washed the day off in my tiny shower—after making sure the blinds were closed—wrapped myself in a robe, and collapsed into bed with my laptop propped on my thighs. Jean Paul hopped up and settled his girth across the keyboard. With some arguing, I maneuvered him out of the way and pulled up a job search engine.

I was qualified for way more than the crappy assistant job I'd gotten at the rehab center six months ago, but something held me back. Every time I thought about applying my movement therapy certification to a real career, fear crept into the back of my head. Pursuing a career meant less freedom. You followed the job rather than your own instinct, and once you started climbing that ladder, it was hard to stop.

The great thing about not having roots anywhere was that I could leave Denver and go wherever I wanted without much worry about tying up loose ends. The apartment was a month-by-month lease. My belongings fit in the smallest moving trailer available to rent. I had no friends or family in the area to miss me when I left, so I opened my job search up to the entire country and scanned through the ones that looked most promising.

Movement therapy, as Trevor so bitterly commented, was on the rise. With the way health was headed in the States, more and more people wanted treatments that assisted the mind as well as the body. From a young age,

I learned the body and the mind were deeply connected. If one was not well, neither was the other, but not many Western health practices took advice from ancient concepts. Movement therapy was one of the few that did.

I scrolled mindlessly through available jobs. A lot of them were similar to the one I'd just left; hospitals or rehab centers needed certified aides or assistants to back up the physical and occupational therapists. As I read through a dozen job descriptions with the same list of duties, I came to terms with something: I didn't want another assistant job. It had been four years since I'd graduated with my advanced degree, and I paid annually to have my certification renewed for a job I didn't have. It was time for that to change.

As much as dance and movement therapy was on the rise, the number of jobs available were low. Most places wanted recreational therapists, who helped patients do things like walk and swim. The movement jobs that *were* available tended to be from niche businesses and small groups, and I didn't do well in cramped quarters.

After a half hour of perusing the job search site, a post caught my attention. A place called the Trevino Center for Health and Wellness wanted to hire their first dance and movement therapist. The responsibilities included formulating a program for the patients, screening and hiring assistants, and expanding the movement therapy sect at the Center. I had never built a program from the ground up, but excitement brewed in my head as I read through the rest of the job post. If I got this position, I'd be my own boss. No Michael or Trevor to tell me what to do, though it was a huge jump to go from measly assistant to

11

full-blown program leader. I didn't have the necessary experience.

I did a quick search on the Trevino Center. It was located in upstate New York, near the Catskills mountains, north of a little hamlet called Lone Elm. I'd never heard of the place. I preferred big cities. The Trevino Center was well-known and liked despite its somewhat secluded location. The Center had been around since the 1920s and grew into one of the most respected private rehabilitation hospitals in the nation. When I thought about it, the name sounded familiar. I was sure I'd read medical articles from doctors and therapists at Trevino before.

The facility looked great. The pictures on the website showed a beautiful historic building, nestled between the trees on the side of a mountain. The inpatient rooms were designed to look homey, rather than the sterile white backgrounds I was accustomed to seeing in similar institutes. One picture featured the Trevino Center covered in a perfect blanket of white snow. Of course, the driveway and the wheelchair ramp had been plowed clean and salted to ensure the safety of patients and employees.

"What do you think, JP?" I asked the cat. "Want to move to Lone Elm with me? It's not really my scene, but if you come along, I might be able to hack it."

Jean Paul lazily lifted his eyelids, glanced at the laptop screen, and promptly went back to sleep.

"What the hell," I muttered to myself. "Don't have anything to lose."

I looked over my resume to make sure it was up to date, wrote a hasty but well-worded cover letter, and submitted both documents to the Trevino Center's website. Then I switched over to the TV show I'd been binge-watching and forgot about the application completely. After all, there was no use worrying about something that might never come to pass.

To my shock, I received an email from the Human Resources office at the Trevino Center two days later. They wanted to set up an in-person interview, but since I was in Colorado and they were in New York, we agreed to a webcam conference instead. My stomach turned as I waited for the call. All of a sudden, I was worried about impressing these people. Getting hired at Trevino would be a huge step forward, a step I wanted to take.

As soon as the video chat application chimed, I hit the Accept Call button. As the screen loaded, I straightened out my collar and made sure the person interviewing me couldn't see I only looked professional on the top. Beneath my polo shirt, I wore pajama pants and fuzzy socks. Right as the video feed loaded, Jean Paul hopped onto my lap and blocked the camera.

"Jean Paul, no!" I struggled to maneuver his slippery body out of the way. He purred happily and butted his head against my face. When I dumped him on the floor, he flicked his tail and meowed loudly. "Shh!"

"Miss Bell?" said a voice from the screen. "Are you there?"

"Yes! I'm so sorry." I straightened the laptop. "My cat's a bit of a loose canon. Hi, how are you?"

The woman on the other end of the video feed had a soft, doughy face offset by the stern purse of her lips.

Behind her was a large window that showed off the mountain scenery.

"I'm well, Miss Bell," she said, her voice not so stern as her lips. "We already spoke on the phone, but allow me to introduce myself. My name is Hilary Noble. I'm Eli Trevino's executive assistant. Eli wanted to interview you himself, but I'm afraid his schedule wouldn't permit it."

"Eli is the owner of the Center?"

The pursed lips returned. "He is our chief psychiatrist, the CEO of Trevino, and yes, the owner of our establishment. Have you not heard of us?"

"I have," I said hurriedly, wondering if I'd already screwed up. " I'm not all that familiar with how private rehab centers are run. I'd love to learn though."

That softened Hilary up a little bit. Her shoulders relaxed as she shuffled through a file on her desk. "Very well. That's no issue. You'll find working for a private company has quite a few advantages. Let's talk about you first. I see you received your advanced degree? That's a great school. How did you enjoy your education?"

The interview took off. I filled Hilary in on my background, education, and my past work experience. Though I'd traveled often, taking temporary jobs rather than permanent jobs, Hilary didn't see it as a fault. She commended me for widening my skill set and therapeutical knowledge. We spoke frankly. I told her that building a program myself had been one of my goals as a therapist. I spoke about the connection between the mind and the body, and how my expertise would benefit all of the patients at the Trevino Center, despite the focus of their care.

"You're certainly earnest," Hilary commented. "I like

that." She dashed a few notes on her legal pad. "That's about all I have for you, Natasha. Do you have any questions for me?"

I hesitated. There was always one thing that weighed on my mind whenever I applied somewhere new. "Do you care?" I asked. "About the patients, I mean. I know it sounds like a stupid question, but it's important to me. The Trevino Center is well-known, sure, but no matter what the health magazines say, the patients' opinions matter more."

Hilary smiled warmly at me. "I can assure you that everyone at the Trevino Center is dedicated to the patients' well-being first and foremost. We would not be one of the best rehab centers in the world if that weren't a fact."

Though I doubted she would have given me any other answer, it still lifted a weight off my shoulders. "That's good to hear."

"It was great talking with you," Hilary said. "We've got a few more people to interview, then we'll be looking over everything to see who might be the best fit. You should hear from me in the next week or two, after Dr. Trevino makes his official decision."

Hilary disconnected the call. I closed my laptop and let Jean Paul hop up again. His fat paws kneaded my stomach like bread dough. I made a loop with my fingers, and he shoved his face through it, over and over, to massage his whiskers.

"Guess we wait and see," I said to the cat.

2

I stuffed a handful of bourbon barbecue potato chips into my mouth right as the phone rang. I licked my index finger clean and slid it across the screen to answer a call from an unfamiliar number.

"Hewwo?" I said, mouth full.

"Hi, Miss Bell? This is Hilary Noble from the Trevino Center of Health and Wellness. We spoke a few weeks ago?"

Here it comes, I thought. I draped my feet across the arm of my chair and leaned my head against the other side. I hadn't heard from Trevino in so long that I figured they'd forgotten about me and hired someone else. I'd already accepted another assistant position at a less reputable rehab center in Denver. Later that day, I was supposed to meet my landlord to sign another month's worth of money away for my apartment.

I finally chewed enough to swallow the potato chips without getting dry bits stuck in my throat. "Hi, Hilary. How are you?"

"I'm well, thank you. I'm calling to offer you the dance and movement therapist position at our facility in Lone Elm. Are you still interested—my goodness, are you all right?"

I thumped my chest, hacking and coughing to dislodge the chips in my lungs. "Y-yes," I gasped. "I'm fine. And yes, I'm still interested."

"Excellent," Hilary said. "We'd like you to start as soon as possible. If I recall correctly, you're living in Denver. How quickly can you make it to Lone Elm?"

"As soon as I can buy a plane ticket."

"By Monday morning?"

It was Friday afternoon. Could I arrange everything— quit my new job, get out of my lease, and make it to upstate New York—in less than three days?

"Monday morning it is. See you then, Hilary."

LONE ELM, New York was not a place I'd heard of before, and as I drove my noisy car into the center of town, the why of it all became obvious. The hamlet was smaller than a postage stamp. I made it from one end of the main street to the other in forty-five seconds, though it would have taken less time if the speed limit wasn't a whopping eight miles an hour. No big box stores or chain restaurants in sight. Lone Elm only contained the necessities: a drug store, a local grocery and farmer's market, a breakfast café that looked popular with the locals, a hole-in-the-wall mom-and-pop restaurant called The Shadows, and—thank goodness—a beautiful inn.

Enormous trees grew around the entire village. They bent over the buildings and streets like lanky nature gods, come to clutch the residents in their leafy fingers. I rolled the windows down and let the cool, misty air cleanse the musty road-trip smell of old fast food, sweat, and cat litter from my car. Jean Paul, confined to a brand-new carrier in the back seat, lifted his nose and let out a plaintive meow.

"We're almost there, boo-boo," I said in the most annoying voice I possessed. I'd been alone for too long. When your only companion was a cat, you lost a certain grip on reality. "I'll let you out soon."

We had been in the car for almost thirty hours. I'd driven all day yesterday with the exception of two one-hour power naps on the side of the road, during which I let Jean Paul stretch his paws and use the portable litter box I'd crafted out of a disposable drip pan. All I wanted to do was check into the motel, get a shower, and take the nap I deserved, but duty called. Though it was Sunday, the Trevino Center for Health and Wellness was open for business, and when Hilary heard of my early arrival, she requested my presence as soon as possible to get all the paperwork in order.

The Shadows Inn—not to be confused with the nearby restaurant—was a gorgeous Victorian dwelling with white siding, a pointed roof, and too many terraces to count. I parked around the side and headed into the lobby. The welcoming scent of cinnamon and nutmeg floated from the kitchen in the back. The inn was tastefully decorated in deep reds, warm browns, and burnt oranges, casting the perfect impression of autumn no matter the season. I caught a peek into the small sitting room to the right. The leather sofas were artfully draped with cozy crocheted blankets. Along the walls, wooden shelves played home to an impressive collection of old books. My fingers itched, longing to explore the library, but the rattle of caster wheels drew me out of my reverie as a teenaged girl with long-brown hair and hazel eyes rolled out from behind the check-in desk in an office chair.

"Hi," she said brightly. She clutched one of the books from the library. *The Fountainhead* by Ayn Rand. Bit of a challenging read for her age. "Are you checking in?"

"Yeah. The last name's Bell?"

She set the book face-down, paying no mind to the broken spine. The book splayed easily, used to such a position. The teenager logged into the laptop on the check-in desk. "Natasha Bell. Gotcha right here. Ooh, you'll be in my favorite room." She reached beneath the desk and unearthed a brass key that looked more likely to open an ancient trunk at the foot of a monarch's bed rather than a room at the local inn, except that it was attached to a neon green macaron key chain. "Room ten. Up the stairs, all the way to the end of the hall. It's the round one with all the big windows you can see from the front."

I accepted the key. "Thanks. Aren't you a little young to run an inn?"

"My mom owns the place," the teenager replied. "I help out in the afternoons and on the weekends. It's not like I have anything else to do."

I gestured to *The Fountainhead*. "Except getting to know Howard Roark. How do you like him so far?"

"He's an ass," she said frankly.

"Baz!" A tall woman, no older than myself, with dark hair and blazing blue eyes appeared from a hidden hallway and hurried over to the check-in desk. "What have I told you about swearing in front of the guests?"

"I don't know. What have you told me?"

The woman tilted her head. "We haven't discussed it, now that I think about it. Anyway, don't." Her blue eyes sparkled as she flashed me a smile. "I see you've met my daughter."

"Baz?" I asked the teenager.

"Don't look at me," said the girl, jerking a thumb at her mother. "It's originally a boy's name, but *someone* was a little too obsessed with Moulin Rouge at the time of my birth."

"I was hopped up on a lot of painkillers," the woman added. She extended her hand over the desk for me to shake. "I'm Lauren. You're in luck. Right after you called, a big wedding party decided to book us. You've got the best room in the house."

"So I've been told." I clutched the key and grimaced. "I forgot to ask. Is it okay to bring my cat inside?"

Baz melted into a puddle. "You have a cat?"

"Yeah, he's in the car, and he's a bit desperate to get out of it."

"We don't usually allow pets," Lauren said.

Baz hung onto her mother's arm. "Oh, please! I've always wanted a kitten."

"Jean Paul's not a kitten anymore," I warned. "He's a chonk. But he is well-behaved," I added to Lauren. "I can keep him in my room to make sure he doesn't bother anyone. I don't have anywhere else to put him. This was all pretty last-minute."

Lauren poked her tongue into her cheek. Baz put on

her best doe eyes, doing all of the work for me. Lauren placed her entire palm over her daughter's face.

"Enough of that," she said. "Jean Paul is welcome to stay as well."

Baz pumped her fist. "Can I get him?" she begged me, bouncing on the balls of her feet. "Is he friendly?"

"When he feels like it." I tossed her my car keys. "Ugly silver Volvo. He's in the back seat."

"Get her bags too!" Lauren called after the teenager as she bounded outside. She rolled her eyes. "Good help is so hard to find." She looked surprised when I chuckled at the joke. "You're new in town, huh? What brings you to Lone Elm?"

"I got a job as a therapist at the Trevino Center for Health and Wellness."

"Oh! Makes sense," she said, typing my debit card information into the system. "Most of the locals who don't own their own business in town work there. So you'll be here a while?"

I sucked air through my teeth.

"No?" Lauren asked. "Your position at Trevino is temporary?"

"It's permanent," I answered, "but I can't say the same for myself. I'm used to big cities, and Lone Elm is—"

"Microscopic, I think, is the word you're looking for." She returned my debit card to me. "Give it a chance. It's quieter than the city, but you'll get used to it, and I hear Trevino has made quite a name. People stay here at the inn, hoping to get on the waiting list."

"There's a waiting list for patients?"

"The Center only has eighty beds."

"Really? The facility looks bigger than that on the website."

Lauren shrugged. "Maybe they're expanding. I've never been up there myself, but my mother was familiar with the place."

"How so?"

"She was committed there."

"Oh." I cleared my throat, taken aback. "I'm sorry."

Lauren's eyes rolled skyward as she waved away the apology. "Nothing to be sorry about. She was clinically insane. Hopefully, it doesn't run in the family."

He's so cute! Baz squealed, barreling through the front door with Jean Paul in one hand and my bag in the other. She dumped the bag on the floor and lifted Jean Paul's carrier up to eye level so she could peer inside. Jean Paul, backed against the far end of his temporary home, let out an unfriendly growl. "Uh-oh, he's mad."

I relieved Baz of the carrier, prying the handle from her tight fingers. "He's scared. He's not used to anyone but me." I set the carrier on the ground and popped open the door. As Baz waited with bated breath, Jean Paul tentatively made his way out of his prison. He looked left and right, confused by the new scenery, then scampered off. His paws slipped across the polished wood floors and he slid into the shadows beneath a red velvet bench adjacent to the check-in desk.

Lauren dipped her head to peer at the cat. Jean Paul's green eyes glowed in the darkness. "Well, now that he's all settled in," Lauren said to me, "we can show you your room as well. Baz? Baz!"

Baz had flattened out, stomach to the floor, in an attempt to lure Jean Paul into the light. She jumped to her feet at the sound of her mother's voice and grabbed my bag. "Right! Follow me, Nat. Is it cool if I call you Nat?"

"That's what everyone else calls me." I waved thanks to Lauren and followed Baz as she dragged my bag up the carpeted steps. I ran my hand across the intricately carved banister. "Try tuna, by the way."

"Hmm?"

"For Jean Paul," I said. "He's a sucker for a little bit of canned tuna. Just a few pieces though. He'll try to convince you to give him the whole can, but it's not good for cats in large quantities. As a treat, it's okay."

Baz lugged my bag over the top step and started down the corridor. "Great! I'll steal a can from the kitchen. Our chef won't mind. God, this is heavy. What's in here, bricks?"

"Books," I said. "I'm starting a movement therapy center at Trevino, so I brought all of my old textbooks with me."

"Movement therapy? Like Tai Chi and stuff?"

"Tai Chi counts, sure," I replied. The little inn's second floor hallway was lined with heavy red carpet and ornate wood doors that led to other rooms. Baz continued to the very end. "But I don't know a whole lot of Tai Chi. The most important thing about movement therapy is getting the patients to enjoy the program safely."

"Cool," Baz commented, dumping my bag at the foot of the last door. "I have no idea what I want to do with my life. I don't want to leave my mom—we're, like, freaky close—but Lone Elm is so boring. Do you know how many people are in my class? Twenty-seven. *Twenty-seven.* Can you believe there are only twenty-seven fifteen-year-olds in the entire town?"

"It's small," I agreed. I gestured to the door with the macaron key chain. "Shall I?"

"Sure, whatever."

I fitted the golden key into the lock. The mechanism grated as I turned it. Baz kicked the door open, and sunlight—misty but bright—poured into the room from a circlet of windows. The turret looked to the street below. There was a balcony, though you had to climb through a window to access it. The queen-sized bed rested right in the center of the turret, facing the windows, its headboard nowhere near the wall. The odd set-up was not warranted by the design of the room—there was plenty of extra space to place the bed in a more sensical position—but Baz answered the stylistic question before I had the chance to ask it.

"The sun comes up right over those trees," she said, pointing through the turret windows. I leaned down to have a look. Beyond Lone Elm's Main Street, the forest took over, level with the second floor of the inn. "Mom likes waking up to the sun, so she stuck the bed here. Personally, I don't like being blasted in the face first thing in the morning. If you want, you can pull the curtains." She tugged on the deep-red curtains surrounding the windows. "They're black-outs, so they'll keep the room completely dark until you want to wake up. Um, what else?" She used her legs to lift my bag onto a large chest near the bed. "If you need anything, dial one on the phone and either me or my mom will pick up. We're not fancy enough to have mini fridges or a snack bar. If you're hungry or thirsty, come down to the dining room. If it's after hours or between meals, check the kitchen. Our chef is super cool once you get past his pretentious *je-ne-sais-*

quois, and if you flatter him, he'll get you whatever you want." She patted her palms against her thighs. "Any questions?"

I checked my watch. I was anxious to get to the Trevino Center. "Do you mind watching Jean Paul, make sure he settles in okay? I have to check in at work, and I don't want him to run off."

Baz's beam was reassuring. "Absolutely! I'll put a few water bowls around the inn for him. Do you have cat food?"

I handed over a bag of dry food and instructed her to fill just one bowl for Jean Paul's easy access. I offered her a ten-dollar bill.

"What's this?" she asked.

"A tip."

Her eyes flickered to my open duffel bag. It was not stuffed with clothes and belongings, as I didn't have many things to begin with. Baz set the money on the dresser. "Mom says I'm not allowed to take tips from the guests. Thanks, though."

She left the room. As I changed out of my road-trip outfit, rinsed my face, and put on a polo, I wondered if Baz's honed perception was a result of nonstop people-watching at the inn.

THE TREVINO CENTER FOR HEALTH AND WELLNESS was a decent drive from the Shadows Inn. The two-lane road curved back and forth to account for the upward slope. Trees crouched over the asphalt and the sun danced through the branches, casting pretty patterns on the windshield. Higher up, mist snaked across the ground and wound around the tires, like twisted fingers of the under-world come to pull me beneath the earth. At last, the trees thinned out and the road widened. Around the final bend, the Trevino Center lay exposed in all its glory.

It looked like the pictures, minus the snow. The parking lot was nowhere in sight, so I pulled into an enor-mous circular driveway, lined with gray cobblestones, that led to the front doors. I parked there, took a deep breath as I checked my reflection in the mirror, and headed inside.

Were it not for the lingering smell of disinfectant, I might have mistaken the reception area for a lobby at a luxury resort. A dolphin-shaped marble fountains gurgled and bubbled in the middle of the polished floors. The seats in the waiting room were made of synthetic leather—it looked expensive, but it was easy to clean. The check-in desk spanned the length of the room, and the secretary behind it wore a black pencil skirt, a white Oxford shirt, and a red ascot embroidered with the Trevino logo. Behind the desk, a three-dimen-sional rendering of the logo hung on the wall. It featured a large lion, rearing on its back legs, with its front paws stretched around an elaborately calligraphed T.

I approached the desk and opened my mouth, but the secretary—who was on the phone—held up a single finger to silence me before I spoke.

"No, ma'am," she said into the receiver. "I'm afraid that's not possible. You'll have to speak to your insurance company. Yes, I understand you're upset, but you signed a form—Ma'am, I'd appreciate if you stopped yelling—" The angry voice on the other end of the line cut off suddenly, and the secretary hung up the receiver with a tired sigh. She looked up at me. "Are you checking in?"

"What? No, I'm the new hire." I shifted uncomfortably from one foot to the other. Compared to the secretary's perfect outfit, my wrinkled polo and creased khakis weren't up to par. "Hilary said to come by and fill out my paperwork today."

Rather than responding, the secretary returned her gaze to the computer. As her typing grew more rapid, her perfectly-lined eyebrows drifted closer together. "Ah, yes. Natasha Bell, our new movement therapist. Have a seat. I'll let Hilary know you're here."

I intentionally placed the fountain between the front desk and my chosen seat, so the secretary wouldn't be tempted to judge my haggard, road-worn appearance and suggest to Hilary that perhaps I wasn't suited for the role after all. The dolphins' cold marble eyes glared at me. I looked away. On the opposite end of the waiting room was an enormous portrait. Curiosity pried me out of my seat.

The portrait featured a slender man, painted from the waist up, with a neatly trimmed mustache, slick dark hair, and beady eyes, one of which was slightly magnified by a monocle. That eye had been painted differently, and if I wasn't mistaken, the silver sheen on the pupil was meant to indicate a cataract. Below the portrait, a small gold plaque sported an inscription: *Elijah Trevino, Founder of the Trevino Center of Health and Wellness, 1922.*

A door I hadn't spotted before banged open, and two women emerged, one with wavy platinum hair, the other a brunette. Both of them wore a heather gray pair of the fanciest scrubs I'd ever seen. They looked more like runway models than nurses or orderlies. Like the secretary's ascot, their outfits were embroidered with the Trevino logo in silver thread.

"He *always* refuses care," the blonde one was saying, rather loudly, to her companion. "It's like, what's the point of spending all this money to stay at Trevino if he won't let anyone flip him over?"

"Because the son doesn't want to deal with him," the other woman replied. "That's what always happens."

"This isn't a nursing home. People shouldn't be allowed to drop off their parents here and take off." The blonde leaned over the desk and batted her eyelashes at the secretary. "Hi, Cameron."

The secretary, Cameron, did not look away from her computer. "What do you want, Imogen?"

"Can you call my four o'clock and ask if she's willing to change her appointment to tomorrow morning?" the blonde requested. "I'd love to get out of here early tonight."

"I'll make a note."

Imogen beamed. "Thanks, doll."

The pair turned away from the desk and headed my way. The darker-haired woman snorted.

"What was that?" she asked Imogen.

"I heard she was a lesbian," Imogen replied in a conspiratorial whisper. "I figure a little flirting doesn't hurt to get what I want."

The other woman glanced over her shoulder. "She doesn't *look* like a lesbian."

"Not every lesbian has to look like one," Imogen said, exasperated. "It's 2019. They can look however they want—oh!"

As they drew level with me, they finally realized their conversation was not as private as they initially assumed. Imogen cast a judgmental eye over me, starting at the tip of my head and traveling all the way down to my worn-out sneakers.

"Are you waiting on a patient?" Imogen asked.

"No, I'm actually waiting on the HR lady."

"*You're* the new therapist? Natasha Bell?"

My lips tightened. "Uh-huh."

The dark-haired woman elbowed Imogen in the ribs, and she lifted her dropped jaw from the floor, pasting a smile on instead.

"Well!" Imogen said. "It's lucky you ran into us. I'm Imogen Hobbs. I'm a physical therapist. This is Ariel—"

"Ariel Cruz," the dark-haired woman said, shaking my hand. "I'm one of the occupational therapists."

Imogen steered me away from the waiting room. "Come with us. It's our lunch break, but we'll give you a quick tour of the place."

I threw a pleading look over my shoulder at Cameron the secretary, but she was busy with another phone call. There was no one to rescue me from Imogen's grasp as she ushered me away from the waiting room. Ariel followed behind us.

"So this is the inpatient care area," Imogen rattled off. "We have fifty beds here, but people hardly stay as long as you'd expect. As soon as one bed frees up, it's filled a moment later. Trevino's waiting list is a mile long." She made an abrupt turn into a small office. Two other workers, startled by our appearance, glanced up. "This is our office-slash-breakroom," Imogen said. "That's Andy and Jewel." The others waved. "You'll get assigned a laptop to work on. Sometimes, the nurses bring treats. Coming, Ariel?"

Ariel had drifted off to pull a container out of the fridge. When she popped it open, the enticing scent of stir fry permeated the room. "I'm going to eat. You go ahead. Nice to meet you, Natasha."

"Nice to meet you too—"

Imogen whisked me away again before I could complete the sentence. "Outpatient PT, speech therapy, the play room for kids, and our entire wing for hand therapy," she said in one breath as we passed each area. "That's what I do. Trevino has state-of-the-art technology, machines no one else in the nation has, and our therapists are some of the best in the world. Not to brag," she added with a grin that indicated she absolutely meant to brag.

We ended up at the intersection of three hallways, and I had no idea how we'd made it there. The signage was no less confusing than Imogen's commentary. Arrows pointed every which way, directing lost explorers to inpatient, outpatient, exits, et cetera. The only thing clearly labeled was a set of doors directly behind us: Ward 13.

An earsplitting scream rang out.

Imogen rolled here eyes as I gritted my teeth. Someone bumped into me from behind, aggressively pushing me out of the way. It was a tiny woman with short black hair, dressed in mint scrubs. She shouldered open the double doors, and the scream intensified without the barrier between us and the patient.

Imogen stuck out her foot, propping the door open so we could look inside. The aide rushed into one of the rooms—a glass window kept us privy to the goings-on—where a young man thrashed against the four-point restraints that kept him glued to the bed. His screams wreaked havoc on his throat and vocal chords, but he went on. The aide bustled with something beside the patient's bed. The young man went quiet and still. The aide brushed his hair away from his face and wiped his forehead with a damp cloth.

"That's Scout Mackay," Imogen said in a low voice. "She's the only aide who has free rein over the entire Center."

"What's this ward? Why was that kid screaming?"

"That's Ward 13," she replied coolly. "The insane asylum."

"We don't call it that anymore." Cameron had appeared from the central hallway, her red heels clicking across the floor. When she linked her arm through mine, relief flooded through me. "I've been looking all over for you. Hilary's ready."

As Cameron led me away, I glanced over my shoulder. Imogen had removed her foot from the door. It swung to and fro before drifting shut, obscuring Ward 13 from view once again.

y meeting with Hilary went as expected. I reviewed my contract, blanched at the idea of spending the rest of my career in one place, and signed at the bottom. The annual salary was more than I'd ever made in my lifetime. We went through every kind of form imaginable, but Hilary emphasized the ones on patient privacy the most.

"Trevino has a reputation to maintain," she had said as I scribbled my messy signature at the bottom of the page, next to the raised gold seal of the Center. "Our patients and their privacy are our first priority. No information should leave these four walls."

I refrained from joking that the massive center included many more than four walls, but Hilary was not the type to enjoy casual humor. Her office was bare of decorations. No family pictures. No desk calendar to take quick notes and appointment times down on. She didn't have a clock. Perhaps time didn't pass in the Human Resources office. It was one of the few rooms I'd entered that didn't have a window. Without the changing of light, you might wonder if the seconds ticked by at all.

"Do you have scrubs?" Hilary asked. She looked me up and down. My face flushed as she pursed her lips at my wrinkled attire. "We don't require them of our therapists, but something appropriate is necessary. Like I said, Trevino—"

"—has a reputation to maintain," I finished for her, smoothing out my pants with my sweaty palms. "I do have scrubs, but they're a few years old. I'm not sure—"

"Never mind." Hilary crossed to a storage closet, bustled around, and emerged with a stack of polo shirts wrapped individually in plastic. "Wear these for now. We ordered them a few years ago. Eli didn't appreciate the color, but it's better you have something with the Trevino logo on it."

The polo was a bright blue-green: a beautiful color if you were standing on the deck of a cruise ship and looking out at the water around a Caribbean island, not so beautiful as a polyester work shirt. Again, the Trevino logo was stitched into the left side of the chest. I pulled the polo out of the plastic and let it unfold.

"They might be a bit big," Hilary mentioned.

A bit big was an understatement. The polo looked more like a dress than a work shirt. The hem reached my thighs and the sleeves covered my elbows. I would appear no more professional in the oversized garment than in my own subpar garb.

"Perhaps you could have it hemmed?" Hilary suggested. "We have an excellent tailor in town. In the meantime, I suggest you order some new scrubs. We all use the same website here so everyone matches."

She slid a catalogue across the desk, and I recognized the fashion-inspired scrubs that Imogen and Ariel had been wearing on the front page. I noticed the prices.

"I might have to wait until I get my first paycheck to order these," I said in a small voice. Heat crept up my neck. "Sorry, but my last job wasn't the most lucrative."

Hilary's pursed lips relaxed. Though she didn't smile, her eyes softened. "I understand, honey." She patted my hand. "I'm happy Eli decided you were a right fit for the company. You seem like a nice girl. I think you'll like it here. Good things await you."

WHEN I RETURNED to the Shadows Inn, Jean Paul had made fast friends with Baz. He lounged next to her on the leather sofa in the library, purring and drooling as she absentmindedly stroked him and forged onward with her book.

"I see the tuna worked," I commented.

Baz abandoned the couch as soon as she saw me struggling to free my arms from the sleeves of my corduroy coat. She pulled it off for me and hung it up in a closet behind the check-in desk. "It sure did. He followed me around the entire time you were gone. How was your meeting?"

"It went well," I said confidently, determined to see the positive side of things. My first instinct was to consider all the things that might go wrong at my new job, but it was time to have a little faith in luck. "Everyone seems nice enough."

Jean Paul leapt off the sofa, stretched and yawned, and sauntered over. After brushing by my legs, he made a beeline for a small bowl of kibble that Baz had set up for him under the velvet bench in the lobby while I was gone.

"I see he's made himself at home," I said.

Baz smiled. "I set up a litter box in the laundry room. It won't be in anyone's way there, and the maids can keep it clean."

"No, I'll do it," I promised. "He's my cat."

She shrugged. "If you want. Are you hungry? It's dinner time. Marcel made coq au vin because we were supposed to have a family of four show up today, but they canceled. Anyway, Marcel's mad because there's no one here to eat his food, so if you're a vegetarian or something, he's *really* going to be pissed—"

I held up a hand to silence the teenager's diatribe. "I'm not a vegetarian, and I love coq au vin. I assume Marcel is the inn's chef?"

"Yes, he's—"

A loud bang echoed from the back end of the inn, followed by a short yell. The double doors at the end of the corridor flew open, and a tiny man in a white chef's coat barreled toward us. Black smoke billowed from the kitchen.

"Incompetence!" cried the chef in a thick French accent, waving his arms to dispel the smoke. "I asked for *one* assistant, *one* American who knows how to cook in this tiny, tiny town!" He shook his finger in Baz's face. "You! Tell your mother I can't work like this!"

"Is something on fire?" I asked. No one seemed too concerned about the smoke drifting lazily from the kitchen. The fire alarm above was silent.

The chef rounded on me. "My meat! That's what's on fire!"

Baz sniggered. I couldn't help but join in. The chef's lip curled upward.

"Fine!" he yelled. "Starve, all of you!"

He turned on his heel, but Baz grasped his elbow. "Wait, Marcel," she said, her tone soothing. "I didn't mean to laugh at your burned meat. Why don't you show me what happened? Do I need to file a damage report?"

"Of course not!" Marcel crossed his arms, though his disgruntled expression faded as Baz comforted him. Without it, his handsome features came to light. He was not much older than me, with a pointed chin, high cheek-bones, and delicate facial hair. Though short, he exuded unmatched energy. "It is only smoke."

"Let's see it," Baz said, leading Marcel away.

As they disappeared, Lauren came out of her office, looking guilty. She made sure the kitchen doors had swung shut before emerging completely. "Baz handles Marcel better than I do," she admitted. "It's best to let him get his anger out all at once."

I wafted the smoke away from the fire alarm with my long arms. "Aren't you afraid something serious happened in there?"

"Honey, if I called the fire department every time Marcel filled this place with smoke, they'd stop coming." Lauren coughed, her eyes watering. "Help me open a few windows, would you?"

DINNER, to my utter shock, was magnificent. Despite the smoke, the coq au vin came out perfect. The chicken fell off the bone, and the vegetables were cooked to perfection. Since I was the sole guest at the inn, I accepted

Lauren and Baz's offer to sit at the same table as them. Marcel's assistant—a mousy teenager who shook every time Marcel called his name—served us. According to Baz, he was one of her classmates at school, and he cooked well when Marcel wasn't looming over him like a storm cloud.

I drank too much wine, recognized my mistake when my head grew woozy, and excused myself from the table. My companions would not let me leave without a napkin full of pistachio macarons, which were apparently Marcel's dessert specialty. Jean Paul followed me up the stairs, meowing with each step. When I collapsed on the bed, he crawled onto my chest, formed himself into a neat loaf, and dozed off.

I smoothed his ears back, enjoying his look of bliss. "Tomorrow's a big day, Jean Paul. First time creating and running a program. Any advice?"

He purred contently. Drool gathered in a blob at the corner of this mouth. When he was particularly comfortable, he turned on the waterworks. I set him at the foot of the bed to avoid the splash zone, laid out my clothes for tomorrow, and went to sleep.

SINCE I WAS the Trevino Center's first ever movement therapist to be hired, I had next to no guidance on what I was supposed to do during my first day. I parked in the driveway again, but Cameron, the secretary, quickly informed me that area was for drop-offs and emergencies only. The parking lot was hidden around the side of the building, so I moved my car and came back inside for the second try at starting my day.

Cameron showed me to the therapists' shared office since I couldn't remember how to get there on my own. Then she emailed me a map of the building in handy pdf form for me to access any time I got lost. Once I was in the right place, Cameron had to return to her proper position at the front desk, leaving me with the lovely Imogen.

"Good morning, Natasha," she said in a bright voice from her desk by the window. Like yesterday, she wore impeccably ironed scrubs. She was the only therapist in the room. The others likely had appointments with patients already. Imogen cast an eye over my oversized polo shirt. "I thought we retired that outfit. Hmm."

I squared my shoulders and set my mouth. "It's all Hilary had for me. I'll get new scrubs too, and then we can all match."

The corners of Imogen's lips turned up. "I like you," she announced, pushing her rolling chair away from the desk. "I've been tasked with getting you started since I don't have a patient this morning. Do you have a plan to get these movement classes started?"

"Uh, I haven't—"

"No?"

"Yes," I said firmly. I drew my files out of my backpack. They were filled with research on movement and dance therapy, as well as my own approach to a start-up program. I'd designed an entire course months ago, out of boredom and the desire to do more than change linens at the rehab clinic. All I needed to do was change it to fit my patients' needs at Trevino. First, I needed patients. "I have it all sorted out. When can I meet my patients?"

Imogen clasped her long fingers together. "You'll have

to recruit some. Your branch isn't required here, so we can't technically make the patients do it. We can only recommend it to them. It's your job to convince them to participate."

The smugness in her voice irritated me. Clearly, she thought hand therapy superior to movement. Meanwhile, I thought all areas of therapy were crucial to the recovery process.

"Sounds great," I said, pasting a smile on. "If you'll point me in the right direction, I'll be glad to do that."

She got out of her chair. "I'm coming with. Can't have the newbie running loose in the Center. You might find our torture chamber!" Her high-pitched laugh trilled annoyingly.

ONCE WE BEGAN TALKING to the patients, Imogen became tolerable. Her cheerfulness, staged or not, was beneficial to those who came to or stayed at Trevino for treatment. We visited the inpatient area first. The people here were either so affected by their ailments that they needed daily attention or they had come to Trevino from far away and paid to stay on site during the course of their treatment.

We went from room to room, and I introduced myself to every patient who wasn't occupied or asleep. To her credit, Imogen let me do the talking as I explained the benefits of movement therapy. A few of the patients immediately declined. These were the bedridden ones, who had not put their feet on the floor for months and saw no hope for themselves any longer. I encouraged them to come to an assembly that afternoon, during which I would explain and showcase some of the things I intended to help them practice. Most of them refused, but hope glimmered in one woman's eyes.

Several patients were excited by the prospect of doing something that appeared recreational. They asked questions about myself and the program, sometimes taking so much time that I had to excuse myself from the conversation in order to move on to the next patient. After I finished talking to everyone in inpatient therapy, I had twenty-three prospective participants.

"It sounds intriguing," Ariel said as we all gathered in the office at lunchtime. The other therapists, save for Imogen, politely grilled me about my intentions for the movement program, making it hard for me to eat my leftover coq au vin in the time allowed. "I'll mention it to my patients as well. I think a lot of them would benefit from something like that."

"Can anyone join?" Jewel asked. She was a middle-aged woman with firm hands and a dry tone that made every word sound sarcastic, whether she intended it or not. "It sounds like a good bit of exercise."

"I don't see why not," I said through a dripping mouthful of saucy chicken. "I need therapists to help out anyway. You're more than welcome to go through the movements with them."

"I'm in," Andy said. Like Jewel, he was in his forties. He had sandy blond hair and a thick Tennessee accent. "Anything to make the day more exciting. Besides, I'm eager to see something new happen at the Center."

Imogen huffed at her corner desk. She had not joined in on the conversation. "We have new things all the time. Last week, they brought in that balloon guy."

"I meant new ways of practicing therapy," Andy

revised. "I'm surprised Eli's mixing it up a bit by hiring you, Nat. Have you met him yet?"

I shook my head and cut a mushy carrot in half. "He seems like a busy guy. Haven't seen him around yet. Are you sure he exists?"

A mutual chuckle went around the breakroom.

"He exists," Ariel assured me. "He mostly works in the psych ward. He's hands-off unless a situation comes to his attention."

"And you better make sure no situations come to his attention," Jewel warned. "He's not pleasant when he's bothered. He's nothing like his father was."

"His father?"

"Elijah Trevino the Third," said Andy. "He died about a year ago—"

"Totally unexpected," Imogen interrupted. "It was tragic. No one thought Eli was ready to take over the Center. There was talk of selling it. We all could have been out of our jobs."

Andy loudly cleared his throat. "Eli was understandably taken aback by his father's death. The man was only sixty-two. I think Eli's done a fair job of managing this place so far."

"Oh, of course!" Imogen agreed instantly. "I was merely stating a fact."

I checked my watch. Lunch was almost over. I'd have to start setting up for my afternoon introduction assembly soon, but with most of my chicken uneaten, I was still hungry. "Which way is the open therapy room?" I asked the group, capping my meal. "I think I'll get started early."

"Down the hall to the left," Ariel said. "Big glass window. Can't miss it."

I thanked her, ducked out of the office, and found the room in question. With a sigh, I sat on the floor and finished my lunch in peace.

FIVE PATIENTS SHOWED up to the assembly. I tried not to let my disappointment show, though Imogen's smirk pushed me to the limit. Thankfully, she couldn't be there for the whole hour, as she had a patient halfway through the assembly. Andy took her place, leaning against the back wall and listening intently as I explained my program in greater detail. I demonstrated some of the movements I intended on using throughout the classes, then showed how each movement could be modified based on a patient's abilities. At some point, I realized how natural it felt to be teaching and moving this way. Despite the small turnout, I was happy.

"That was great," Andy said, once we had returned all the patients to their rooms after the assembly. "Are you sure you've never done this before?"

"Positive," I replied. "But I've been planning something like this ever since I graduated from my Master's program. All I needed was an opportunity."

He high-fived me. "I'm glad you found it here. Trevino's great, but the patients get restless. This should help." He walked me back to the therapy room. "Do you need help cleaning up? I can—" He caught a glimpse of the wall clock and sucked in air through his teeth. "Actually, I can't. I've got a patient in five minutes."

"It's fine." I waved him off. "I got it covered."

In an hour, I'd made plenty of mess in the therapy room. I'd used almost every assistance tool available to show the patients how much variety was possible during my classes. Now, the room was littered with colorful stretching bands, large inflatable exercise balls, and other items. Whistling happily, I began to organize everything.

A moment later, Scout Mackay—the aide who had bumped into me yesterday outside Ward 13—appeared in the doorway. She surveyed the mess.

"I'll do that," she said, taking a handful of assistance bands from my grip. "The therapists like things arranged a certain way."

In some ways, she reminded me of Marcel. She was small, barely five feet tall, but she exuded aggressive energy. Her black, chin-length hair hung as straight as a pin around her pointed face. She had a small mouth, a wide nose, and narrowly spaced eyes, as if her creator had accidentally calculated her facial proportions wrong before depositing her on the earth. With one look, she could silently command you to move out of her way, which I did so.

"I was going to clean up," I said. "I think I remember where everything goes."

She swept past me and hung up the assistance bands on the wall, a different place from where I'd found them. "This is part of my job. The other therapists like to have time to write their notes."

"I can clean up after myself."

Scout threw a wry look over her shoulder. "You're new, aren't you? Were you an aide before?"

"Yes."

"It shows," she said. "Don't worry. You'll become as pompous as the others soon enough."

I recognized the dismissal and let myself out of the room. For a moment, I watched Scout clean up. She worked at lightning speed, and she seemed comfortable alone. She was right. I had plenty of things to do and little time to do them. My first day only had an hour and a half left.

The office was busy and loud. The other therapists had finished with their last clients and were now working on their documentation. Somehow, they managed to complete paperwork and hold multiple conversations at the same time.

"No, you have to soak them in the moonlight first," Jewel was saying to Andy. Andy, looking skeptical, held a handful of blue stones with ancient runes engraved on them. "Just try it! It's good energy."

Imogen's voice pierced through the air as she complained to Ariel. "And then I was all, 'No, Dorian. That's not the way it works.' And then he was all, 'I'm the patient. I can refuse treatment!' Ugh, like, what are you even doing here, Dorian?"

I gathered my potential patients' files and sat at the desk and laptop that had been assigned to me earlier that day. Within minutes, my concentration was wrecked. With so many voices competing around me, I couldn't focus on the task at hand.

"And then he puked all over my brand-new scrubs!"

Imogen made a horrible retching sound to accompany her story, and that was the end of the line for me. I picked up the laptop and the files and excused myself from the office.

I wandered around, searching for a quiet place to work. First, I returned to the therapy room, but it was locked and I didn't have a set of keys yet. Then I pulled up the pdf map on my phone and spotted something called the "overlook" on the west side of the building.

The overlook, it turned out, was an enormous balcony that spanned the length of the Center's left side, the view from which was unparalleled. A beautiful lake stretched all the way to the base of the greater mountains, the caps of which soared into the sky. The sunset cast a pink glow over everything.

I stepped outside, gaping at the view. A chilly breeze nipped at my nose and ears, but until the sun went down, it would be bearable. Since there was nowhere to sit, I settled cross-legged on the deck itself, propped the computer in my lap, and began to work.

As I was finishing up, I heard the sliding door to the balcony shift open. A man in his early thirties came outside. He wore black slacks, a dark green shirt unbuttoned at the collar, and a look of exhaustion. His eyes caught mine, and he blinked in surprise.

"Oh," he said. "Sorry. People aren't usually out here at this time of day." He peered at the open files around me. "Odd place to work, isn't it?"

"I can go," I offered, stacking the files. "I'm finished here."

"Nah." He sat on the deck too. "You must be Natasha Bell. I'm Eli."

Nerves rattled in my stomach. I did not expect to meet Eli Trevino whilst sitting on the ground outside with a stack of patient files that technically should not have been removed from the therapists' office.

"How was your first day?" he asked. "What do you think of the place so far?"

"It's great," I replied honestly. "I've never worked in a facility as nice as this one before. I'm excited to get started."

"We're excited to have you on board."

For such a young guy, he'd already accumulated wrinkles around his eyes and mouth. It didn't help that his dark hair contrasted so heavily with his fair skin. The difference highlighted the subtle bags beneath his green eyes. Despite his obvious fatigue, he was the nicest-looking psychiatrist I'd ever seen.

"Any questions?" he asked, though his expression begged me not to come up with any.

My inquiry popped out of my mouth before I had a chance to wonder why I was asking it. "What's it like working in Ward 13?"

Eli smiled wryly. "You've heard the gossip, huh?"

"No, not much. Just curious."

"It's rewarding," he answered. "But it's hard. Ward 13 gets a bad reputation because of the stigma attached to mental health, but I'm doing my best to dispel that stigma. Ever since my father—" He trailed off, looking across at the mountains. "I'm doing my best."

"Eli?"

A slender blonde woman, wearing a sleek black dress and fiddling with diamond earrings, appeared at the balcony door. She waved Eli to his feet.

"What are you doing out here?" she demanded. "We

have to be at this charity dinner in five minutes. Where's your tie? Come on!"

Eli shared a secret eye roll with me, making me smile, before the blonde woman took him by the hand and led him away. I shivered, collected my things, and headed inside to find Imogen waiting for me.

"You're not supposed to take files out of the office," she reprimanded. "Something could have happened to them."

"Got 'em all right here. Nothing to worry about it." I tried to walk by her.

"He's married, you know," she called after me.

"Who?" I asked without turning around.

"Eli."

"Good to know. Thanks, Imogen."

I waved my thanks. From what I could tell, she cared more about this crucial information than I did.

4

———————————

*A*s the weeks passed by, I settled into a comfortable routine. My room at the Shadows Inn began to feel like home. Once, I perused potential apartments in the dining room to have Baz rip the newspaper out of my grasp and demand I stay for as long as I needed. I suspected the teenager was more attached to Jean Paul than she was to me, but I did notice Baz often asked my advice when her mother wasn't around. Lauren was one of the best landlords I could have asked for. The inn was impeccably cared for, the food was excellent thanks to Marcel, and I didn't have to hand over an arm and a leg to afford my place there. Furthermore, Lauren always provided excellent conversation, especially when she told stories of past guests who stayed at the resort.

"This guest swore up and down that Marcel had served him heavy cream in his coffee," she was saying one early morning as we had our regular breakfast of omelets and coffee together. "Apparently, this guy was counting calories and could only drink skim milk. You know

Marcel; he scoffs at skim milk. He doesn't order it for the kitchen, so I knew that Marcel was lying like a rug as he repeatedly told this guest it was *not* heavy cream." She chuckled to herself. "I don't know how he kept a straight face. I sure couldn't."

Laughing at the visual, I refilled my coffee cup halfway. "I wish I could have seen that."

"If you stick around long enough, you'll witness our antics at some point." Lauren pushed the creamer across the table for me, and I added a dollop to my drink. "How's work so far? Do you like it?"

"It's great," I said. "I was nervous about starting this program, but I get more confidence with each class that I teach."

"Are there more patients participating now?"

"Yes, we opened up the movement therapy classes to outpatient as well," I answered. "So my schedule is full."

Lauren lifted her mug to tap against mine. "I'm glad to hear it. I have to admit. I never had the highest opinion of the Trevino Center."

My brow furrowed. "Why's that?"

"It's my own fault," Lauren sighed, sitting away from the table and cradling her coffee in her lap. "When my mother was committed, I made no attempts to see her. We didn't have the best relationship. I eased my guilt by blaming Trevino for her disappearance."

"Did the Center do something?"

"No. I drove up there once, knowing full well visiting times were over," she replied. Her eyes glazed over. "The Center, of course, turned me away and told me to come back tomorrow. I never did, and I used that experience as an excuse not to try again." She cleared her throat and

49

returned to the present. "Anyway, I'm glad you're doing well there. Speaking of which, aren't you going to be late?"

It was half past six, and the drive to Trevino took at least a half hour.

"If that damn road through the mountain wasn't so winding, I could make it there in five minutes." I chugged my coffee, ate a danish in three bites, and brushed the crumbs off my scrubs. I'd finally gotten ones to match everyone else at the office and retired the ugly sea water polo shirts. "Can you remind Baz to cut back on Jean Paul's dry food? He's gained three pounds since I moved here, and I'm scared he might become inert matter."

"I'll take care of it." Lauren shooed me off. "Go, go!"

THE FIRST CLASS of the day was seated yoga. It was one of my go-to routines for my patients because it was easy on their bodies but still made them feel better. Also, it helped my wheelchair patients not to feel left out. As I led the class through modified poses to stretch the side body, shoulders, neck, and arms, Andy and Jewel watched from the back and assisted when necessary. I liked the two older therapists. Though they were as conversational as the others, they were far less interested in gossip than Ariel and Imogen. They didn't make me feel as if we were all competing for some unknown prize. For whatever reason, Ariel and Imogen always acted like proud peacocks around me, spreading their feathers for all to see.

"They're threatened by you," Andy had muttered to me once, after witnessing a curt interaction between me and the others. "They see how good you are at your job, and it scares them. Rumors have been going around that Trevino is looking to cut back. Money problems."

"Cut back?" I asked. "Why would the Center have hired me if they were trying to save money?"

Andy shrugged. "Got me beat, but keep an eye on your competition. Especially Imogen. No one's ever seen Eli take an immediate liking to anyone like he has to you. That bothers Imogen."

Since I was hired, Eli made frequent appearances in the therapy wing. To me, it seemed normal for the boss to make sure his employees were working as expected, but I soon learned this was unnatural behavior for Eli. Usually, he remained ensconced in either Ward 13 or his office. Often, he visited my classes to observe, but he never said anything. He simply nodded his head, smiled, and went on his way. In Imogen's book, this evidently meant he was favoring me.

"Why is it my problem if something bothers Imogen?" I asked Andy.

He chuckled. "Perhaps you haven't noticed, but Imogen is the unofficial queen of the therapy office. It's best to get on her good side. Otherwise, she can make things uncomfortable. I suggest getting to know her. She's a tough cookie to crack, but she's gooey in the center."

I wrinkled my nose. "Not sure I want to crack her, to be honest."

He laughed at that.

"SPREAD THE FINGERS as wide as possible," I instructed in my motivational voice. "Reach for the sky! High, higher, as high as you can go! Now come down softly and breathe out." I demonstrated at the front of the class, seated in the same stiff-backed chairs as everyone else. I brought my palms together. "Palms to your heart, everyone. Let's take a moment to appreciate the time we've taken out of our day to move together. Would anyone like to share an appreciative thought with the class today?"

Lenny, a stooped man in his eighties with more mobility issues than I could count, was the first one to croak, "I appreciate not being dead!"

Everyone laughed, and I cracked a smile. "Thank you, Lenny," I said. "Anyone else? Appreciative thoughts? Maybe an inspirational quote?"

A woman with tight blonde curls raised her hand. She was one of my original patients and attended my classes every day. I'd watched her improve slowly but surely over the past couple of weeks.

"Yes, Carol?" I called on her.

"I'm appreciative of you, Nat," Carol said, smiling softly. She was a quiet soul who did not often speak, so I leaned in to listen. "Thanks to you, I'm being discharged earlier than expected."

A wave of emotion washed over me. My lower lip trembled, but I clasped it between my teeth before my patients could notice. "That's amazing! I'm so glad to hear that, Carol."

"She's not the only one," another patient, Marty, chimed in. "I was supposed to be here for another six weeks, but Andy is so impressed with my progress that he wants to send me home in five days!"

Andy grinned from the back of the class and nodded to confirm it. Other patients expressed similar sentiments. Though not all of them were able to be discharged early like Marty and Carol, each and every one who attended my classes regularly stated that they hadn't felt so happy and energized in months.

I waved my hands to quiet the class. "Thank you so much, everyone. It means a lot to me that these classes are efficient. Let's close it out with a moment of silence and reflection."

At the end of each class, I encouraged everyone to clear their thoughts and meditate on their goals thus far. The length of the moment varied. Sometimes, the class was so quiet and contemplative that I let them go on for ten to fifteen minutes. Other times, it was almost impossible to achieve silence what with all the fiddling and wheelchairs squeaking, so I kept it short.

Normally, I took the time to do my own reflection. I silently reviewed what I thought had gone well during the class and what seemed difficult for each patient. Later, it would help me to note those struggles for future reference. Today, though, I found it difficult to focus on my work. My heart jumped like a giddy pony galloping through a field of wildflowers. I kept peeking through my eyelids to admire my patients. I was so proud of how far they had all come in a few short weeks.

After the reflection, I dismissed the class. Andy and Jewel began helping everyone back to their rooms. Scout, as usual, came in to clean up. We nodded to each other, and I got out of her way. Since that first day, I didn't bother trying to help. Scout made it clear she preferred to work alone.

Lenny cornered me in the hallway on my way back to

the therapists' office, or rather Jewel cornered me by pushing Lenny's wheelchair into my path.

"He wouldn't let me take him back to his room," Jewel said. "He said he wanted you to do it."

"Damn straight!" Lenny said, his voice croaking like a frog's. If I had to guess, Lenny spent most of his youth blowing through cigarette packs. "It's our tradition. Isn't it, Nat?"

I grinned. "Since when?"

"Don't you stand me up, young lady!" Lenny said, wagging a finger in my face even though he was smiling. "I'm too old, and my heart can't stand it!"

"I got it," I told Jewel. Taking control of Lenny's wheelchair, I began to roll him back to his room. "How was class for you today, Lenny?"

Part of the job was not picking favorites. I gave equal time and attention to all of my patients, but I couldn't help but gravitate toward Lenny. A lot of older people at Trevino had resigned themselves to their fate, but Lenny refused to be one of them. No matter how his body betrayed him, he always had a smile on his face.

"I can lift my left arm higher than I could last week!" he informed me proudly. "Look!" With obvious effort, he raised his left hand to the level of his ear and set it down again with a long out breath. "See?"

"Wow, Lenny," I said, genuinely excited. "Soon, you'll be out of this chair and salsa-ing down the hallway."

"Ooh, do you offer salsa classes?"

I smiled. "Not yet. My dance sessions are more therapeutic and interpretive. It's all about getting comfortable with your body and creating a flow."

"I can flow!" Lenny attempted one of the dance moves

popular with teenagers on the Internet these days, where he pumped his arms, slowly, from one side of his wheelchair to the other and gave a feeble hip thrust. "Look at me. I'm a-flowin'."

"You sure are. Here's your room, sir."

Lenny's room was in the long-term nursing area of the Center. He had one of the best views out his window, the same view of the lake and mountains from the balcony upstairs. It was decorated with every manner of origami animals. Books of colorful folding paper were stacked on the shelf in the corner. With his slow, sausage-like fingers, it took Lenny over an hour to fold anything into a recognizable shape, but he did it without help.

"What are you going to fold today?" I asked as I helped him transfer from the wheelchair to the comfortable armchair he liked to sit in by the window.

"What would you like me to fold?"

I gazed around the room. "I don't see a giraffe in here yet."

"A giraffe…" Lenny muttered. His fingers worked with invisible paper on his lap, as if he were figuring out in his head how to create what I'd asked. "I'm sure I could do it. Hand me those papers, eh?"

I put the book of folding paper in his lap and patted his hand. "No extra ice cream today. The nurse said your blood sugar's been spiking."

"Psh!" He feebly waved this off. "We're all going to die some day!"

I rolled my eyes and left Lenny to his origami. In the hallway, I glanced into the room across the way. A woman lay in bed, staring at the ceiling with a vacant expression. I tapped on the door jamb, and she tilted her head to look at me.

"Oh, Nat," she said. "It's you."

I came into the room. "Missed you in class today. Too tired?"

The woman, Bonnie, was only thirty-nine years old, but she had suffered a major stroke that made much of her body foreign to her. When she spoke, she rolled the words around in her mouth like clothes in a washing machine. I was one of the few therapists, other than the speech specialists, who understood her on the first try. As such, I was also one of the few therapists she cooperated with.

"Exhausted," she admitted. "Done."

"May I sit?" She nodded, so I perched on the edge of her bed. "The yoga bores you, doesn't it?"

She didn't reply, but I saw the answer in her eyes.

"Don't worry," I said with a smile. "I'm not offended. Why don't you try my dance class instead? I think you'll like it."

Bonnie returned her gaze to the ceiling. "I don't know, Nat."

"I have one this afternoon at two," I told her. "That gives you enough time to eat lunch and take a nice nap. What do you say?"

"I know you mean well, but I don't have the motivation today."

"You don't have to make any promises to me," I said, patting the covers as I stood up. "Take some time to think about it. Have a nap. If you feel well enough to come, I'll see you there. If not, no hard feelings. Sound good?"

Bonnie managed a feeble smile. "You're annoying."

"I know."

I TOOK the long way back to the office, eager for some time alone with my thoughts before I had to bear the daily lunchtime extravaganza. This path through the Center passed by the Center's business offices. I waved hello to Hilary, who waved back. Then I glanced into the largest office—Eli's—which sat in the direct center of the building's architecture. Oftentimes, it was empty, but every once in a while, I caught sight of the same well-dressed blonde woman who had come to fetch Eli after our first meeting. She was his wife, I presumed, but if that was the case, why did she always appear to be working at his desk?

She was there today, her long mane slicked back in a fantastic ponytail. She wore a plum-colored satin pantsuit with a plunging neckline. A diamond pendant dangled from a long necklace and settled against her chest to show the amount of skin there. Though the outfit was not profane in any way, the woman looked like she might be more comfortable at a fashion magazine's office than at the Center.

As I passed, rolling my feet from heel to toe so she wouldn't hear my footsteps, the woman murmured ferociously to herself.

"What is he *doing?*" she said, resting her forehead in her hand as she flipped through some sort of book. "Hemorrhaging money, that's what he's doing. Jesus—"

A floorboard beneath my foot creaked, and the woman glanced up right as I darted beyond her line of vision. I made the first turn around the closest corner, even though this hallway didn't lead back to the therapists' office, and waited. As I listened, the woman's heels clicked into the hallway. A few moments later, they retreated to Eli's office, and the door shut behind her.

"I HEAR your patients are practically flying home."

Imogen's statement took a few moments to reach my ears. I was distracted by my lunch—leftovers courtesy of Marcel again—and a mindless game on my phone I played as an excuse not to participate in the usual conversation at this time of day.

"Huh?" I said, pulling my focus from my phone.

"Your patients," Imogen repeated, blinking pointedly at me. "I heard a few are being released early. I hope you don't mind I won't be recommending any of mine leave therapy before their courses of treatment are finished."

Of course, this wasn't about my movement program's success. It was about Imogen.

"I suppose I wouldn't release them either if I felt my work hadn't allowed them to progress as much as I hoped," I replied in a light voice. Behind Imogen's fake smile, Andy made a slashing gesture across his throat. I coughed and changed my tone. "Imogen, isn't your birthday coming up? Are you doing anything fun? What are celebrations like in Lone Elm?"

Imogen's manner pulled a one-eighty. She forgot about our inane rivalry in favor of her best subject: herself. "Don't you worry, Natasha," she said. "We celebrate as well as the city girls. Have you ever been axe throwing?"

"Sounds dangerous."

"It's a controlled environment," Andy said. "There are targets."

"And booze," Imogen added.

"So we're back to dangerous," I commented.

"It's fun," Ariel chimed in. "You'll see."

A knock on the door interrupted the conversation. Eli stood at the entrance. Imogen dropped her fork. Lettuce from her salad plopped to the floor and sprayed caesar dressing across Ariel's scrub pants.

"Hi, everyone," Eli said. "How's it going?" Everyone muttered a polite response. Eli nodded. "I wanted to drop by and congratulate you, Natasha. Two separate patients sought me out to tell me what a positive effect you've had on them in the last few weeks. That's never happened here before."

Imogen's face dropped. I tried not to laugh. "Thank you, Eli," I said.

He cleared his throat nervously as everyone stared at him in awe. "That's all. Have a great rest of your day, everyone. Natasha, keep up the good work."

"I will. Thanks."

As Eli left, Andy and Jewel turned to me with wide eyes.

"Wow," Jewel said. "I don't think that's ever happened before."

"It's not that big of a deal."

Imogen, regaining her composure, wiggled her shoulders and sat higher in her seat. "Nat's right. Eli's trying to be more present in all areas of the Center. He complimented me the other day too. Privately."

I wrangled my expression into submission, not daring

to turn Imogen's adverb into a joke. "I'm sure he did, Imogen."

"Back to axe throwing!" Ariel said brightly. "Are you coming with us, Nat? It's going to be a blast."

"Tonight?"

Ariel nodded.

"Is that all right with you, Imogen?" I asked. "It's *your* birthday after all."

The war on Imogen's face was valiant enough to break swords and shields. Her lip trembled. Her nose wrinkled. Her eyes narrowed. Would she call a draw?

A smile spread from one end of her cheeks to the other. "Of course it's all right! Therapist night! Woohoo!"

AFTER WORK, I picked up a birthday card at a local shop and a gift certificate for the café. I'd noticed Imogen always came in with a cup of coffee from that place each morning. After changing out of my scrubs, I met the rest of the therapists at a bar called Good Times between Lone Elm and the next town over. It turned out axe throwing wasn't a daily event. The bar set up the targets once a month, and the excitement drew quite a crowd from all around.

Imogen promptly ordered drinks. Two vodkas later, she sang like a canary. Mostly, she moaned about her patients, though I had to hand it to her; she never broke patient confidentiality by mentioning any of their names. If Imogen was the queen of therapists, Ariel was her lady in waiting. Ariel talked less, but she was by no means quiet. Her conversations were less patient-based and geared more toward which reality television star was causing drama in Hollywood now.

Less enthused to talk about work and the Kardashians, I drifted off to share a table with Andy and Jewel. We toasted to a good day's work, threw some axes, and enjoyed each other's company. I learned a few things about my coworkers. Andy, it turned out, was born and raised in Memphis but had moved to New York City to be with his girlfriend after several years of long distance. When they broke up, he found the job at Trevino and decided to stay there. Jewel, out of the current employees, had worked at Trevino the longest. According to Andy, she had knowledge of Trevino's inner workings, though she never shared it with anyone else. Eventually, Andy and Jewel dissolved into a conversation of their own, and though they didn't mean to exclude me, I found myself nursing a bottle of beer all by my lonesome.

When Imogen drunkenly stepped up to the line to toss axes, I got out of dodge. Across the room, I noticed Scout drinking at a table alone. I stopped by the bar and ordered another round of Scout's drink from the bartender. It was soda water. I had it sent over anyway.

When the bartender pointed at me through the crowd and Scout turned to look, I raised my bottle in thanks. She lifted the soda water in a return salute.

5

The next morning, great joy was brought to me in the form of Imogen's hangover. I'd stopped after a few beers, but Imogen's vodka-fueled birthday rage had gone on for hours. She drooped over her desk, her hair limp and unwashed, with last night's mascara smudged across her eyelids. Ariel arrived, looking slightly fresher, and handed Imogen a pack of makeup-removing wipes.

"Good morning, Vietnam!" Andy boomed as he came into the office. Imogen and Ariel winced. "Ooh, it's a war zone in here. What's the damage, ladies?"

"Lower your voice," Imogen said through clenched teeth.

Leaving the other therapists to duke it out, I skipped off to Lenny's room. It was almost time for morning class. Usually, Andy helped Lenny to my movement sessions, but I'd decided to surprise him that morning. When I reached his room, however, it was empty.

Lenny's bed was freshly made. His armchair was gone,

and the wardrobe was free of his clothes. Most disturbing of all was the lack of origami animals. I spotted a crumpled piece of paper in the wastebasket, plucked it out, and smoothed it. It was a half-completed origami giraffe.

"He passed last night," a voice said behind me. It was Scout, on her way to do her morning rounds. "While we were all out at the bar."

My throat closed up. "Quickly?"

"In his sleep."

"Okay. Thanks, Scout."

I TAUGHT my classes that day with remarkably less enthusiasm than usual. The seated yoga class was too quiet without Lenny's funny comments. My sadness was contagious. Soon enough, all of the therapy patients were moping around, not just in the movement sessions but in everyone's sessions.

"What's gotten into them today?" Imogen demanded at lunch. She'd regained some composure with the help of an electrolyte drink and a fresh face of makeup, though she dared not eat anything in case the leftover alcohol in her system wanted to rebel further. "All three of my patients refused treatment this morning."

"Lenny died," Jewel informed her. "Everyone's feeling it."

"The old guy who hits on everyone?" Imogen's lips puckered. "So what? Weren't we waiting for that to happen anyway?"

"Don't you have any compassion?" I snapped. "Lenny was a person too. He lived here for last few years of his life. We were the only family he had."

63

"We?" Imogen questioned. "Honey, you've only been here a few weeks. What would you know about connecting with *our* patients?"

Andy rolled his chair between mine and Imogen's desks. "Let's take a break," he suggested. "Everyone's a little on edge. It won't do us any good to bicker."

As usual, I abandoned the therapists' office early to set up the room for my next class. The first person to arrive was Bonnie, who hadn't come yesterday as I'd asked. She walked alone, leaning heavily on a cane, without a therapist to guide her.

"Did you make a break for it?" I asked, hurrying over to help her. "I could have gotten Andy to help you."

She shooed me away and shuffled to a chair by herself. "I'm tired of needing people to help me. Isn't that why I'm here? To learn to do things for myself again?"

"Yes," I agreed. "But until you can, it's safer to do them with supervision."

The walk from her room to the dance class had caused her forehead to dampen with sweat. "Did you know I'm a mother of three? Little boys. Eleven, eight, and three. Every time they visit, they ask me when Mommy's coming home. I don't know what to tell them."

"If you don't mind me asking, why aren't you in outpatient care?" I said, continuing to set up the room now that Bonnie was stationary.

Her eyes lost what little shine was in them, which happened when Bonnie was feeling discouraged. "I would be a burden to my husband. As it is, he works full time *and* takes cares of the boys. I can't ask him to take care of me too."

"I think he might have a different opinion," I said. "I'm sure he'd rather have you at home, and your kids would do."

Bonnie shook her head. "You don't understand."

"Maybe I don't."

She studied me as I hooked my phone up to the speaker system to play music. "What's wrong with you? You're usually perkier."

I heaved a sigh. "Lenny died."

"Aw, honey. That's the way life goes."

"I know." I pretended to fiddle with the phone cord, but I was actually keeping my gaze away from Bonnie so she couldn't see my watering eyes. "But Lenny was one of the first ones to join my movement classes. He had so much faith in himself to get better, and then he didn't get the opportunity."

"You'll affect plenty more people at Trevino," Bonnie said. "Hell, I'm here, aren't I?"

BONNIE, as it turned out, was a magnificent dancer despite her unfortunate restrictions, though I wasn't basing my opinion on any sort of actual dance talent. It had more to do with the way she lost herself in the move-ment and the music. For the entire class, her eyes remained bright as she jerkily pranced across the room, bobbed to the tempo, and waved her cane like a conduc-tor's baton. She was the sole bright spot, the thing that got me through the class.

Ten minutes before the end, Eli came in to watch. Try

as I might, I couldn't hide my lackluster teachings. During the reflection, I was the one who fidgeted too much, distracting the patients from their meditations. I ended it early and turned away from Eli to help Bonnie.

"That was wonderful," Bonnie said breathlessly, using her cane for support as she spun around. "I didn't think I could move like this anymore."

"Make sure not to overexert yourself," I warned her. "I'm sending someone to check on you later. You're going to be sore tomorrow, for sure."

"Oh, don't be a killjoy."

Bonnie allowed Andy to escort her back to the room, but I had a feeling it was because Eli hadn't left yet. I hoped he would go, but he waited until the last patient was gone before approaching me.

"Is it safe to say you are also experiencing post-traumatic stress from Imogen's birthday extravaganza last night?" Eli asked, a note of teasing in his voice.

"No, I lost a patient."

Eli sobered at once. "Leonard Buskin. He was a good man. I was sad to hear of his passing."

My eyes threatened to drop tears. I noticed Scout in the hallway, waiting for us to finish so she could come in and clean.

"Natasha, patients come and go," Eli said, drawing my gaze upward to his soft expression. "It happens all the time, and when it does, you can't allow it to affect your treatment of other patients. This is part of the job."

I sniffled. "I know, but it's the first time it's happened to me."

"I understand." Eli shuffled from one foot to the other. "I came to ask you a question. Would you consider putting together a program for the patients in Ward 13?"

I looked sharply at him. "They aren't therapy patients."

"To my knowledge, movement therapy is effective in treating a number of mental ailments as well as physical ones," Eli said professionally. "Do you disagree?"

"Of course not," I replied. "I did the research myself. Sorry, I guess I thought you had to be specifically certified to work in Ward 13."

Eli smiled. "You *are* specifically certified. Are you interested?"

I hesitated. One of the things Imogen and Ariel liked to gossip about most were the goings-on behind the doors to Ward 13, and the news was almost never good. The worst of the worst were sent to Trevino for mental health treatment, and though I was never one to believe the stigmas, the talk was severe enough to scare me. Not to mention, every time I walked past those double swinging doors, someone was screaming behind them.

"Can I think about it?" I asked Eli. "Or this is a mandatory assignment?"

He held up his hands. "Take all the time you need. It's not mandatory, but I will kindly take this opportunity to remind you that you signed a contract. If I recall correctly, you did agree to create programs for all patients in this facility, not just the ones you favor."

My cheeks turned pink. "I don't favor anyone. Let me think about it, and I'll let you know how I might proceed with a program to fit the needs of those in Ward 13."

"That's all I'm asking." He made to turn away but paused. "I'm sorry about Lenny. You should know that every time we lose a patient, I take it personally."

He walked away, shoulders slightly more rounded than when he'd appeared at the end of my class. I looked after him, wondering if the other employees didn't give Eli Trevino enough credit.

WHEN I ARRIVED home at the Shadows Inn, Marcel was, as usual, in a mood. A family of six had been staying at the inn for the past week. Not only did their children have various diet restrictions, but they weren't particularly clean. Additionally, random items that belonged to the inn had gone missing, like valuable books and fountain pens from the library. All in all, the family's stay had been stressful for the chef, the maids, and Lauren, and we were all keen for the sextet to check out. Unfortunately, we had one more day to get through.

"Preposterous!" Marcel roared from the kitchen. His voice echoed through the dining room and lobby, scaring the couple who'd come for a romantic getaway off their early dinner. "I do not keep such ingredients on hand! Dairy-free, gluten-free, egg-free? I cannot work like this!"

Something shattered, and the couple hurried off with wide eyes. I peeked through the swinging doors into the kitchen. Marcel was alone, except for his assistant, who was glued to the far wall to avoid Marcel's throwing arm as the chef tossed metal pan lids across the room like flying discs.

"Whoa!" I caught Marcel's elbow and confiscated the lid he meant to launch next. "Let's take some deep breaths, Marcel."

"I cannot breathe!" he retorted, snorting through his nose. His finger quivered as he pointed upward to the larger rooms above. "Did you hear what they requested for dinner tonight? Macaroni and cheese! I do not make macaroni and cheese, but when I do, I expect it is made with *macaroni* and real *cheese!*"

I wrinkled my nose. "What the hell do they expect it to be made of then?"

He waved his arms excitedly. "Exactly!"

Behind him, the assistant chef shook his head vigorously. I'd accidentally egged Marcel on rather than calming him down.

"Marcel, you are a professional chef with years of experience," I reminded the fuming Frenchman. "There is no challenge you can't rise to. What do you need from the store to make this fake mac and cheese? I'll be happy to get it for you."

Marcel's lip twitched. "I suppose I can write up a list."

"Excellent."

ARMED with Marcel's list of odd ingredients, I took my coat from the closet behind the check-in desk. Jean Paul wound himself around my legs in figure eights and complained loudly. Since I'd started my job at the Center, we hadn't spent a lot of time together. I supposed that was why he'd recently taken to sleeping on my face at night.

"Sorry, buddy," I said, bending down to smooth him from head to tail. "I'll play with you when I get back."

"Where are you going?" Baz, who'd walked in through the back door, asked. Her cheeks were pinker than usual, and her eyes had a watery look to them, but it wasn't cold enough outside yet to warrant such physical reactions. "Can I come?"

I held up the list. "Marcel needs a few things from the market, and your mom is out running errands already. You're welcome to tag along, but don't you do homework around this time?"

Baz crossed her arms and wiped her nose on the sleeve of her puffy jacket. "I don't want to do homework right now."

If she wasn't an A student with phenomenal SAT scores, I might have recommended she stay at home. As it was, she looked like she needed a break.

"All right," I agreed. "Come on. You can pick out some treats for Jean Paul."

THE LOCAL GROCERY store bustled with customers. The pre-dinner time slot was the busiest of the day, as everyone needed to get those last few ingredients they'd forgotten during their previous shop. Baz and I made a game out of locating the strange items on Marcel's list, as they weren't things either of us shopped for often.

"Tapioca starch," I read off.

"Baking aisle," Baz guessed.

"Hmm." I looked up at the signs above each aisle, but none of them included substitute flours. "I'm going to go with the gluten-free shelf. Break!"

We separated, each going to check if our check was correct. I scanned the small shelf of gluten-free items, but tapioca starch was not among them. However, a blue box of something else caught my eye.

"Got it!" Baz appeared at the end of the row, holding a bag of tapioca starch high above her head in triumph. "Five points for me."

I held up the blue box. "I got the gluten-free macaroni. I get five points too, right?"

"That's not fair. We weren't looking for it yet."

"Oh, come on."

"Fine. Three points."

"Fair enough." I marked our winnings on the top of Marcel's list. When I finished, I caught Baz staring at something behind me. Turning around, I saw a girl in a cheerleading outfit with a long braid at the end of the aisle. "Who's that?"

Baz stepped to her left so I blocked her from view of the girl. "No one."

"Yeah, right. Is she the reason you were crying when you came?" I asked. "What happened? You want me to go punch her?"

"No, don't!" Baz's eyes began to water as a tall boy joined the cheerleader and slung his arm around her shoulder. "Forget about it. Can we get out of here?"

"We still have to find nutritional yeast."

"I'll get it."

She ducked in the opposite direction of her classmates. As I turned on my heel, a familiar blonde woman knocked into me. My basket dropped from my grasp, scattering Marcel's groceries across the floor.

"Oh, God," said the woman, kneeling to pick up my items. "I am so sorry! I was in such a rush. I didn't see you there."

"I can relate." I swapped the crumpled box of macaroni for a new one off the shelf. "Don't worry about it. We all have days like that."

She swept her long ponytail over her shoulder. "I'm starting to feel like all of my days are like this." She paused to examine my face. "Wait a minute. You look familiar. Do I know you?"

"I work at Trevino. I've seen you around there."

I might not have recognized her were it not for her unmistakable hair. Instead of a silky suit or tight-fitting dress, she wore dark wash jeans and a red-and-orange flannel top. In this attire, she blended in with the locals without trouble.

"Oh!" the woman said, clapping her palm to her forehead. "You're Eli's new therapist! He talks about you all the time." She offered her hand. "I'm Lindsay Trevino, Eli's wife."

We shook hands, then she grabbed a random pack of gluten-free crackers and put them in her cart. After staring at them for a moment, she returned them to the shelf. "You must think so poorly of me. I usually make a point of introducing myself to all of the new employees. After all, I'm the one who signs your paychecks."

"You work there?" It made sense, considering all the times I'd seen her in Eli's office.

"I have for years," she answered. "Since Eli's father died last year, I've been picking up extra duties to help Eli."

"I heard about that," I said. "I'm sorry for your loss."

Her brow softened. "Yes, thank you. Eli was more affected than I was, but I did work closely with his father. Things haven't been the same since, which is why I'm running around like a chicken." She leaned in and lowered her voice. "Speaking of chicken, what do you know about pot pie? It's one of Eli's favorite meals to eat when he's feeling down. I thought I'd surprise him, but I'm not the world's best chef."

"You can short cut it with canned creamed soup and

frozen mixed vegetables," I suggested. "And top it with biscuits if you don't want to bother with pastry crust."

"That's genius!" Her eyes lit up. "Why don't you join us for dinner?"

"I don't think—"

"Please," Lindsay pleaded, grasping my forearm. "Let me make up for my horrible behavior at work. Besides, you seem to be full of cooking knowledge."

Baz reappeared, waving a small container. "Found the nutritional yeast. Let's get out of here."

I shot Lindsay an apologetic look. "Maybe some other time?"

Baz glanced between us. "If you guys have plans, go for it. I can take the ingredients back to Marcel on my own. Hey, Mrs. Trevino."

Lindsay smiled warmly. "Hi, Baz. How's school going?"

"It's going." She peeked into Lindsay's basket. "Chicken pot pie? I like it with biscuits."

Lindsay clapped me on the shoulder. "I'll have Natasha bring you some leftovers."

DESPITE THE DINNER HOUR, Lindsay's work phone kept her busy. As she dashed around the kitchen, she kept the phone pressed to her ear, arguing with the caller. When she hung up one call, another one came in. The fifth time this happened, she spilled a can of creamed soup across the countertop. The phone dropped from her ear and plopped into the soup. As Lindsay swore under her breath, I took pity on her.

"Go," I whispered, grabbing a roll of paper towels from the counter to clean up the mess. "I'll take care of it."

"Are you sure?" She plucked her phone from the soup with two fingers and wiped off the front. "Thank goodness it's water resistant."

"I'm sure. Take your call. I can manage this."

She mouthed her thanks and returned her attention to the phone. "Yes, I'm here. No, I won't sign those papers."

As Lindsay disappeared into another wing of the house, I blew out a long sigh. The last thing I expected to do tonight was make dinner for the Trevinos in their beautiful home. The place was like a modern-day castle. Though I wasn't much of a cook, I envied the massive kitchen with its sleek stainless steel appliances and several square footage of counter space. Floor-to-ceiling windows looked out on the mountains. The sunset cast purple light across the dining room table.

Eli arrived home as I slid the completed pot pie out of the oven and placed it on the counter. He placed his briefcase on the counter and looked in either direction.

"I'm sorry," he said. "I thought I hired you as a therapist, not a personal chef."

I chuckled. "I ran into Lindsay at the grocery store. She invited me to dinner."

He eyed the browned biscuits atop the pot pie. "She invited you or she ordered you to make it for us?"

"She had to take a call."

"I see. My apologies. I'll remind her that our employees at the Center are not required to serve us at home."

I shrugged. "It was no problem. I volunteered anyway."

Lindsay came in, tucking her phone into her pocket. "I am so sorry." She kissed Eli's cheek. "Hi, honey. Your accountant is as dumb as a bag of rocks." She noticed the chicken pot pie on the counter. "That looks wonderful, Natasha! What would I have done without you?" She squeezed my hand like we were old friends then bustled off to the cabinets. "We need plates. And wine. Lots of wine."

AFTER DINNER IN THEIR COMPANY, I decided I liked Eli and Lindsay Trevino. As we ate, their professionalism fell away, leaving normal people in the wake. We talked little of work and instead shared stories from other facets of our lives. I heard tales of Eli and Lindsay's early dating days and shared some of my tamer adventures as well. What I liked most about them was the spasmodic nature of their relationship. They never quite appeared to be on the same page, but neither one of them seemed concerned about it.

"Tomorrow, we have that golf event at the country club," Lindsay reminded Eli over the chocolate ice cream she'd dug out of the freezer for dessert. "I laid out your blue tie."

"I thought that was on Friday?"

"I wrote it in your schedule book for Thursday."

"I don't look in my schedule book."

"Whose fault is that?" Lindsay planted a kiss atop Eli's head as she collected his empty crystal bowl and put it in the sink. "Blue tie. Tomorrow at four. Don't forget."

"Natasha, remind me," Eli joked. "Otherwise, she'll have me killed."

As I laughed, I caught sight of the kitchen clock and hastily stood up. "It's ten already? Jean Paul is going to be furious with me."

"Boyfriend?" Lindsay ventured curiously.

"My cat."

They both chuckled. Eli collected my coat from by the door.

"Let me drive you home," he offered. "It's a long walk."

6

*J*ean Paul refused to affiliate himself with me that night. He pranced off to cuddle with Baz instead. In the morning, he played hard to get, but I did manage to pet the end of his tail before leaving for work. As soon as I walked into the office, Imogen pounced on me.

"What was it like?" she demanded. "Is their house enormous? Someone said they had the same interior decorator as Cher. Is it true all the door handles are made of crystals?"

I ducked around her and hung my coat on the back of my desk chair. "What are you talking about?"

Imogen crossed her arms. "Everyone knows you went to the Trevinos' house for dinner last night. It's all over the Center."

"Wow, news spreads fast here."

"Don't act like you didn't go."

I sat down, scooted my chair closer to the desk, and logged in to my computer. "I'm not. I did go."

Imogen sat on my mouse pad, making it difficult to navigate the documentation system. "Under what circumstances? The Trevinos never have employees over at their house. Eli doesn't like to mix work with pleasure."

I almost rolled my eyes. "His wife literally ran into me at the grocery store and invited me over to apologize. That's all. Eli seemed fine with it."

Imogen's huff rustled the hair on my arms. "It's strange. That's all. Are you going to fess up or not?"

"What's she confessing?" Ariel asked, coming into the office. Andy and Jewel arrived behind her.

"Natasha had dinner with the Trevinos last night," Imogen announced. "At their *house.*"

Ariel's eyes widened. Andy and Jewel stared blankly at each other.

"So?" Andy prompted.

"So she's gotta have stories." Imogen turned back to me. "Come on, Natasha. Be a pal. What's their house like? Is Lindsay as big of a bitch as everyone says? What did you eat? I heard that famous chef from the city comes and cooks for them once a week. Was he there?"

"No famous chefs," I said loudly as I shoved Imogen off my mouse pad. "No celebrity interior designers. Lindsay was incredibly pleasant and welcoming, as was Eli. It was a nice evening. The wine was vintage."

Imogen gasped. "Expensive?"

"I'm not sure." Everyone was staring at me, so I turned away from my computer to address them all. "It wasn't a big deal, okay? It was nice to talk to them outside of work. They're human beings, not business robots."

"Shocking," Ariel said.

After that, Imogen abandoned her line of questioning

to discuss the matter further with Ariel. I could hear them whispering from the corner, and every once in a while, I caught sight of them peeking at me while I worked. As I ignored them, Andy and Jewel rolled over to me.

"Well?" he asked, grinning. "Are you going to give us the real story or not? What were you doing at the Trevinos?"

I caught sight of Lenny's name on my computer screen. I'd forgotten to remove him from the list of patients that attended my class. His file, and all my notes on his progress, should be backed up somewhere for future reference. Sadness stole over me.

"What's going to happen to Lenny?" I asked Andy and Jewel. "He didn't have any family left, right? How does that work?"

If Andy was disappointed that I didn't want to gossip about the Trevinos, he hid it well. "We have a memorial service at the end of each year to honor the patients we lose. Lenny will be included in that."

"What about his assets?" I said. "What happens to his things?"

Naturally, it was Imogen who answered. "He donated everything to Trevino," she answered. "I heard the aides talking about it this morning. He wrote a will and everything. All his money went to the Center. I suppose he considered us his family."

I decided not to throw her comment from yesterday into her face. "Did anyone know anything about him? I wish I had the chance to ask him more."

"I worked with him most," Jewel said. "He immigrated here from Finland when he was a child. His mother and father owned a department store back home before they died, but he didn't want to inherit the business. He wanted to be a poet."

I smiled sadly. "That sounds like Lenny."

Jewel opened the drawer to her desk and took out a handful of origami animals. "Here. I rescued a few of these out of the trash. He wrote inside them."

THE ORIGAMI ANIMALS sat beside my computer all day. I didn't have the heart to unfold them and ruin Lenny's careful work. Besides, I wasn't sure I had the right to read his private poetry. To me, if someone folded up their words so they couldn't be seen, it was for a reason.

I made an effort to put more pep in my classes today, hoping it didn't seem forced. My mind kept wandering off. Mostly, I thought about Lenny. For all the talking he did, he hadn't spoken much about himself. I never got the impression he had enough money to make any significant donation to the Center, but when I saw Lindsay in the halls around lunchtime, I learned otherwise.

"It's terrible," she said, her eyes gloomy. "I hate when patients die, but it couldn't have come at a better time. We needed the generosity of his donation. God, is that awful of me to say?"

When I wasn't thinking about Lenny, I picked apart my dinner with the Trevinos last night. Did Imogen have a point? The more the rumor mill churned, the more I understood the oddity of Lindsay inviting me over. According to most employees, no one had ever seen the Trevinos outside of work or related events.

"They seem so normal," I said to Bonnie that afternoon. After exerting so much energy the day before, she hadn't been able to attend my class, but I visited her while she rested in bed. "Am I being paranoid?"

"I think you're letting Imogen get to your head," Bonnie said, tapping her temple. "I know girls like her. They feed off other people's insecurities. I would know. She asks me to repeat myself three times, and I'm sure she understands me."

Outside Bonnie's room, Scout passed by.

"What about her?" I asked, nodding to the aide.

Bonnie craned her neck to look. "The aide? Doesn't talk much. I prefer it that way though. Small talk makes me want to strangle someone."

"Imogen acts like she has rabies." I watched Scout unload a fresh batch of folded sheets in the linen closet across the hall. "Why do you think that is?"

Bonnie shot me a loaded look.

As usual, I completed my notes for the day out on the balcony. I relished each minute. Soon, it would be too cold to stay out here for so long. I'd have to suck it up and write my notes in the office with the rest of the therapists.

I kept my favorite of Lenny's origami creations on my clipboard. It was a small purple whale, and it reminded me how important it was to find joy in the little things. When the sun began to sink toward the mountains, I set aside my notes and went to the railing to watch. The sky was different in Lone Elm than in the city. The colors were deep and vibrant, and the light of the dying sun sparkled on the lake below. I took in a deep breath, savoring the fresh mountain air.

A shout echoed below the balcony, and a flash of

movement caught my eye. A patient tore across the Center's side yard, toward the lake, his medical gown flowing out behind him like a cape. A burly man in classic Trevino scrubs sprinted after the patient and tackled him to the ground. The patient struck the aide across the face. The aide's grunt floated up to the balcony.

"Hurry!" he growled.

Scout caught up to the wrestling pair. As the large man held down the patient, Scout took something from her pocket. I peered down at them, trying to get a look at what was happening, but the aide's broad shoulders blocked my view.

The patient went limp. The muscled aide lifted the patient from the ground. His clinical gown was stained green with chlorophyll. Together, the aide and Scout took the patient inside. Right before she disappeared beneath the balcony, Scout glanced up. I pedaled backward, unsure if she'd seen me or not.

"Natasha?"

I jumped at the sound of my name. Ariel raised an eyebrow.

"Calm down," she said. "I wanted to remind you about the employee meeting tonight. We do it at the end of every month to talk about our patients' recent progress."

"Yeah, sure. I'll be there in a minute."

Ariel stepped out onto the balcony, looking closely at my pale face. "Are you okay?"

"Um." I stalled and glanced across the yard. There was no sign of the struggle. "I think a patient tried to escape. Scout and this other guy tackled him."

"That happens all the time." Ariel tied her long hair into a messy bun and waved me inside. "It was probably someone in Ward 13. They're always trying to make a break for it. You'd think Eli was torturing them down there."

I WAS quiet throughout the employee meeting, my head filled with thoughts of the almost-escaped patient in Ward 13. While Imogen led the discussion about our most promising patients and what we could change to become more efficient, I stewed in my distraction.

"Natasha?" Imogen finally prompted. "Anything to add? As our newest addition, we'd like to hear from you."

I pulled myself back to the current moment, taking a second to process Imogen's question. "You're asking me for suggestions?"

Imogen shifted from one foot to the other. "You have a fresh perspective. It's welcomed here."

I leaned forward in my seat and caught Imogen's eyes. "In that case, I don't think it's appropriate to talk about patients behind their backs. It creates a hostile environment, and if we don't respect our patients, how are we supposed to treat them effectively?"

Imogen's cheeks turned pink. "I don't think any of us are speaking poorly of our patients, but let's all take Natasha's suggestion into account, shall we?"

Andy stifled a snigger, and Jewel disguised a laugh with a coughing fit. Only Ariel had the gall to look offended on Imogen's behalf. I sat back, satisfied.

When the meeting came to an end, I sensed someone standing behind me and turned to face Imogen and Ariel. Despite the tension between us, the two of them managed to put on friendly faces.

"We're going to the Shadows Restaurant for dinner," Imogen informed me. "They have a prime rib special they only run once a month. You're coming with us."

I put on my coat. "Thanks for the invitation, but I have plans with Baz tonight."

Ariel's brow furrowed. "Your landlord's teenaged daughter?"

"She's having classic high school romance problems," I explained, "and I promised I'd get her out of her funk tonight. Maybe some other time?"

"Sure you don't want to hang out with some people your own age?" Imogen asked.

"We're dying to hear more about the Trevinos," Ariel added. "Eli's such a mystery."

That explained the invitation. After subtly insulting Imogen during the meeting, I couldn't understand why she'd want to have dinner with me.

"I don't want to let Baz down," I said.

Imogen rolled her eyes and walked away. "Whatever."

"Some other time," Ariel said.

I DID HAVE plans with Baz, but we weren't scheduled to meet until later that night. I dawdled in the office until the other therapists had gone home. Then I found my way down to the basement of the Trevino Center. The air below ground was as cold as it was outside, and for good reason: the only thing on this floor of the Center was the morgue.

Maybe it was macabre to want to visit Lenny after he was gone, but I needed closure. This was the only way I could think to get it.

The morgue attendant was a skinny guy with a thin neck and hollow cheeks, who looked unlikely to be able to haul bodies to and fro. He also had quite the poor attitude.

"You want to see a patient?" he asked with a dull expression. "Why? You can't therapize a dead dude."

"It's personal."

"Then it's not my problem," the morgue attendant replied. "This isn't a funeral home. I'm not gonna pull a body out of the freezer so you can say goodbye."

I caught sight of the name on his badge. "Listen, Ernie. I meant it my trip was personally *professional*. As Leonard's therapist, I have the right to check on his motor functions after death."

Ernie stared at me. "Motor functions. After death. You do know what you're saying, right?"

"Can you just pull him out?"

Ernie sat back on his metal stool and crossed his arms. "What's in it for me?"

"What do you want?"

He looked me up and down. "A date."

"Keep dreaming. I'll give you twenty bucks, and you can take yourself out though."

Ernie sucked in his bottom lip, considered the offer, then extended his hand. "It's a deal."

"I don't shake with morgue attendants," I said. "The smell of death is bad enough without having to touch you."

In a quick gesture, he turned the proffered handshake into a hair-smoothing move instead. If he had more hair, it might have been convincing. Ernie slid off his stool and gestured for me to follow him into the adjacent room.

The temperature dropped again, as did my stomach. Two bodies lay on the slabs in the freezer.

"Not your boy," Ernie said of the bodies.

They were both women. "I can see that."

Ernie yanked on a square metal door. The table inside rolled out, exposing Lenny's pale, stiff body. "Here he is."

I forced myself to walk over and look at Lenny. Death had a way of making every face unfamiliar. Gone were Lenny's pink cheeks, toothy smile, and crinkled eyes. His skin sagged off his bones and sank into his eye sockets.

"How did he die?" I asked Ernie.

Ernie examined a label on Lenny's table. "Natural causes, it says."

"What about the autopsy?"

"There wasn't one," he answered. "No family to order it. Why so curious anyway? He was an old dude."

"He seemed fine," I murmured.

"People die, man," Ernie said. "It's the one human condition you can always count on."

THE CENTER WAS quiet when I returned to the upper levels. The day staff had gone home, and the night staff, who had a knack for moving invisibly, took over. As I passed Ward 13, I noticed Scout at the end of the hallway. She carried an armful of medication bottles and didn't see me as she turned the corner. Did she ever get tired and go home or was she a robot Eli had invented to patrol the Center's corridors during all hours of the day?

Scout wasn't the only one at Trevino after hours. Eli was in his office when I walked by. He stooped over his desk, fingers entangled in his hair. I knocked lightly on the glass door, and his head shot up. When he saw me, he relaxed and waved me in.

"I thought you were supposed to be at some event at a country club," I said as I took a seat in one of the leather chairs opposite to his.

His jaw dropped. "Oh, God. I completely forgot." He rooted through the desk drawer for his phone and groaned at the screen. "Six missed calls from Lindsay. She'll kill me for this."

"Say you got caught up with work. That's the truth, right?"

Eli pinched the bridge of his nose. "It's the same story over and over again. She's getting tired of hearing it. What are you doing here so late anyway?"

I lifted my shoulders. "I felt like I wasn't done for the day. Reflecting on things, I guess."

"On Ward 13?"

"How do you figure that?"

He swiveled one of his computer monitors around to show me a set of security videos. The live feeds flipped through different angles, except for one camera in the bottom left corner of the screen that remained fixed on the doors of Ward 13.

"I saw you stop by," Eli said, swiveling the screen back toward himself. "Have you given any more thought to my proposal?"

"Honestly?"

"Preferably."

I let out a sigh. "Working in Ward 13 scares the crap out of me. I grew up in a tough environment. A lot of the people and kids I interacted with had untreated metal health issues."

"The key word there is untreated," Eli pointed out. "Our patients in Ward 13 aren't raving lunatics. No one facing mental health challenges should be treated as such."

"I don't have anything against working with them."

"Then what's the problem?" He tossed a stress ball from hand to hand. "I think this program would be great for my patients. They need something stimulating."

Harsh memories from my childhood swirled through my head. If Eli knew more about me, he might not want me to have anything to do with the patients in Ward 13.

"I want to meet the patients first," I bargained. "I'll need to evaluate them to determine what measures I need to take to teach them."

Eli nodded. "Easy enough. You can shadow me tomorrow."

7

*E*li started his day at dawn, so I arrived at his office with bleary eyes and a cup of black coffee that Marcel had made extra strong for me. Eli pointed to the cup.

"Is that for me?" he asked.

I pulled it out of reach. "Hell no. You expect me to be functional before the sun comes up? I need every drop of this."

He laughed, pulled on his white coat, and grabbed a clipboard. "Fair enough. Let me give you a rundown of what we do each morning. Gulp that coffee. You won't be able to bring it into Ward 13."

While Eli spoke, I caffeinated myself at a dangerous rate. Thankfully, Lindsay had sent Eli to work with an extra donut that day. When he offered it to me, I used it to ease my scalded tongue between sips.

"Every morning, I do rounds," Eli explained. He flipped through the papers on his clipboard. A closer look showed patient names and a checklist for things like medication, current temperament, and diet changes. "It's pretty simple. I ask how each of my patients is feeling, and we do what I like to call a mini-sesh. The patients have a few minutes to tell me whatever's on their mind. If it's something I can address promptly, I do so. If not, I put a note on their chart to remind me to bring it up in our session later. These are my notes on patient files." He patted the top of an enormous cabinet. "The Center's official documents are all electronic, but I prefer to write by hand and scan my notes in later. This cabinet stays locked at all times, but if you need access to my notes for whatever reason, I'll find a way for you to read them."

Eli straightened his tie, smoothed his hair, and gestured for me to follow him. He took the stairs at a rapid pace, but his shoulders remained level and his voice unbothered by his gait. "I finish my rounds at lunch, eat, and then begin private therapy sessions in the afternoon. I see most patients two to three times a week, depending on their current state and how much time I have on my hands. At least once a week, I skip rounds in the morning to catch up on private sessions."

Out of breath at the bottom of the stairs, I asked, "Isn't there another psychiatrist who could cover for you?"

"We have a psychologist," Eli answered as the heels of his loafers clicked across the lobby's marble floors. He nodded a greeting to Cameron at the front desk. "She picks up the slack when I can't get to everyone, but I'm the only one who can prescribe or alter medication. I prefer it that way."

We passed the therapy wing. My usual office was empty this early in the morning. Part of me longed to sit at my normal desk and get started on my regular routine, but disappointing my boss and one of the biggest names in psychiatric treatment wasn't on my to-do list that morning. I hurried to catch up with Eli.

"Do you treat with anything other than medication and talk therapy?" I asked him, trying to match my stride to his. With his long legs, it seemed impossible.

"The Center wouldn't be so renowned if we didn't." He peered at me from the corner of his eye. "Are you interested in psychiatry?"

"Just curious. What other kinds of treatments do you offer?"

"Cognitive and dialectal behavior therapies, naturally," Eli answered. "Those are the building blocks of what I do. We also do electroconvulsive therapy and something called transcranial alternating current stimulation. Have you heard of it?"

"I don't think so."

"It's promising for sufferers of major depression who haven't had much luck with other types of treatments," Eli explained.

"Aren't those types of treatments controversial?"

We arrived at the entrance to Ward 13, but Eli answered the question in the hallway before we entered. "Not as much anymore," he said. "Like most things in my field, there is a stigma attached to ECT because of its rough history, but it's safer these days. There's nothing I won't try to help my patients. Are you ready?"

I nodded. Eli placed his hands on the doors to push them open then hesitated.

"I should warn you," he said. "This is going to be different than your average day on the therapy floor. It's best to stay vigilant."

A lump formed in my throat, but I nodded again anyway. Eli propelled himself into Ward 13, and I followed on his heels.

I hadn't seen inside the psych ward since my very first day at the Center. I'd forgotten that it was just as beautiful as the rest of Trevino. Sunlight flooded the main hall, reflecting off the white walls and dark wooden accents. The high ceiling made everything seem open and airy, and large windows invited the mountainous scenery inside.

The main difference between this ward and the other ones was the amount of privacy the patients received. In the therapy wing, each person had the option of drawing a shade across the small window that looked into the hallway. Here, the rooms were practically made of glass. You could see right into each patient's living quarters and monitor what they were doing at any given moment. The attached bathrooms had a short wall, but no door, to afford the user an illusion of privacy.

"Welcome to Ward 13," Eli announced, spinning around with his arms spread wide like Fraulein Maria on top of a hill in Austria. When I raised my eyebrows at him, he clapped his arms to his sides again and cleared his throat. "We have thirty beds, and they're always occupied. There's a waitlist to be treated."

"So I've heard."

THE RUMORS about Eli that had circulated in the therapy wing proved themselves wrong. As I watched him work, it became obvious he had an instinctive knack for the job. First off, he spoke to his patients without condescension or superiority. He knocked and allowed them to answer before entering. He sat on a stool by the patient's bedside to be on the same eye level as them, and though he stuck to a basic script, he made sure the patient led the conversation.

What surprised me most was not Eli's good nature as a doctor, but rather the general age of his patients. Though some adults were present, the majority of Ward 13 occupants were teenagers.

"Good morning, Wilson," he said, stepping into the next room on his list. "How are you this morning?"

I observed the patient, a young man around seventeen or eighteen, from the doorway. He did not answer Eli's question. He lay flat on the bed, no pillow, and stared at the ceiling with a blank expression.

"Scout!" Eli called into the hallway.

The aide appeared from another room. "Yes, sir?"

Eli indicated Wilson's non-responsive state. "Did we run into some issues earlier?"

"He was hostile when we attempted to check his vitals." Scout detached a clipboard from the outside of Wilson's room and handed it to Eli. "He threw his food tray at me. When neither me or Dashiell could calm him down, we administered a sedative."

Eli shone a small flashlight into Wilson's unseeing eyes. "How much did you give him?"

"It should wear off soon," Scout answered vaguely. "The details are on his chart. Anything else, sir?"

"Any other problematic patients this morning?"

"Rooms fourteen and twenty-six."

We had already been to room fourteen, which belonged to an older woman with severe dementia. She'd been admitted to the Center for an experimental treatment, but she often thought she was living in a different era. According to Eli, her subsequent panic attacks often turned violent.

"Toby," Eli muttered under his breath. To Scout, he added, "I'll check on him next."

As Scout left, I spoke up. "Eli? I couldn't help but notice how many of the patients seem to be sedated in one form or another. Most of the ones we've seen were lethargic. I assume that's from the medications?"

Eli checked Wilson's chart, his index finger locating the medication he was given and the dosage. "Not everyone. Many of these patients suffer from depression as well as their main diagnosis. It exhausts them."

I chewed my tongue, unsure if I bought this explanation or not. "Eli, if I'm going to teach a movement program to these patients, I don't want them to be sedated. I want them to be free to do as they please during class."

He smiled grimly as he brushed by me to return the chart to its place outside the room. "As I said, the patients aren't sedated unless necessary. Seeing as this is a psychiatric ward, we do rely on sedation at certain times, for the safety of our patients and ourselves."

"I understand that," I said, "but there's no point in leading dance or movement classes when they're all a moment away from unconsciousness."

Eli regarded me from his tall height. I stood firm. "All right," he said at last. "I'll take your request into consideration. I get where you're coming from. It will be a case by case basis though. I won't risk my patients' safety."

"I never asked you to."

We continued down the hall, and Eli's task of rounds in the morning began to bore me. This was the reason I had chosen a branch of physical therapy. I preferred to work with the mind *through* the body, rather than drill my patients with a series of unending questions that most of them didn't want to answer. Eli's compassion grew stale as the morning wore on. When we arrived at room twenty-six, he had next to none left.

The curtains, located outside the room so the patient didn't have the choice whether or not to draw them, were closed. No one could see in or out of the dark room.

"Before we go in here," he said, "I want to warn you of the patient inside. He's not a good kid. He might be the most problematic patient we've ever treated here. He throws things, he insults people, and he does whatever he has to do to make you doubt yourself. Don't listen to him and stay out of arm's reach. He's restrained, but he's crafty, and I don't want you to get hurt on your first day on this floor."

The hair on my arms rippled as goosebumps arose on my skin. What kind of teenager could make a grown man with years of experience in his field grow stiff in the neck and shoulders as Eli did now? As he reached for the door, he went light on his feet, bending his knees a little, as if expecting a great impact upon his entrance. With a deep breath, I followed him inside.

The patient was asleep. The glow from a single fluorescent bulb in the adjoining bathroom cast a yellow sheen across his young face. He was no older than fourteen. His wavy golden hair lay across his forehead, in dire need of a trim. The insides of both arms were bruised, marks of how many times he'd been stuck with needles.

His lack of muscle made his cheekbones and elbows sharp and pointy. Around his wrists, he wore padded manacles that secured his arms to the bed. Everything else about him was hidden beneath a thick, weighted blanket.

Without ceremony, Eli flicked on the overhead light, flooding the room with brightness. The teenager did not stir.

"Toby," Eli said flatly. "I know you're not asleep."

The patient breaths flowed rhythmically in and out. His eyes flicked back and forth beneath their lids, a sign of REM sleep.

"Maybe we should check back later?" I tentatively suggested.

"He's faking it." Eli banged his clipboard against the end of the bed. "Toby!"

Still no response.

"I think he's asleep," I said. "But you should probably check his meds if he's this deep in it. I don't think it's natural for him to—"

The teenager shot straight up from his pillows, yelling like a madman. His face turned bright red as he rattled the chains that kept him restrained. I leapt away from the bed, heart pounding, and pasted myself against the far wall. The teenager's yells dissolved into laughter.

"Oh, God," he said, doubled over with glee. His restraints were long enough to let him wipe tears of laughter from his eyes. "You should have seen your face!" he told me. "You were like—agh!" He waved his hands and pulled a horrible mocking impression of my startled expression. "That was priceless. Phew!"

"Ha, ha," I said dryly.

"Told you," Eli muttered to me. He raised his voice.

SECRETS IN THE WOODS

"Toby Gardner, this is Natasha Bell. She's a movement and dance therapist."

Toby scoffed. "That's a thing? That's stupid."

"It's proven to be very effective—"

"Effective, my ass," Toby interrupted. "You're telling me *dancing* can cure me? Hey, Doc, here's an idea. Why don't you admit there's nothing wrong with me?"

"Toby, we've discussed this," Eli said. "You wouldn't be here if the treatments were working. The type of disorder you have can be very dangerous."

Toby let out a raucous laugh and pointed to himself. "I'm dangerous? Are you kidding me? You're the one torturing kids, probably because you like wiping your nose with money."

"Toby—"

"What about you?" Toby asked, turning his attention to me. "What are you doing here? Don't tell me you feed into all this bull crap about Trevino being the best psychiatric hospital in the nation. The doc here's an effin' quack."

"Watch your language," Eli reprimanded sharply.

"Or what?" Toby challenged. "You'll put me under again? That's what you always do when you're feeling threatened, right? Knock out the people who aren't buying your dumb story?"

The muscles in Eli's jaw jumped as he clenched his teeth together. A red blush crept up his neck. He had handled the other difficult patients with grace and patience, but there was something about this teenaged boy that got under his skin.

"Toby, I'm making the rounds with Doctor Trevino today to promote a new program for Ward 13," I said, trying to give Eli some time to recover from his lack of professionalism. "We'll explore things like dance, yoga, Tai Chi, and boxing—things that challenge the mind and body to keep you healthy. I'd like to start this program next week. Would you be interested in something like that?"

Something flickered in Toby's eyes. At first, I thought it might be curiosity, but it morphed to devious mischief. "*Would you be interested in something like that?*" he repeated in a squeaky imitation of my voice. "Do you know what I'm interested in? Getting the hell out of here!"

He thrashed against his restraints, pulling so hard that his wrists went red beneath the cuffs. With each breath, he let out a piercing howl. Veins protruded from his neck as his face turned bright red. I half-expected his head to explode as I stopped myself from covering my ears.

"Scout!" Eli bellowed into the hallway. "A little help in here!"

Scout rushed in, a syringe in hand. Toby swung at her, but she stepped nimbly under his short-range punch. He grabbed a pen from the front pocket of Scout's scrub pants and stabbed her arm with it. A tiny dot of blood and ink welled up on her skin.

Scout grimaced and twisted the pen out of Toby's grasp. He convulsed, screaming louder as she grabbed the meaty upper part of his arm, plunged the needle into the muscle, and depressed the syringe. Tears streamed from Toby's eyes as he caught my gaze across the room.

"Please," he begged hoarsely. His eyelids drooped. The tranquilizer was kicking in. "I don't belong here."

He passed out, slumping across the pillows. His head lolled to one side, stretching his neck into a position that would cause cramping when he woke up. Scout made no effort to move him. Rather, she pressed a disinfectant wipe over the small wound in her arm.

"My fault," she said before Eli could ask whether she was okay. "I should have checked my pockets before I walked in. Let me go clean this up."

Eli checked Toby's pulse. With the teenager asleep, Eli's cool head returned. "Toby is the perfect example of why you need to stay vigilant in this ward. A patient can turn uncooperative and violent at any moment. If you're not careful, you could get hurt."

"Why is he so angry?"

Eli scribbled something in his personal notebook. "You heard him. He's convinced he doesn't need to be here. He thinks we're out to get him." He closed the notebook. "By the way, he's not eligible for your program. I don't want him anywhere near the other patients."

Eli left. I waited until his footsteps faded down the hallway before adjusting Toby's head so that he rested more comfortably against his pillows. In unconsciousness, the rage had gone from the teenager's face. All I saw was a boy who needed help.

"We'll see about that," I muttered to myself.

AT DINNER with Lauren and Baz that night, I looked up between courses and noticed both mother and daughter staring at me.

"What?" I demanded. "Do I have risotto on my face?"

"Quiet determination, more like," Lauren said.

"Really?" Baz scrunched her nose as she examined me. "I was thinking murderous intent."

Lauren swatted Baz with her napkin and said to me, "You seem to be lost in thought. Usually, our dinners are chattier than this."

"Sorry," I said, setting my fork down and leaning back to stretch my stomach. "This Ward 13 thing is getting to me. I can't stop thinking about it."

"Everything okay?" Lauren asked, one brow raised.

I gazed across the room, my mind anywhere but the present. "I can't help but think that if I had real parents, they might have sent me somewhere like the Center."

Baz lifted her eyebrows. "Dude, are you a nutcase?"

Lauren smacked Baz again, this time with more force.

"It's fine," I said. To Baz, I added, "I never knew my parents. I grew up in the foster care system and got unlucky with guardians. After a certain incident, they said I was too dangerous to foster and sent me to a juvenile detention center."

Baz's eyes grew wide. "What did you do?"

I caught a glimpse of Lauren's expression. She, too, was curious, but I could sense something else as well: judgement or fright perhaps. Either way, I didn't want to share my story.

"It doesn't matter," I told Baz. "My record was cleared when I turned eighteen. All I'm saying is I could have ended up in Ward 13 if things had been different, but I'm not so sure it would have been better for me." I turned to Lauren. "Did you know it's mostly kids in there? I'd guess seventy percent of the beds belong to teenagers."

Lauren calmly sipped her wine. "Last year, the Center advertised their abilities to treat at-risk youth with new, innovative therapies. They've been flocking here ever since."

. . .

LATER THAT NIGHT, I lay in bed, stroking Jean Paul's soft coat while he rumbled against my neck. No matter how much I tried to relax, I couldn't go to sleep. My eyelids remained stubbornly open. Jean Paul complained as I rolled out of bed, but as I sat on the cushioned window seat with my laptop, moonlight streaming in, he curled up beneath my legs and fell back to sleep.

I logged in to my work account and pulled up Toby Gardner's file. The diagnosis code confused me. He was being treated for narcissistic personality disorder, a diagnosis that often meant the patient had an exaggerated sense of self-importance and required constant attention. The only possible symptom I'd seen in Toby that morning was the way he insulted both me and Eli in an attempt to make us feel less than him. Was that what it was though, or was Toby just a teenager trying to defend himself?

I scrolled through Toby's file, lost in thought. He was admitted to Trevino after an altercation with his stepfather, a rich businessman from New York City. Toby's home address was smack in the middle of the Upper East Side.

Out of curiosity, I exited out of Toby's file and clicked on other teenagers who had been admitted to Ward 13. Felicity Swann, sixteen, had been admitted for suicidal tendencies. Her family also lived on the Upper East Side, and her father owned one of the biggest publishing companies in the business. Wilson Knicks, the seventeen-year-old who had been sedated that morning, came from Martha's Vineyard and old money. His mother owned a company that managed several expensive department stores.

It went on. Each teenaged patient in Ward 13 had been sent there by wealthy parents or guardians. Technically, it checked out. The Trevino Center was a private practice with an inscrutable reputation. Less fortunate people couldn't afford to be treated there.

I pulled up Trevino's official website and navigated to their donation page. The parents of those in Ward 13 were seriously committed to their children's well-being. In addition to treatment fees, they had all donated a minimum of ten thousand dollars each to the Center, dedicated to "research for treatment of dangerous youths."

8

When I accepted Eli's proposal to create a program for Ward 13, I hadn't considered how much work I'd be adding to my already-full schedule. In addition to my classes for the physical and occupational therapy patients, I had to study more patient files, research disorders, and find time to schedule classes for Ward 13 as well. A full two weeks passed before I worked everything out. Thankfully, Eli didn't push me to move faster, but the other therapists noticed my harried existence.

"Are you okay?" Andy asked me one day. He watched me scribble a note so furiously that the paper tore beneath my pen. "Why are you mad at the notebook?"

I balled up the torn sheet and tossed it into the garbage then stretched my arms overhead. My back popped, and I groaned. "I'm swamped. I'm supposed to start teaching a class in Ward 13 tomorrow, but I don't know how I'm going to get all these notes done before then."

Andy flipped through my notebook. "All you have to

do is type them up?"

"Yeah, but it'll take me a while. I'm not the fastest typer."

"I'll do it for you," he offered. "It's no big deal, and it's not a breach of confidentiality," he added, seeing my mouth open to ask the question. "All your patients are already my patients, remember? We share this information anyway."

"You'd really do that for me?" I asked.

"Sure. It's no problem."

"Wow. Thanks, Andy."

Imogen made an insufferable kissing sound. When I threw a sharp glance at her, she desisted and pretended she'd been working on her computer instead of eavesdropping this entire time. As soon as I looked away, she and Ariel sniggered.

"Ignore then," Andy said under his breath. "They're jealous because I always finish my work early and I never do *them* favors."

Something about Imogen's teasing stayed with me for the rest of the day and into the next morning. I'd pushed all my morning classes in the physical therapy ward to make room for Ward 13 at the beginning of the day. It was better to get the thing that made me most anxious out of the way first, so I wouldn't have to spend hours ruminating on it beforehand. Despite my preparation, I felt jittery when I met Eli before the class.

"Ready?" he asked, looking me over with an arched eyebrow.

I shook my hands out. I'd skipped my morning coffee, but even without caffeine, I vibrated like a guitar string. "Let's do this."

"You look nervous."

"I'm fine."

Eli stepped between me and the door of the ward. "If you don't feel comfortable with this, I don't want you in there. These patients are like dogs. They can sense when something's not right, and they will try to take advantage of you. I did as you asked and kept the ones in your class off sedation, so you *have* to be confident in there."

I squared my shoulders and set my face. "I said I'm fine."

I skated around Eli and entered the ward myself. It was louder today than my first visit. The patients had more freedom than they were accustomed to. They chatted loudly, calling for each other across the hallways or shouting to the aides. They moved around in their rooms instead of laying in bed.

Wilson did pike push-ups with his feet propped on the bed. Thankfully, the Center had provided him with a pair of sweatpants because a clinical gown would not have covered all of his assets. He was a powerful kid with bulging muscles. His file said he'd been on the weight lifting team at his high school before he was committed to Trevino. Eli almost knocked on his door, but I stepped in front of him to do it myself.

"Hey, Wilson," I said casually.

Sweat dripped into his eyes as he turned to look at me, but he didn't abandon the exercise. "Hi. It's Doctor Bell, right?"

"She's not a doctor," Eli grunted.

"You can call me Nat," I said. "Or Natasha. Are you ready for class?"

Wilson finished his push-ups, planted his feet on the

floor, and rose to his full height. He towered over me. "I've been looking forward to it. Am I coming with you?"

"You sure are."

For safety purposes, Eli made me promise to bring the patients to the designated Ward 13 therapy room one at a time and to always have someone—himself or another aide—with me in case things got out of hand. As we led Wilson down the hall, I felt no danger. He walked right next to me while Eli watched from behind, and though the teenager's looming height and powerful build should have been intimidating, all I sensed from Wilson was eager determination.

"Here we go," I said, holding the door to the therapy room open for him. "Once everyone gets here, we'll get started. Until then, you can stretch or warm-up. Whatever you like."

Wilson's gaze drifted to the far corner of the room. There, an enormous man in mint-colored scrubs stood like a bodyguard, his hands clasped behind his back. He made no greeting as we came in. When he caught Wilson's eye, the teenager looked away.

"Dashiell's here for your safety," Eli muttered to me. "He'll keep an eye on things."

"He can stay until the class starts," I said. "Then I want him gone. This is supposed to be fun for the patients. They don't need to be watched."

"I disagree—"

"We're doing this my way, Eli," I reminded him firmly.

His lips tightened as he looked down at me. "Fine."

WE COLLECTED four additional patients from around

Ward 13, all of them between the ages of thirteen and eighteen. They weren't all as cooperative as Wilson. Wilson, himself, grew loud and excitable once we had everyone in the same room. Their voices bounced off the walls and echoed back as they talked and gossiped. They made quite a racket for five teenagers, but I reminded myself that they probably hadn't been allowed to socialize like this in several months.

When the time arrived to start class, I pointed at Dashiell then pointed at the door. He glanced over my shoulder, where Eli stood. Eli nodded, and Dashiell abandoned his post. Eli gave me one last look, as if to say I better know what I'm doing, before exiting too.

I clapped my hands sharply to get the class's attention. Two boys and three girls had shown interest and been approved to take my class: Wilson Knicks, Felicity Swann, Joshua Malloney, Rebecca Callahan, and Alexis Blackwell. On paper, they were depressed, anxious, or violent teenagers with harmful tendencies. In this room, they were human beings with a blank slate.

"Good morning, everyone!" I called over their overlapping voices. "Welcome to your first dance and movement therapy class. I'm sure you're all wondering what we might be doing in here…"

Not one of the teenagers appeared to care what they were doing here. They paid no attention to me at all, continuing to talk to each other instead. I tried again.

"If I could have your attention," I shouted. The class looked up at me. "We're going to start class off with something called the BrainDance. It's a nice little warm-up that'll get the blood flowing and start the good chemicals in your brain moving. How about we all get in a line?"

The teenagers shuffled into a straight line, exchanging glances and muttering to each other. Once they were settled, I turned on the music. It was nondescript lo-fi electronic music, the kind I listened to when I needed to focus or study. The beats were slow, but the music was interesting enough to nod your head to.

"Here we go," I said. "First thing we're going to do is breathe. Inhale, reach your arms up. Exhale, let it all go."

They followed along, watching me for cues. I ignored the sniggers and nervous giggles that arose.

"Good," I said. "Now, we're going to move into some core stuff. You're going to curl up and hug yourself as tight as you can!" I bent over and pulled my arms close to my body. "Then you're going to come up and expand as far as possible." I reached up and spread my arms to lift my chest. "Make sure you breathe with the movements. Come on, everyone join in."

The teenagers half-heartedly did the moves. They glanced at each other to make sure everyone looked as ridiculous as they did. On his way down, Joshua—the youngest in the group—made a gross farting noise out of the side of his mouth. The group burst out laughing.

"Nice," I said dryly. "Let's stick to the dancing, okay? Try again. Inhale up, and exhale as you bend over."

"Did you hear that, Wilson?" Rebecca Callahan asked in a staged whisper. "She asked you to bend over. Isn't that sexual harassment?"

I clenched my teeth, but Wilson cast Rebecca an annoyed look. The other three laughed under their breath.

"Let's focus on ourselves," I suggested. "Come on up. Moving on to some tactile warm-ups. Tap your arms in time to the music. Tap your shoulders, belly, and thighs. Then brush them all. Arms, shoulders, belly, thighs—"

"This is stupid," Joshua exploded. "It's for kids!"

"Anyone can do the BrainDance," I said. "It's beneficial for everyone."

Joshua sat down and crossed his arms. "It's for babies. I'm not doing it."

"Then maybe you shouldn't be in this class."

Wilson raised his hand. "Miss—I mean, Natasha. Josh kind of has a point. I feel pretty stupid doing this."

"So do I," Felicity chimed in.

"I don't have to voice my agreement," Rebecca added. "Just look at my face. This is dumb."

"What about you, Alexis?" I asked the last girl. "Do you think this is stupid too?"

Alexis, the second youngest member of the group, shrugged. "I don't care. As long as I can get out of my room for a little bit, you can do whatever you want up there."

There was the truth of it all. These kids didn't express interest in the dance program because they wanted the opportunity to improve. They wanted to get out of the rooms Eli kept them locked in.

"The BrainDance is not just for babies," I told the class. "We'll be doing it as a warm-up before every class, so you might as well get used to it. I suggest you forget about what you look like and focus on what it feels like. Loosen your muscles. Open your mind—"

"Quack!" Joshua coughed. He puts his fists in his armpits and flapped his elbows like wings. "Quack, quack, quack!"

"That's enough," I said.

"Quack!" Rebecca joined in. "Quack, quack, quack!"

"Enough," I repeated louder.

Alexis began quacking too, and while the eldest of the group—Wilson and Felicity—didn't add to the duck imitations, they also didn't help to calm anything down. They drifted aside, laughing and whispering to each other as the three younger teenagers made fools of themselves.

Joshua grabbed one of the pillows stacked in the corner of the room. I'd planned on using them for a short meditation session at the end of class, but Joshua had different ideas. He ripped open the fabric, pulled out a handful of feathers, and tossed them into the air.

"Whoa!" I attempted to pull the pillow out of Joshua's grasp but only succeeded in ripping the fabric further. Feathers rained down as if a chicken had collided with a firework overhead. "Put it down, Joshua!"

"*Put it down, Joshua!*" the child mimicked. "Quack, quack, quack!"

Alexis and Rebecca seized pillows of their own, and before I could stop them, had yanked out the filling and thrown it about. Their loud quacking rang in my ears. As I reached for Rebecca's pillow, she tossed it to Alexis. When I rounded on Alexis, she threw the pillow to Joshua. Around I went like the monkey in the middle, all while the teenagers laughed at me.

When I stepped forward again, the bottom of my shoe slipped across the feathers that coated the ground. I fell backward hard. All of my breath whooshed out of my lungs when I hit the floor. Pain radiated through my tailbone and up my spine.

The teenagers burst out laughing. All except for Wilson, who rushed toward me. When I felt his hands at my elbows, I swatted him away, scared of him. He raised his palms in innocence and let me stand up myself. I ran from the room.

In the hallway, I slammed into Dashiell. My head bounced off his massive pecs. If he hadn't caught me, I would have fallen over.

"What happened?" he asked in the deepest voice I'd ever heard. He examined my red, teary face. "What did they do?"

"Not listening," I managed to get out, despite my humiliation. "Throwing things everywhere. I slipped and fell—"

Dashiell picked me up and set me aside then marched into the therapy room and closed the door behind him. I sat on the floor against the wall and put my head between my knees. I couldn't believe I'd let a bunch of teenagers get the better of me. I expected them to be a little bit of trouble, but I should have been able to handle it. Imogen's laughing face popped up in my memories.

It could have been worse. The kids weren't violent. They were bored and disruptive. I had to make them see this class was a good thing. We could come to an agreement. Of that, I was sure.

I wiped any hint of moisture from my eyes, smoothed my hair, and shook out the front of my scrubs so they weren't so wrinkled. As I did so, Dashiell emerged from the room, looking no worse for wear.

"They're all yours," he said.

"Uh, thanks."

With a fresh perspective, I re-entered the classroom, determined to handle the teenagers with more grace this time around. My vigilance turned out to be unnecessary.

ALEXANDRIA CLARKE

The feathers had been swept into the corner of the room to be picked up later. Wilson, Joshua, Alexis, Rebecca, and Felicity all sat cross-legged in a straight line with their hands folded in their laps. They kept their heads forward, and only their eyes darted to look at me. As I passed Joshua, his entire body quivered. In fear. What had Dashiell said to them?

"Let's make a deal," I suggested quietly. "Alexis said it already. The reason you all are doing this is to get out of your rooms. I respect that, and I respect you. That being said, I can't let you come in here and do whatever you want for an hour." When I paused, no one interrupted me. "If you do what I ask in here, you get to keep an hour of relative freedom. If you misbehave, it's back to your rooms, where Scout or Dashiell will likely dope you up with something you don't want to be on so you can stare at the ceiling like a zombie for the next eight hours."

Wilson's throat bobbed as he swallowed. He shook his head ever so slightly.

"It's your choice," I announced. "Enjoy your time in here or lose it. It's that simple. Would anyone like to leave?" No one replied. "Good. Get on your feet. Let's try the BrainDance again."

All five of them stood up.

I was happy to see the teenagers smiling after the hour had passed. Once we finished the warm-up, I decided to mix things up and taught the teenagers how to shadow box. They threw punches and kicks with reckless abandon while I rounded the room and corrected their form and posture. Wilson ducked and swirled around an invisible opponent. Joshua wildly lashed out, his limbs like jelly as his entire face scrunched up in concentration. I half-expected the girls to be dainty. Rebecca and Felicity were, but Alexis performed the exercises with as much gusto as Wilson. By the end of the hour, everyone was sweating and out of breath.

I escorted the teenagers back to their rooms with Scout's help. No one gave me any trouble, though I suspected that might have something to do with the Scout's easy access to tranquilizers. We dropped Wilson off last.

"Nat?" he asked softly as I made to close his door. "Thank you."

"Anytime, Wilson. I'll see you at our next class."

I withdrew into the hallway and noticed Toby standing at the window to his room, peering at me without shame. I waved. He raised a hand but couldn't seem to figure out how to make his fingers move.

"Can I talk to him?" I asked Scout. "I'll make it quick."

"Sure. He's half-under."

Toby moved away from the window as I knocked on his door and pushed it open. "Can I come in, Toby?"

He lowered himself to sit on the bed. Halfway there, he lost control of his legs and plopped down. "Do whatever you want," he said groggily.

I glanced over my shoulder. Scout watched from across the hall.

"I think you should come to one of my dance classes," I told him. "What do you think?"

Toby looked up at me. His pretty blue eyes were glazed over, and his face sagged in a way that suggested he had limited control over the muscles beneath his skin. He nodded weakly to Scout through the window. "They won't let me."

"What if I convinced them?"

He let out a noise that might have been a chuckle if he wasn't so drugged. "Good luck. Maybe. I'm tired."

"I'll leave you be. Get some rest."

In the hallway, I walked over to Scout and asked quietly, "What do you know about him? Anything you can tell me?"

Scout shrugged. "He's the worst one in here. Worse than Wilson, and that kid can get crazy." She leaned in to create more privacy between us as a nurse walked by. "Look, I can get through to most of these patients, but Toby's a lost cause. Don't waste your time."

"Was he the one who tried to run away?"

Scout froze. "What?"

"I saw you and Dashiell chasing a patient," I said. "Was that Toby?"

"You must be confused."

"I am not."

Scout pulled away from me. "What you're doing for these kids is great, but don't push it. You don't have full privileges in this ward. Don't act like you do."

She left before giving me time to react to her subtle threat. I watched her saunter off then returned to the therapy room and cleaned up the feathers before my next class.

I LED one more class in Ward 13, this one for adults. It went well, and I didn't need Dashiell to command the older patients' attention. Unlike the teenagers, their diagnoses usually involved Alzheimer's or dementia with side effects that ranged from wandering off and getting lost to becoming violent due to not understanding their situation. They performed the BrainDance obediently, but instead of shadow boxing, I led them through the little bit of Tai Chi that I knew. The art form was good for establishing balance and helping the elderly to catch themselves should they happen to fall.

After lunch, I returned to my usual physical therapy patients and taught another three classes. Then I whittled away at my notes in the office, typing and typing. With so many patients, I had an immense amount of paperwork to complete. Andy, Jewel, Imogen, and Ariel all left before me. The sun set, and the office turned purple then black. I didn't realize I'd forgotten to turn another light on until the bright computer screen made my eyes water.

A janitor came by to polish the floors. Shortly after, I heard the familiar click of Eli's loafers across the tile. He peeked into the office.

"Natasha?" he said, surprised. "What are you still doing here?"

"Notes," I replied wearily. "I didn't have time to do them earlier."

Eli rested a hand on the back of my chair. "Please go home. You can do this tomorrow. You've had a long day."

I rubbed my eyes and logged out of my work account. "Can I ask you something?"

"Sure."

"I want to work with Toby."

Eli pursed his lips. "Is there a question in there?"

"Everyone says he's hopeless," I said, "but I don't believe that. He's here for treatment, right? He should have the same opportunity as anyone else in that ward to take my class. I think it would be so good for him. He needs this, Eli. He needs something to hope for—"

Eli held up his hands to stop me. "I think you're right."

Stunned, I let my next argument slip away. "Really?"

"Dashiell told me you handled your morning class well," Eli said. I kept my face impassive. Perhaps Dashiell had left the bit about the kids chasing me from the room with pillows out of his story. "The reason parents bring their children here is because I refuse to give up on them. We've been treating Toby for almost a year, and we've seen no progress. It's my hope this class of yours triggers a breakthrough with him."

"You won't be disappointed," I promised him.

"I have conditions," he warned. "Number one, you have to work with him privately. I won't have him around other students until he can behave appropriately. Number two, he will always be under some kind of sedation. Don't argue with me," he added when I opened my mouth to do just that. "I can't tell you how many times Toby has attacked a member of the staff, including myself." He rolled up the sleeve of his shirt to show me a strange scar on his forearm. "He grabbed me with a syringe and stabbed me. Condition number three," he went on, covering the scar again. "Toby will be patted down before he enters the room with you, you can use no props or assistance tools that might double as a weapon, and Dashiell will stand right outside the door and monitor your sessions through the window as he sees fit."

"That was three conditions."

He frowned. "Take it or leave it, Natasha."

"I'll take it," I said hurriedly. "I'll take it."

9

*T*oby was silent as Dashiell unbuckled the restraints around his wrists, helped him to his feet, and guided him down the hallway. His eyes were clearer than the day before. Eli had kept his word; he hadn't sedated Toby with anything other than daily mood regulators prescribed to keep Toby's personality disorder at bay.

As I followed behind Toby and Dashiell, I examined the boy from top to bottom. He was too thin, as if he'd refused to eat more than once. He had no muscle mass. His shoulders curved inward and his winged scapula protruded through his thin white T-shirt. I made a mental note to ask Eli why Toby hadn't also been prescribed physical therapy to help his imbalanced body.

I'd dressed the therapy room with the same equipment I used for the regular classes. Pillows, soft exercise balls, and some padded angled supports. I also included a standalone punching bag that sprang back when you hit it. With enough force, the entire thing was meant to topple over.

"Thanks, Dashiell," I said, holding the door open for him once Toby was inside the therapy room. "We'll be okay."

Dashiell cast a wary eye over Toby. "Are you sure, Miss? I can stay, just in case."

"That won't be necessary."

He turned his back to Toby and lowered his voice. "Perhaps you're not familiar with the boy's case, but—"

"I'm familiar," I said at a normal volume. "Please follow Eli's directions. He said you were to stand outside and supervise from there."

He relented, but not without giving me a look that plainly said how stupid he thought I was for risking alone time with Toby. In the hallway, he stood at the window and peered inside, his heavy brow scrunched.

Toby loitered in the center of the room, swinging his arms around his waist to experiment with his temporary freedom. His eyes darted sharply to the windows that led outside, the equipment on the floor, the door to the hallway, and Dashiell's shadowy face.

"If I didn't know better, I'd think you were looking for a way out of here," I commented. I pretended to be absorbed in my notebook. "Can't imagine why you'd want to do that."

"That was sarcasm, right?"

"Something like that." I sat on the floor, extended my legs, and made myself comfortable. "From what I gather, you're not happy here at Trevino. You say you don't belong here."

Toby glared at me. "This was a trick, wasn't it? Say

you're going to let me out of my room, but all you're doing is shrinking me more."

"No, we're here to do some exercises," I told him. "I was looking at you on the way here, and we definitely need to find some stuff to help you build strength. I could get you into the physical therapy ward—"

"No!" he shouted. "I won't give you a reason to keep me here any longer."

"Toby, I read your file," I reminded him. "Your parents have committed you indefinitely. You can't leave the Center until Eli sees marked improvement in your condition."

"I don't have a condition," he snarled.

"Your file says differently."

He crossed his arms. "Do you believe everything you read on paper?"

"I generally believe medical diagnoses done by my superiors, yes."

"Then you're as stupid and worthless as they are."

I raised an eyebrow. "Let's pull back on the hurtful words."

"Why should I?" Toby demanded. He paced across the room. "None of you believed me when I tried to tell you nicely."

"You were nice?"

He cast a dirty look at me. "I don't belong here."

"So you keep saying."

Toby fell silent. I let him pout, even when his thighs began to wobble because he hadn't stood up for sustained periods in months. He refused to sit, though his eyes flickered to the beanbags stacked against the walls. The tremble continued down his calves.

"Have a seat," I said, taking pity on him. "On the floor, please."

Were it not for his fatigue, I doubt he would have obeyed. As it was, he sank into a cross-legged position with obvious relief.

"Good." I scooted closer to him, but not so close that I wouldn't have time to react if he lashed out. "I usually start these classes with a standing warm-up, but you look tired. We can do it sitting. I want you to breathe in and reach your arms overhead." I demonstrated the move, which looked like the top half of a sun salutation routine. "Then exhale as you come down and fold forward over your legs. With me, this time."

He remained stubbornly upright while I went through the motion again, arms wrapped tightly around himself.

"Feeling silly?" I asked lightly. "Don't worry. No one's watching except me, and I'm not judging you."

Toby jerked his head toward the hallway. "He's watching."

Dashiell's mouth hardened as we looked toward him. I waved him off. With some reluctance, he backed away from the window and stood on the opposite side of the hall so his face wasn't so visible to Toby.

"There," I said. "Better? Don't be embarrassed."

"Who said I was embarrassed?" he challenged. "I just don't want to do it."

I let my arms float to my sides. "Listen, I've been through this with the other kids. If you don't do the exercises, you have to go back to your room. You might as well appreciate the time you have with me because you're not going to have the same type of freedom anywhere else in this place."

Toby let out a scoff. "You think an hour with you constitutes freedom? Are you effin' crazy?"

"Language," I reminded him.

He popped to his feet. "I'll say whatever I damn well want!"

"That makes you sound like a housewife arguing with her husband, but so be it."

His lip curled upward. "I heard the others talking about you. They said you're a fake. They said this dance therapy thing is complete bull crap."

"Really?" I cocked my head like a curious puppy and put on an oblivious expression. "They rather seemed to enjoy our session yesterday. Wilson did exceptionally well. By the way, how are you able to overhear conversations when you're locked in your room all day?"

It was bait, and I felt guilty for it afterward. What with all the rumors surrounding Toby, I should have expected his reaction. He snapped, and he snapped hard.

"You don't know me!" he roared, spit flying from his mouth. His yell made my ears ring. A malnutritioned body like Toby's shouldn't be able to produce such a deep, echoing boom. "You don't know anything about me! You think you do because you've read my file? It's a piece of paper full of lies! You're helping them. *You're helping them!*" His voice and finger quivered as he pointed to the door and, beyond it, Dashiell. "You want to help me?" He drew in the shivering finger and jabbed it into his own chest. "Then get me out of here!"

His chest heaved, his lungs working extra hard to propel his rampage as far as possible. His gaze roved the room again, and his hand twitched with extra energy he needed to expel. I offered him my notebook.

"Here," I said. "Throw this."

He reached for it then drew his hand back, one eyebrow arched in question. He thought I was trying to trick him.

I brandished the notebook. "Take it. I'm serious. Chuck it as hard as you can, but don't hurt yourself. Your shoulders don't look like they're in the best shape."

He took the notebook with surprising gentleness. Then he turned away from me, pulled his shoulder back, and threw the notebook with as much force as he could muster. A feral yell ripped from his throat as the notebook slammed into the opposite wall and landed pages-down, spine broken on the floor. Toby panted, his shoulders shrugged up to his ears.

"Felt good, right?" I asked. "Do it again. Throw something else."

He didn't need much more encouragement. He lifted a beanbag from the floor and hurled it away from himself, bellowing like a bull. Then he reached for a smaller bean bag meant for tossing at a target and threw that too. It exploded against the wall and showered the room with plastic pellets. The destruction spurred Toby on. He threw one thing after another until the room was in complete disarray.

I watched from my seat on the floor, staying alert in case Toby turned his anger on me. Never once did he throw something in my direction. He made a point of keeping me out of his line of fire. Once, Dashiell poked his head through the door, wearing a look of alarm, no doubt in reply to the noise Toby was making. I shook my head and shooed him out before Toby noticed his presence.

After several minutes, Toby's anger died off and fatigue replaced his adrenaline. When he angled his arm to throw another bean bag, his entire body shook. He let the bag drop to the floor. For a solid minute, he stared around the room, taking in the mess he'd made.

He said nothing as he picked up my notebook, arranged the pages so it closed neatly again, and handed it to me. I accepted it. Looking into his face, I saw the haze in his eyes had gone away. His blue irises, usually dulled by medications, shone excitedly with an emotion I couldn't place at first.

"What did you just do to me?" he asked.

Relief, I realized. Toby had relief in his eyes.

"HE DOESN'T NEED IT," I argued to Eli for the tenth time.

For the past several weeks, since I started working with Toby and the other Ward 13 kids, Eli had been avoiding me. I'd finally hunted him down in the office. Eli, sick of my opinions, kneaded his temple.

"The meds are bogging him down," I pressed. "They're holding him back during our therapy sessions. At least consider lessening his dosage."

"We have been over this, Natasha," Eli said. "You are Toby's therapist. I am his doctor. I decide whether or not he's ready to have his medications altered, and I haven't seen any improvement."

"But I have," I reminded him. "He's different during our sessions. He pays attention to me. He respects me. He performs the movements with enjoyment, and it's because he's not hopped up on sedatives—"

Eli slammed his hand on his desk, making me jump. I

stepped backward and studied the lines of fury around his mouth. I'd never seen him lose his temper before.

"Toby may exhibit positive changes in your sessions," he said quietly, "but he has not shown any similar changes outside of the therapy room. He still behaves abhorrently to me, Scout, Dashiell, and the other aides."

"Did you ever consider he resents you for not believing in him?" I asked dryly.

Eli's gaze snapped sharply to mine. "He slapped Scout across the face yesterday. Did you know that?"

I swallowed hard.

"I didn't think so," Eli said. "You aren't looking at the full picture, Natasha. Toby is manipulating you. He's trying to make you an ally, and it's working. You're in here arguing for his case while every other person who deals with him argues against you. Don't you see the problem in that?"

My teeth clenched. "You know what I see? A boy who needs someone to listen when he speaks. Someone who believes that when he says he doesn't belong here, maybe it's true. I see a boy who needs help."

"As do I," Eli assured me. "But we have to work together to ensure he gets that help." When I didn't reply, Eli sank into his leather chair with a sigh. "Natasha, it boils down to this. Either you work *with* me or I'll recommend Toby no longer attends your sessions."

"That isn't fair."

"Maybe not," he said. "But if your sessions are interfering with my treatments, I'm afraid I'll have no choice. Is that understood?"

I locked my face into place to prevent a scowl from forming. "Yes, sir."

. . .

MY DISAPPOINTMENT with Eli carried over into other aspects of my life. That weekend, I went apple-picking with Baz, Lauren, and Marcel. Marcel's side business—he sold seasonal pies to the locals—had picked up as the weather grew colder. Everyone wanted an apple pie after dinner, and according to Marcel, they sold better if the apples were freshly picked.

I lagged behind the group as we marched through the orchard. Though the sun shone overhead, it was still too cold for my taste. The wind bit my nose and seeped through my coat. I drew my hood up and tightened the drawstrings so that the least amount of skin was exposed to the breeze.

Up ahead, Baz balanced on a ladder and used a long-handled pick to gleefully separate ripe apples from the trees. Marcel stood below her, holding a basket to catch the fruits, but he couldn't keep up with her rapid-fire pace.

"Slowly, slowly!" he commanded in his ridiculous accent. "I am not as fruity as you!"

"I beg to differ!" Baz called back, dropping another bunch of apples from the tree.

While Baz and Marcel argued, Lauren fell back to walk with me. "Not in the mood to climb any trees?" she asked.

"Not really."

"You've been distant lately," she remarked. "Baz said you were supposed to help her with a school project, but you didn't show up."

I groaned and rubbed my forehead. "I completely forgot about that. I'll apologize to her."

"She's not offended," Lauren said. "She can see you're

distracted. Is everything okay? We've missed you at dinner."

Since I'd been teaching more classes, I hadn't made it back to the inn in time for dinner. My customary meal turned into begging Marcel for leftovers or raiding the kitchen late at night for scraps.

To make matters worse, Jean Paul had come down with a mysterious illness. When I'd taken him to the vet during my lunch hour, we discovered he'd been eating one of the plants that Lauren kept in the library. The leaves were toxic to cats. The vet had to pump his stomach, and I stayed up the entire night to watch him vomit greenery. Mercifully, Lauren put the half-eaten plant on a higher shelf where Jean Paul no longer had access to it, but I couldn't help but wonder if the cat had purposely made himself sick to get my attention.

My work-life balance was seriously out of whack. I spent almost every waking hour at the Center. I barely spoke to or saw anyone beside my patients. Andy and Jewel had given up on socializing with me. Ensconced in my own work, I became invisible in the therapists' office. Twice, Imogen sat on me because she hadn't realized I already occupied the most comfortable rolling chair.

"I'm having trouble with a patient," I admitted to Lauren. "Eli and I disagree over the course of treatment. He says the patient is manipulating me, but I think it's the other way around."

Lauren's face hardened as she crossed her arms. "Hmm."

"What?"

"Oh, nothing."

I stopped her in her tracks as she made to follow

Marcel and Baz to the next tree. "You were going to say something. What, you agree with Eli? You don't even know the patient or the case."

"Relax," Lauren said. "I'm on your side. I've experienced arguing with the Trevinos before. I know what it's like to attempt advocating for someone there."

My shoulders dropped. "Your mother? I thought you never visited her."

"I didn't," she replied. "We had a tough relationship, but that didn't mean I wanted her to be miserable. I received updates on her condition, and I disagreed with how she was being treated. In the end, it didn't matter."

"Why not?"

"Because Elijah Trevino—the former," she added, "was determined to do what he thought was right. I suppose his son inherited his stubbornness. I eventually gave up. You know the rest of the story." She noticed my forlorn expression and grasped my elbow. "That all came out with the wrong intent. I meant to say you should fight for your patient. By the sound of it, you spend more time with him than the rest of those doctors and aides combined. Your professional opinion matters, Natasha. Don't let a rich boy fool you into thinking it doesn't."

ON THE FOLLOWING MONDAY, I met Dashiell in Ward 13 for our regular schedule. We freed Toby from his room and escorted him to the movement studio. Dashiell excused himself, and I began leading Toby in the exercises. Halfway through, he stopped moving.

"No offense," he said, "but did your cat die or

something?"

Confused, I answered, "Uh, no. Why?"

He pointed at me. "Because your face looks like that." He lifted his palms. "Again, no offense."

I attempted to rearrange my expression into a smile, and Toby shuddered.

"That's worse," he said.

I threw a bean bag at him. It hit him squarely in the chest, and he caught it in his hands. "Get back to work, kid."

"Aren't you supposed to be helping?"

I got to my feet. Since Eli refused to let Toby work with a physical therapist, I'd started including extra exercises to help his posture. This included working out with resistance bands. I helped Toby get into position for face pulls.

"Keep your shoulder blades glued down," I said, using my palms to flatten his scapula to his back. "Don't let them hunch up when you pull. Go ahead."

He tugged the resistance band toward his face, fighting to keep his shoulder blades in the right place. I adjusted his posture, and he tried again.

"How have you been feeling lately?" I asked as he continued the set. "Have you noticed any changes since you started working with me?"

"My body feels better," he replied. "I used to ache all over, especially my back and chest, but since we started working out, it's not so bad. I still get sore, but in a good way."

"That's great. What about your mood?"

His grip slipped, and the resistance band snapped back violently. With a calm hand, I picked it up.

"I'm fine," he said shortly. "Give me the band."

I fiddled with the band. "Can I ask you a personal question? It might make you upset, but I feel like I need to know."

Toby's brow scrunched inward, as it often did when he thought I was invading his personal privacy. "You can ask," he growled.

"I've seen remarkable improvement in you," I told him first. He deserved to hear it. "When you're in here, it seems like you're dedicated to getting better."

He went through the motions of the face pull, using an invisible resistance band since I still held the one he'd been using. "I guess."

"Eli tells me your behavior hasn't changed beyond the movement studio," I said. "I heard you slapped Scout the other day. You won't eat unless a certain nurse brings you food. You continuously talk back to Eli and belittle him. You lash out against Dashiell—"

"I get it," he snapped.

"When we first started classes, you asked me to help you out of here," I reminded him. "I'm trying to do that, but you need to do your part too. Why won't you show the rest of them how well you're doing?"

I offered him the band. He resumed his exercises.

"I hate them," he puffed unexpectedly in the middle of his set. Though I'd stepped back from helping him, his form was perfect. "Doctor Trevino, Scout, Dashiell. I hate them all. I hate most of the nurses, except Misty. They talk to me like I'm crazy and stupid. They make me take so many medications that I can't feel my tongue in the morning." He finished the assigned number of pulls but kept going. "I feel dead inside, like my brain is flat-lining. The only time I feel normal is in this room."

"That's twenty-five," I said, taking the resistance band out of his grasp. "Take a break."

He wiped sweat from his forehead as I filled a paper cup of water for him. He drained it in seconds, so I filled another.

"Another personal question," I said. "How did you end up at the Center to begin with?"

His expression darkened. "You first."

"What do you mean?"

"I can tell you've got deep, dark secrets of your own." He jerked his chin at the long sleeves I wore beneath my scrubs. "I've seen those scars on your arm. Why don't you start with that?"

I ran my fingers across the raised, jagged bumps on my skin. Unlike Toby, I'd let go of my past. It no longer affected my daily life, which was why I felt comfortable sharing it with him.

"My parents died when I was a baby," I started. "Car crash. Tragic. Blah, blah, blah. There was no one to take me in, so I got stuck in foster care. My guardians got worse and worse over the years. So did my own behavior."

Toby sat on the floor, listening intently.

"I got into a lot of fights," I went on. "When I was thirteen, I went to this middle school in a pretty bad area of town. One of the girls there had it out for me. During study hall one day, she pulled a knife on me." I rolled up my sleeve to show him the scars. "I have another one in my stomach. I almost bled out."

Toby whistled. "Tell me you at least got a few punches in."

"I did more than that," I admitted. "I outsmarted her. I took the knife, and in self-defense, I stabbed her."

The color drained from Toby's face as he saw the truth on mine.

"You killed her."

"She died in the ICU," I told him. "The paramedics couldn't save her."

He rolled to his feet and tugged his fingers through his hair. "What happened to you afterward?"

"I got lucky," I said. "I wasn't tried as an adult. There were enough witnesses to say that I'd acted out of concern for my own safety. Still, I ended up in a juvenile detention center for the better part of my high school career."

Toby stared at me, mouth open.

"You can ask," I said.

"Ask what?"

"What it feels like to kill someone."

He swallowed the lump in his throat. "Well? What does it feel like?"

"Empty." I threaded the resistance band through my fingers, needing something tactile to distract me. "Kind of like how you say you feel when you're on all those medications."

Toby sat down again. This time, he kept more space between us. I knew enough about body language to understand he was scared of me.

"How did you get from there to here?" he asked. "You don't see a whole lot of teenage murderers going to college to become therapists."

I let out a laugh. "The whole incident struck a chord with me. I realized if I kept acting the way I'd been acting, I'd never be happy or be at peace. In juvie, you have a right to an education, so I got my GED. My personal essay got me into five different colleges and won me a scholarship." I indicated a headline with my hands. "It was called *I Was a Teenaged Criminal.*"

Toby snorted. "You're kidding me."

"I'm not," I promised. "Of all the things I've done in my life, I'm most proud of my ability to move on from what happened to me when I was thirteen. You can do the same."

Toby hugged his legs into his chest and rested his chin on his knees. "You know, my family wasn't always rich. My real dad left my mom before I was born. I grew up in this crappy apartment in Brooklyn before Brooklyn got cool."

I sat against the wall, breathing quietly. Now that he was talking, I didn't want anything to interrupt him.

"Everything was fine," he said. "I liked my school and the neighborhood. Then the company my mom worked for got bought by a bigger company. The guy who owned it took a liking to her. Next thing I know, she's married to this rich douchebag and wants to move out of our home to some penthouse in the city." He pinched a tear that hovered on his eyelashes. "From the beginning, the guy didn't like me. You can imagine what it was like when Mom told me he was going to be my stepfather. At the wedding—"

The door burst open and Eli stomped in, his face beet red. "Natasha, can I see you outside?"

"We're not done with our session."

"*Now.*"

I apologized to Toby and excused myself from the room. "Eli, what's going on—?"

Suddenly, he was in my face. "What the hell do you think you're doing?" he demanded. "This isn't story time, Natasha. You're not here to pad the boy's ego. You're not *friends*, for God's sake."

Stunned, I had no ready reply.

"You're a professional," Eli said, jabbing his finger into my shoulder. "Act like one."

He stormed off.

*T*iming had never been my strong suit. Right as I was returning to the therapists' office to finish my notes, Imogen and Ariel were on their way out. I nodded politely as we swept by each other. Usually, they flounced off without issue, but Imogen must have seen weakness in my expression that day.

"Not so fast," she said, stretching her arm across the doorway so I couldn't get in. "This isn't healthy, Natasha. I spoke to Hilary in HR, and she said no one works as many hours as you do. Is it true you're last to leave the building every day?"

I rubbed my temples and sighed. "I don't know. Probably. The night nurses get here before I leave."

"I don't think it's fair," Ariel said. "Aren't you paid hourly?"

"No," I answered. "Salaried. Just like you two."

"In that case, it's unjust," Imogen added. "Eli shouldn't expect you to keep up this pace. It's inhuman. You're coming with us." Panic flooded through my veins as

134

Imogen linked her arm in mine and marched me away from the office. "Ariel," she called over her shoulder. "Grab her things. She needs her coat. It's freezing outside."

"I'm fine, really," I said, trying to pry my arm out of Imogen's grasp. "I have some important work to catch up on. You don't need to do this, ladies."

Ariel caught up with us, draped my coat across my shoulders, and took up my other arm so I was trapped on both sides. "Don't try to argue," she said. "You're coming to dinner with us, no matter what."

"Really, I already have plans!"

They ignored my lies and marched me beyond the sterilized halls, into the lobby, and past the front desk. As we emerged from the Center and into the wind, my coat dropped off and landed on the cold stone driveway.

"I'll get it!" I cried, wrenching my arms free of the other therapists.

A manicured hand reached for my coat at the same time as I did. Lindsay Trevino met my gaze as we stood up, each with a handful of the ratty fabric. In contrast, she wore a beautiful tan peacoat over a white Oxford shirt, tight black pants, and heeled boots that made her several inches taller than me.

"Going out?" she asked quizzically. She waved to Ariel and Imogen. "I thought we had plans tonight."

"We do?"

Lindsay lifted a perfectly waxed eyebrow in the direction of the therapists behind me. "Don't we?"

I caught on. "Yes! Yes, we do. I was just trying to tell Imogen and Ariel about—"

"Our coffee date," Lindsay finished as I stuttered. She

looked over my shoulder. "Sorry, ladies. You can have her some other time, I promise."

Imogen's draw dropped as Ariel's eyes widened. I hid a grimace. Tomorrow, they would no doubt pester me with endless questions of why Lindsay Trevino would ask me to get coffee with her. Today, I was simply appreciative of a night without their company.

"Shall we?"

Lindsay linked her arm in mine. This time, I went willingly. She raised a hand at the driveway's curb, and a valet attendant pulled up in an expensive Mercedes.

"In you get," Lindsay said, ushering me toward the passenger seat. She tipped the valet guy as she exchanged seats with him. "Thanks, Paul."

The attendant, maybe twenty years old, pocketed the cash with a grin and touched his hat. "Anytime, Miss Trevino."

As the heated seat warmed my butt and back, Lindsay pulled out of the driveway. I turned around to wave at Imogen and Ariel through the back windshield. They wore identical stunned expressions.

"Phew!" I faced front again and yanked off my gloves. The car was already so warm that I didn't need them. "Thanks for that."

Lindsay smiled. "You looked like you were being carted off to war."

"I'm not a people person," I said hastily, hoping Lindsay didn't think ill of me for avoiding the other therapists. "I do better on my own. Imogen and Ariel are nice enough, but—"

"Nat, relax. I don't require you to get along with every

single person you work with." She rolled her eyes. "Heaven knows I don't."

"Thanks again, anyway," I said. "You can drop me off at the edge of town if you don't want to go all the way to the inn. I know it's out of your way, and I don't mind walking."

She cast me a mischievous glance out of the side of her eye. "Did you think you were getting out of coffee with me?"

"Uh, I—" I stuttered, as confused as Imogen and Ariel as to why Lindsay had singled me out twice. "Coffee's great, but I haven't had dinner."

"Good thing the café serves food."

THOUGH I WOULD NEVER ADMIT it to Marcel, the teenaged barista behind the counter at the local café made a better cappuccino than he did. Then again, I favored coconut milk to dairy milk, and Marcel refused to use it. Little did he know, it altered the flavor of the coffee in the best way.

"Hmm." I closed my eyes and inhaled the steam coming off the foam. "Smells great."

The windows of the café fogged at the corners. Crystals of ice formed on the outside of the glass. The sky darkened into a never-ending gray blanket. It would snow soon, perhaps before Thanksgiving next week.

Lindsay picked up her herbal tea from the counter, set it on our table, and shrugged out of her fancy overcoat. "God, the cold makes my bones ache. Beware of getting old, Natasha."

"I think it's a pretty safe bet we're around the same

age," I said. "Just because you've done more with your life than I have doesn't make you older than me."

Lindsay scoffed and looked off into the distance through the window. The streetlights twinkled on. A group of middle schoolers in the park across the street glanced up, said their goodbyes, and separated. A sad smile touched my lips. They had parents to tell them to come home when the streetlights came on. To them, it might have been annoying. To me, it would have been a blessing.

"I haven't done more," Lindsay said.

"I haven't seen you around much lately," I replied. "I can only guess that means you're working away."

She stirred sugar rocks into her tea and kept stirring long after they dissolved. "Things at the Center are rough. Eli—" She glanced up. "I suppose I shouldn't be talking about it to an employee."

I leaned forward. "Does this have anything to do with Eli's increasingly horrible moods?"

Her shoulders dropped in relief. "You've noticed too?"

"He's been difficult to work with lately," I mentioned. "At the beginning, he seemed receptive to my ideas, especially with the patients in Ward 13, but recently... He yelled at me this afternoon. Told me to be more professional with the patients."

Lindsay made a face. "You're kidding. Out of all our therapists, you're the one with the most compassion."

"Maybe compassion doesn't always translate well with this job," I sighed.

The barista called my name, and I went to the counter to collect the ham and cheese panini I'd ordered for dinner. Lindsay's food came up right after, so I grabbed her plate too.

"Thanks, I'm starving," she said as I set a cup of soup and a side salad in front of her. She crunched up a packet of saltines and dumped them on top of the soup. "I'm sorry about Eli. He's under a lot of stress. We all are."

I took a bite of my sandwich and chewed thoughtfully. "Would I be prying if I asked about the financial state of the Center?"

She bristled uncomfortably but retained her composure. "It's amazing how quickly rumor spreads, isn't it?"

"That usually happens because the rumors are true."

Lindsay rested her face against her closed fist, pushing the skin of her cheek up toward her eye. "Your job isn't in trouble, if that's what you're wondering."

I *had* been wondering. I liked Lone Elm. For the first time, I felt like my work meant something. More than that, I had found an odd sort of family in Lauren and Baz. Despite my initial reservations about moving to a small town, I found myself not wanting to leave it. But that wasn't the only reason I was curious about Trevino's monetary issues.

"It's not that," I said. "It's more about Eli. When he's stressed, he doesn't treat his patients or his employees as well as he should. I don't meant to tattle on him, but I do think he's allowing his emotions to interfere with his medicine."

"Aren't you worried I'll tell him you said all of this?" Lindsay asked.

I shrugged. "If you do, he has two ways of looking at it. He can either examine his current routine and correct himself or decide I'm wrong and punish me. Either way, his actions define *his* character. Not mine."

Lindsay set down her spoon. "I envy your self-confidence. If only someone had taught me that sort of lesson when I was younger."

"I learned that one myself," I assured her. "It comes from years of being on my own, a self-preservation tactic, if you will."

"I don't doubt it." She blew across the surface of her soup. Cracker crumbs scattered over the table, but she paid it no mind. "If I confide in you, would you be so kind as to keep it to yourself? The last thing I need is for mine and Eli's business to become gossip."

I mimed zipping my lips shut.

She let out a long sigh. "He's dropped the ball on the business side of things. I've practically been running the Center on my own. It's a good thing I interned under Eli's father before he passed. Otherwise, we might be completely lost by now."

"You interned at Trevino?"

"You don't know the story? I thought everyone did." She fished a piece of cheesy broccoli out of her soup. "One of those fancy New York magazines did a piece on us."

"Power couple of the year?"

She laughed. "Something like that."

"I didn't read it."

"I'll start at the beginning then," she said. "I majored in business and received an internship to work at Trevino right out of college. I was young and hadn't the faintest idea what it was like to run an enormous rehab center. Elijah—Eli's father—was the best mentor I could have hoped for. He saw promise in me, and he taught me everything about the Center."

"That's how you met Eli, I'm guessing."

She nodded. "He was fresh off his degree. You can probably understand why I fell so hard for him. He was handsome and intelligent, and I liked his family. Work relationships were frowned on, so we snuck around for a year. When his father found out, I was afraid he might resent me, but Elijah was ecstatic. Within another year, we were married. I was sure the rest of our lives would pan out as I'd pictured."

"But something changed?"

Her mouth drooped at the corners. "Elijah's death last year was unexpected. It threw everything out of orbit. The plan had always been for me and Eli to take over the Center, but we didn't expect it to happen so soon. We weren't ready." She tapped her spoon against the bowl, and the clink of metal against ceramic echoed through the café. "Eli took it particularly hard. He hasn't been the same since."

"I'm sorry," I murmured. "That must be tough on the both of you."

She pasted on a smile that didn't reach her eyes. "We're muddling through. Anyway, without Elijah at the head, we lost a lot of funding. Investors pulled out when they realized how little experience Eli had with money. I've had to beg others not to do the same." She left her soup and studied me from across the table. "Hiring you was my idea. The Center needed something new to boast about. I can't thank you enough for being as efficient as you are. You're helping me save this place."

A blush crept up my neck and into my cheeks. "Please.

If it weren't for this job, I'd still be washing linens and refilling wipe canisters in Colorado."

"Look at it as a two-way street then," Lindsay said. "How are you liking it at the Center so far? It's been almost two months since you arrived."

"I love it," I answered, as I always did when someone asked. "It's a dream come true to do what I'm doing, and I've seen so many improvements in my patients."

She lowered her voice. "What about in Ward 13? How are the patients there responding to your program?"

"Slowly but surely," I told her. "Wilson's insomnia is getting better, and Scout told me she was able to lessen his dosage. Alexis has pulled a complete one-eighty. Toby" —I let out a sigh— "is still Toby, but I'm hoping I break through to him soon."

Lindsay cleared her throat. "Toby Gardner?"

"He's a good kid," I said earnestly. "He works so hard in our sessions, and I don't see many symptoms of his disorder. I keep wondering if he was diagnosed improperly. We got to talking the other day—Eli interrupted us— but if I had to guess, Toby experienced a trauma in his past that has made him behave this way. Eli thinks—"

"Stop there," Lindsay said shortly. Her head swiveled to make sure the other café patrons weren't listening in. "First of all, we're in public. You are putting this patient's privacy in danger by speaking about him so frankly. Secondly, I like you, Natasha, but you are not a psychiatrist. Stick to Eli's diagnosis. Don't undermine him. These kids are struggling, sure, but that doesn't mean they're beneath tricking you to get what they want."

The hairs on my arm stood up. These days, I was used

to Eli speaking to me in such a superior tone. From Lindsay, it sounded foreign.

"My apologies," I said curtly. "I'll check my behavior in the future."

Lindsay softened, her shoulders slumping. "I'm sorry, I didn't mean to go all boss lady on you. Toby is an important patient of ours. If we take too many risks with him, we could jeopardize his health and the Center's reputation. I need you to keep a close eye on him, closer than the other patients."

"Like I said, he's made significant advancements in his treatments," I replied, in a quieter tone. "If his health is imperative to the Center's reputation, then both you and him are on the right track."

"That's good to hear." Lindsay checked her watch. "I should get you home soon. You probably have an early day tomorrow."

I wrapped the other half of my panini in foil and stuffed it in my pocket for later. "Don't worry about it. The inn is right up the street. I don't mind walking."

"Are you sure? It's freezing."

I tugged my gloves on. "I don't mind. It helps clear my head. See you tomorrow?"

"See you sometime," she said. "I'm swamped with work."

I patted her shoulder. "Let me know if you need anything. I'm happy to help."

She placed her hand over mine. "That means a lot to me, Nat. Thank you."

Outside, my hair lashed against my face in the wind. I jammed a beanie over my head and yanked my hood up, pulling as much fabric as possible around my skin. With my vision obscured, I ran right into a tall, black-coated being.

"Oh, sorry!" I craned my neck and spotted a familiar face. "Dashiell, hi. I didn't know you existed outside of work."

Inwardly, I smacked myself for saying something so stupid, but Dashiell grinned. I'd never seen his teeth before. The expression looked more feral than friendly.

"I can assure you I exist beyond the walls of the Center, Miss Bell." He straightened my beanie, which had gone cockeyed when I'd run into him. "Get home safely."

"I will, thanks."

Dashiell sidestepped me and went into the café. I took a few steps forward before curiosity itched my neck. I glanced over my shoulder and watched as Dashiell took my seat across the table from Lindsay. They bent their heads together, becoming absorbed in conversation almost instantly.

TWO WEEKS PASSED WITHOUT INCIDENT. Perhaps Lindsay did pass on my words to Eli, because he became much calmer in my presence. When I spoke about the patients, he made an obvious point to listen to me. Though I was hesitant to talk about Toby again, it felt necessary. Mostly, I spoke to Lindsay about him. She wanted daily updates on his condition, which she passed on to Eli. In general, Eli was more receptive to my ideas and thoughts on Toby, so much so that Toby himself began to notice.

"It's better," Toby said to me, sweating after a hard session. "Doctor Trevino stopped babying me. His voice is different when he talks to me, like he respects what I want more. I haven't taken sedatives in nine days."

Toby's marked improvement became the talk of the Center. I couldn't go anywhere without someone congratulating me.

"It's a miracle," one of the nurses told me in the hallway once. "I thought that kid would be stuck here forever. You should be proud of yourself."

"I'm proud of him. He put in the work."

The only person who didn't seem so happy with my connection to Toby was Scout. She'd begun avoiding me in Ward 13 unless I requested her help with my other patients. Occasionally, I caught her staring at me from across the room. When I made eye contact with her, she quickly looked away. Though Toby no longer needed to be on a constant watch, Scout spent an inordinate amount of time near his room, as if she expected him to revert to his psychosis at any moment.

Thankfully, Toby remained consistent, so much so that when Eli approached me with a certain piece of news, it didn't come as a surprise.

"He's making tremendous strides in our sessions," Eli said. He'd called me to his office to talk privately. "I have you to thank for that, and" —his face flushed red— "I must apologize for my previous behavior. If you hadn't spoken to Lindsay, I never would have given Toby the chance to get better. Rest assured, I've learned from this experience. I won't dismiss your opinions again."

"That means a lot to me," I replied. "I was simply advocating for the patient."

"As you should." Eli shuffled papers on his desktop.

"You should be happy to hear that I approved Toby's discharge."

Emotions warred within me. On one hand, Toby's release was the best news I could have hoped for. It's what we've been working toward the past few months. On the other hand, I would be sad to see him go. Of all the patients I had, I'd connected with him the most.

"That's great," I managed to say. "When is he leaving?"

"His parents are coming to pick him up tomorrow morning," he said absently, distracted by a spreadsheet with several confusing figures listed on it. "Feel free to bid him goodbye and good luck tonight. I have to address this."

Dismissed, I backed out of Eli's office and took the stairs to the lobby two at a time, my footprints echoing loudly across the marble. The Center was quiet. It was after normal work hours, and everyone but the night nurses had gone home. I picked up my pace, hurrying toward Ward 13, as if Toby's parents might come early and take him away tonight.

As I approached the ward, a terrified yelp echoed through the corridor. My job turned into a run. I burst through the doors and followed the agonized cries right to Toby's room.

He sobbed freely, his face red and streaked with tears. His hair stood on end as though he'd been pulling it out strand by strand. His favorite nurse, Misty, sat at his bedside with a box of tissues.

"What happened?" I demanded, rushing in.

"He's been like this for an hour," Misty said. Her face bore marks of crying too. Her eyes were bloodshot and watery. "He won't tell me what's wrong. I called for the aides—"

I stepped past her and took Toby's hand. "Hey, buddy. It's me. It's Natasha. Everything's going to be okay. You're okay."

Toby shook his head, and a fresh wave of tears ran down his cheeks. "I don't— I can't— Please don't make me—"

So overcome with emotion, he couldn't get a full sentence out. Scout and Dashiell arrived, no doubt replying to Misty's call. Dashiell reached for the restraints to secure Toby to the bed—he hadn't needed them in weeks—but Toby screamed, hugged his arms to his chest, and flipped over to hide himself from everyone in the room.

I shoved Dashiell away from Toby's bed. "He doesn't need those. Everyone, get out. Get out! It's stressing him out."

Dashiell and Misty read enough rage and severity in my tone to leave the room. Scout, on the other hand, drew closer. Toby's breathing quickened as he looked at her from beneath his pillow.

"He's having a panic attack," Scout said. She moved past me, approaching Toby's bed with such quiet steps that he didn't react to her. "The medication will calm him."

"I don't think—"

"It's better for him this way." The familiar syringe came into view. She flicked it to get the air bubbles out and drew Toby's arm away from his chest. Numbed to everything, he let her. "He might hurt himself otherwise."

I sucked in a breath as I watched the needle go in.

Scout pushed the plunger, forcing the medication into Toby's arm. His eyes drooped and his body went slack, face pressed against the pillows. Scout gently turned his head so he could breathe freely.

"Don't worry, kiddo," she muttered to him. "Everything will be all right tomorrow."

I tossed and turned all night, upsetting Jean Paul so often that he finally hopped off the bed and meowed at the door until I got up and let him out. Until dawn, I sat in the library and stared off into the distance, my head flooded with thoughts. Something wasn't sitting well with me, and it wasn't until the sun peeked in through the crack in the curtains and shone right in my eye that I realized what it was.

Lauren emerged into the foyer, wearing jeans and a plaid flannel shirt instead of her usual slacks and floral blouse. It was a Friday, after all. "You're up early," she said, noticing me in the library. "Everything okay? I heard Jean Paul sneak into Baz's room last night."

"One of my patients is being released today."

"That's great!" She studied my furrowed brow and downturned lips. "Is that not great?"

"Something tells me he's not ready to go home yet," I muttered. "I get the feeling he won't be safe."

Lauren leaned against the arched wall that separated

the library from the lobby. "What are you still doing here then? Go tell that to your boss."

I CHANGED into my scrubs and ran outside to find my car completely buried in snow. The night had dumped several feet of the stuff over Lone Elm, and though the town was picture perfect, it was the last thing I needed. Thankfully, the roads had been plowed, so Lauren gave me a ride up to the Center. As we drove around the last bend, I spotted a tall, familiar figure hurrying along the side of the road.

"There's Eli," I said. "You can drop me off next to him."

Lauren slowed the car. "Why is he walking?"

Eli glanced over his shoulder as he saw the car approaching, but he didn't pause as Lauren hit the brakes to let me out. I thanked Lauren and rushed after Eli as she turned around and headed back down the hill.

"Eli, wait up," I called, slipping on a patch of ice. "I want to talk to you about Toby. I know his parents are coming to pick him up today, but I don't think he's ready to go home. You didn't see him last night. He went into a blind panic. He was scared, and until—"

"You haven't heard yet, have you?"

Eli's mouth was set in a hard line, and the corners of his eyes wrinkled with worry and anger. Still, he refused to slow his pace.

"Heard about what?" I asked.

Red and blue lights reflected off Eli's pale visage. I whipped my head around and caught sight of the ambulance and police cars parked outside the Center. The other therapists and day nurses stood outside in a clump, whispering to each other and craning their necks to get a look past the emergency vehicles that blocked the entrance to the building. A chill ran down my spine that had nothing to do with the fresh snow.

"I've got to go," Eli said shortly, jogging toward the mess. "We'll talk after."

Heart pounding, I joined the therapists' huddle. For once, Imogen and Ariel were quiet. Andy held Jewel on one side and wrapped his free arm around me. Hilary and Cameron sat on the curb with Misty, Toby's favorite nurse, who sobbed freely as the other women attempted to comfort her. My stomach dropped.

"What happened?" I asked in a hoarse voice.

"Someone killed themselves," Imogen answered promptly. Even in a situation like this, she wasn't to be outdone. "In Ward 13."

The sudden urge to vomit rose in my throat. I swallowed it back. There was no need to panic, not right away. Maybe the victim was someone I didn't know, someone I'd never worked with—

I spotted Eli in the midst of the blinking lights. He rushed over to a pair of unfamiliar people, a pretty woman in her early forties with wavy gold hair and an older man in a blocky suit with a nose like a monkey's. The woman was beside herself. She threw herself into Eli's arms, sobbing as she pounded against Eli's chest. Eli patted her back. He was close to tears himself, but he kept them at bay.

The older man appeared unbothered, or perhaps a little annoyed. As his companion embraced Eli, his eyes shifted skyward in a half roll, as if he were trying to contain his irritation. The emergency lights flashed, and he covered his face. When a paramedic passed close to him, he seized the emergency worker and pointed to the lights. The paramedic glanced up and shook his head. Had the man really asked the paramedic to turn off the lights because he was inconvenienced by them?

A team of paramedics emerged from the Center, wheeling a stretcher. Everyone fell quiet and spun around for a look at the victim, but there was no body, only a pile of unused medical materials. The golden-haired woman let out a fresh sob. Her supposed spouse patted her once on the shoulder. I studied them with a sinking heart. Then my gaze dropped to Misty, who was still inconsolable. My denial reached its peak, and I flowed down the mountain of realization.

I took off, making a run for the Center's front door.

"Natasha, wait!" Andy called after me. "Don't go in there!"

No one could stop me. I tore past Eli and the mismatched couple, several paramedics, and a crowd of police officers who didn't seem to be busy doing anything. One of them tried to grab me and failed. I sprinted into the lobby and made a sharp turn toward Ward 13. My ice-covered boots slid across the polished floor, and my feet flew out from under me. I went down hard, all of my weight coming down on my left wrist. It cracked under the pressure, but the pain went unnoticed. I pushed myself up with my other hand and kept running.

The doors to Ward 13 were propped open to make way for emergency services. The patients had been locked in their rooms. Many of them stood with their noses pressed to the windows, peering out into the corridor to see what had happened. I made a beeline for Toby's room and thundered inside.

Everything was covered in blood. The sheets, the walls, the floor. It was a sea of red.

Scout caught me before I collapsed. Her grip was powerful for someone so small. She hauled me out of the bloodied room and set me on the floor. I grabbed her sleeve and yanked her closer to me.

"Where is he?" I croaked. My vocal chords worked so hard and yet seemed so inefficient. "Where's Toby?"

Remorse flitted like a hummingbird through Scout's dark eyes.

"In the morgue," she replied.

Ward 13 swam around me. My vision blurred. I blacked out.

I AWOKE IN THE EMPLOYEES' clinic, a small room outfitted with an examination table and basic first aid materials. Every once in a while, someone visited to fetch a Band-Aid for a paper cut or a painkiller for a headache. I doubted any of the therapists had collapsed and needed to recover here before.

I felt hungover. My head weighed heavily on my neck. My tongue seemed thick enough to block my throat. As I sat up, I felt as though someone had replaced my organs with rocks and mud. Perhaps that morning had been a terrible drunken nightmare.

The truth scooped me up like a dump truck and spat me out again. The blood-covered room flashed before my eyes, no matter if they were closed or open. Scout's reply —those three words—echoed over and over in my head. *In the morgue.*

Toby was dead. He'd killed himself. After an entire

year at Trevino—supposedly the best mental hospital in the nation—and on the brink of his release, Toby committed the one true crime any person could commit against themselves. But why?

Imogen came into the clinic. She smiled softly, without hint of her usual smirk. "I came to check on you," she said. "Are you okay? Scout said you had quite a shock up there."

I covered my eyes with my hands. "I don't think I can work today."

"You have other patients scheduled."

"I'll see them tomorrow."

Imogen came closer and took my hands away from my face. When I looked up at her, she wore a surprisingly soothing expression.

"I know this is hard," she said. "But your patients are counting on you. They need you as much as Toby did."

I furiously wiped an escaped tear away from my cheek. "Why didn't the paramedics take him to the hospital?"

"I overheard Eli speaking to the parents," Imogen said. "Are you sure you want to hear this?"

"Tell me."

"He was dead before the paramedics got here," she murmured, squeezing my hand. "There was too much blood loss. No point in taking him to the hospital. Eli convinced the parents to keep the body here."

"Why?"

"My guess is for legal reasons," she replied. "With Toby here, Eli and Lindsay can control the news about his death. If he's transferred to a hospital, his records will be much easier for the news to get ahold of."

"Does it matter?" I sniffed. "He's dead either way."

She raised her eyebrows. "Sometimes, I forget you haven't been working here that long. The Center is the best rehab facility in the country. You'd think that means our patients come first, but in reality, the Center's reputation is what's most important to Eli and Lindsay."

"Eli isn't like that," I said. "He cares about his patients."

"I'm sure he does," she agreed, "but he cares about the Trevino family name more."

IMOGEN, bless her uncharacteristic mood swing, got me through the first part of my day. She walked me to each of my classes, supervised the patients during sessions, and helped me teach. When she wasn't available due to her own therapy appointments, she assigned someone else to take her place. Andy, Jewel, and Ariel watched me around the clock, ensuring I wouldn't fall apart in front of my patients.

My last class before lunch was interrupted when Eli and an armed police officer entered the therapy room without prior warning. Imogen rushed over to them before I could say anything, and though she tried her best to usher them out, it wasn't working.

"They want to talk to you," she muttered to me so my patients wouldn't hear our conversation over the music. "In Eli's office."

"After the class ends," I replied.

"Eli said now. He asked me to take over."

I let out a heavy sigh and waved my hands to get the class's attention. "Everyone, Imogen is going to finish up with you. I'll see you next week."

The dancers groaned at my departure. Eli's expression was hard as I met him and the officer at the door.

"What's this about?" I asked.

"Not here," Eli said sternly. "In my office."

"As you know by now, Toby Gardner committed suicide last night," Eli told me once the three of us were safely tucked in his office, away from prying eyes and curious ears. "We're trying to get to the bottom of the situation."

By "we," I assumed he meant the Center and the police, but the officer in question didn't do anything other than stand in the corner of the room with his hands resting on his belt.

"What happened?" I asked in a whisper. "What did he do to himself?"

"That information is confidential right now," Eli answered. "Anything you can tell me about your sessions with Toby might help."

"I told you everything. I thought he was doing better."

"What about this morning?" he questioned. "You had mentioned that he wasn't ready to go home."

I pinched the skin of my wrist to divert my emotional pain to something physical. That way, I wouldn't start crying in front of my boss or the surly police officer in the corner.

"When I visited him last night, he was distraught," I said quietly. "He was screaming and crying like he'd seen a demon. He couldn't even talk, Eli. Scout had to sedate him again."

"Did he mention anything to you before that?" Eli asked. "You had a session with him earlier that day, right?"

"Yes, and he seemed fine."

Eli paced behind his desk, throwing nervous glances at the police officer. "So he didn't say anything about harming himself? He never dropped any hints that he was thinking about doing this?"

"Eli, I'm telling you, he was getting better," I insisted. "Is it possible he didn't do this to himself? Could one of the other patients broken into his room?"

Eli shook his head. "There's no way. Our lockup procedures are flawless. Thank you, Natasha. I'm sorry this had to happen to one of your patients. That's the risk of working in Ward 13."

"But I—"

The police officer finally spoke up. "We'll need to investigate this Ward 13, to make sure the other patients are getting proper treatment."

Eli wore an affronted look. "What does this have to do with the rest of the patients?"

"A boy killed himself in your ward, Dr. Trevino," the officer replied. "You don't want it to happen again, do you?"

"No, of course not."

"Then it's prudent we look into this case—"

The door to the office flew open and Lindsay stormed in. "There are reporters swarming the front lawn!" she spat, her face and neck bright red. "This cannot be happening, Eli. We need a plan—" She stopped short when she noticed that Eli had company. "Oh, hello, Officer. Natasha. I didn't see the two of you."

The officer tipped his hat. "I'll be downstairs with my team if either of you need me."

"We won't," Eli replied shortly. "And until I see official

paperwork, you don't have access to my wards. If my patients see the police, it might upset them."

The cop smirked. "We'll play it by ear."

Lindsay sank into a spare chair and flipped her hair over her shoulder. When she spoke, she addressed both of us. "What are we supposed to do? His mother is beside herself. Can you imagine? She thought she was going to be picking up her cured son today, and all we have for her is a body bag."

I flinched, unable to picture Toby zipped away in a dark plastic coffin. Eli took notice and shot Lindsay a warning stare.

"We need to do some damage control," Eli said. "Lindsay, call our PR guy. What's his name? He's good at getting the press to back off. Natasha—Nat?"

I yanked myself out of my terrible thoughts. "Yes?"

"Continue with your day as you usually would," he ordered. "Don't speak to the reporters outside. Don't talk to Toby's parents."

"They might want to speak to me. Did you tell them I worked with Toby?"

"They don't know who you are," Lindsay said as she massaged her temples. "So keep quiet until we figure out how to handle this."

"You can get back to work," Eli said. "We'll let you know if anything comes up that you need to be aware of."

FOR THE REST of the day, my mind wandered to Toby every two seconds. It was a hundred times worse than when Lenny died. At least Lenny had passed because of his age. He was as happy as one could be for someone whose life was limited to a rehab facility. Toby's death, on the other hand, felt like a mystery. Admittedly, I'd only known him for a few months, but in that time, he had gone from a hostile, hurtful patient to a kind-hearted, caring boy determined to do better by himself. Then, all of a sudden, he was gone. It didn't make any sense.

The other therapists made a point of helping me throughout the day. Andy helped me type up my notes again, so that I could leave the office on time. As we were all getting ready to go, Imogen held my coat for me so I could easily slip into the sleeves, Ariel grabbed my phone and slipped it into my pocket before I forgot it on the desk, and Jewel offered me a ride home since I didn't have my car again.

"Actually," Imogen said. "Is anyone interested in dinner out? I'm not in the mood to go home yet. I need a distraction from today."

Surprised by my own mouth, I answered, "I'm in."

"My kids are waiting for me at home," Jewel said apologetically.

"I'm out too," Ariel added. "Got a date tonight. Not that I'm much in the mood."

Andy sighed heavily. "You go ahead, ladies. I'm exhausted."

So IT ENDED up being me and Imogen at the Shadows Restaurant, something I never expected to happen. We got a booth in the back, tucked away from the happy, chatty patrons. Imogen sat on the same side as me, and I oddly appreciated the comfort of her closeness. We ordered a bottle of wine to share and an appetizer.

"This is only the second time I've seen you outside of work," Imogen remarked, a few glasses in. A spot of pink shone brightly on each of her cheeks. "Not much of a people person, are you?"

"Never have been."

"Why did you decide to come out tonight?"

"Because otherwise I would have had to be alone with my thoughts."

She rested her chin on her fist and scrutinized me. "You're good at that normally?"

"Normally."

The server stopped by the table to deliver a diatribe about the weekly specials, which neither me nor Imogen wanted to order. When she went away at last, Imogen sank further into her seat.

"It's horrible, isn't it?" She flattened out her straw wrapper and stuck it to the condensation on her water glass. "It's not the first time something like this has happened, but it's never been a kid before."

I set aside my wine. "People have killed themselves at Trevino before?"

"Of course," she said. "It's a psych ward, and some people can't get better, no matter how hard they try."

"I don't think that's true."

She waved me off with her napkin. "A different subject for a different day."

"Did Eli and Lindsay say anything to you today?" I asked her. "They're acting so weird."

Imogen refilled her wine glass even though she hadn't finished what was inside. "I bet. Toby was one of our highest profile patients."

"He was?"

"Didn't you read his file?"

"Yes. It didn't say anything about—"

"His stepfather is Banks Billings," Imogen interrupted. "The Wall Street guy? He's a billionaire. He promised Eli he'd donate a million dollars to the Center if we could 'fix' Toby."

My jaw popped open. "Are you serious?"

Imogen nodded. "From what I hear, the Center needed that money. I doubt we're getting it now. Eli and Lindsay will have to figure out another way to pay off their debts. Not to mention, it's terrible publicity. The Trevinos can't possibly pay their publicist enough to smooth this over. The rumors will start soon enough, and that'll hurt the Center even more."

"Are you worried?" I asked. "About losing your job?"

"You should be worried," she said, slurring her words slightly. The appetizer hadn't arrived yet, and she was drinking on an empty stomach. "You were closest to Toby. If they need a scapegoat, you're the obvious choice."

"Eli and Lindsay wouldn't do that."

She lifted an eyebrow. "You really think you know them that well?"

"I thought you worshiped the ground Eli walks on."

Imogen let out a giggle then a hiccup. "I like Eli, but everyone knows he's not the man his father was. Hell, if Elijah was still running the Center, this probably never would have happened. Or if it did, we never would have heard about it."

The appetizer arrived, and the crispy calamari bits distracted Imogen from explaining her last statement. The wine hit me a few minutes later. My head swam in the warm red Malbec, and we dissolved into conversations about less important things. Imogen complained about an ex-boyfriend for the rest of the meal, and I blessedly welcomed her life story. This was exactly what I needed from tonight.

AT THE INN, the wine's numbing effects wore off by midnight, leaving me alone in my room to stare at the ceiling. Jean Paul hadn't bothered sleeping next to me that night. I suspected he favored Baz's bed to mine these days. When it became obvious that I wouldn't be sleeping anytime soon, I threw off the covers, went to my work bag, and pulled out my handwritten notes on Toby. Maybe I'd missed something during all our sessions together.

I sat on the window seat and read by the light of the moon. The first few pages were crammed with messy, hasty handwriting. I'd jotted down so many assumptions about Toby that ended up being untrue. As I read further, things became clearer. Not once had I written that Toby seemed like he wanted to harm himself. In fact, I'd documented the opposite. As our sessions went on, I wrote more and more about Toby's improving mood, his continued cooperation, and that he'd begun opening up to me emotionally.

As I set the notebook aside, confused by its contents, something fluttered from between the blank pages and landed on the floor. I picked it up and peered curiously at it. It was a Polaroid picture with worn edges. I recognized the child in it right away. Toby, around the age of three or four, laughed in the arms of an unfamiliar, handsome man. They shared the same nose and mouth, so the man could only be Toby's real father. My smile wavered. How had this ended up in my notebook? I flipped the picture over and gasped.

Someone had written a note on the back: *Trevino kills. Find out the truth.*

he picture of Toby haunted me through the night and the next day. The mysterious message on the back was all I could think about. Who had put that photo in my notebook? I kept it on my person at all times. It seemed impossible that anyone could slip something inside it without me noticing. Moreover, who would write something like that? *Trevino kills. Find out the truth.* First off, I had no evidence that the Center was up to no good. Second, what truth was I supposed to be exposing, *if* the message was even meant for me?

Lauren, on her way to refill another guest's coffee cup, glanced over my shoulder. "Cute kid."

I hurriedly tucked the photo into my pocket and returned my attention to breakfast. Marcel had made Belgian waffles with fresh berries and homemade whipped cream, but my stomach flipped over too frequently to consider enjoying the meal. My tongue seized as I popped a particularly sour blackberry between my teeth.

"Nephew?" Lauren guessed when I didn't reply.

"Family friend," I lied. I couldn't bring myself to tell Lauren what had happened the day before. First of all, I didn't want to talk about Toby's death, and secondly, the mysterious picture was driving me insane without having to talk about it. I had no desire to pick apart its potential meaning with Lauren.

After all, the whole ordeal was starting to feel like a mean prank. The more I thought about it, the more obvious it seemed. Imogen's atypical behavior yesterday raised my eyebrows. Never before had she made such an attempt to help me, but she spent every free minute by my side. She was the only one who had been close enough to my notebook to slip the picture inside, but to what purpose? I intended on finding out.

"Nat!" Lauren snapped in front of my eyes. "Hey, you're freaking me out."

"Sorry," I said, pulling myself back to the present. "I have a lot on my mind. Can I have more coffee?"

"Your cup's full."

I looked down. Indeed, I hadn't touched my beverage yet. "Oh."

Lauren shook her head and rubbed my shoulder. "Let me know if you want to talk about it. I can tell there's something going on with you."

"Don't worry about me." I pulled on my coat and poured the mug of coffee into a to-go cup. "Tell Marcel thanks for breakfast."

Lauren walked to the lobby with me. "Before you go, can I ask a favor? Baz has a research paper due next week, and she's decided to write it on the history of mental health care in America. She asked if you might be able to rustle up anything useful at the Center." She caught sight of my downturned lips and added hastily, "It's okay if you can't. I can take her to the library to find something else."

"I think the Center has a library somewhere," I said, zipping up my coat and steeling myself for the cold winds and snow outside. "I'll see what I can find."

THE DRIVE up the hill felt indicative of the day to come. My car groaned with every turn, struggling to make it up the incline. Though the road had been cleared, a thin sheen of ice had settled on the asphalt. My old tires, almost absent of tread, slipped and slid across the pavement. I pitied the large truck—no doubt an outpatient or another employee—driving up to the Center behind me. The one-lane road provided no option for them to dodge around my slow, ailing vehicle.

When I parked, I neatly avoided the eye of the truck driver and headed inside. Today, I was the last therapist to arrive at work. The others already sat at their desks or arranged materials for their sessions.

"How are you doing, Nat?" Andy asked in a worried tone when I walked in. "Yesterday was a tough one."

I put on a mask of professionalism. "I'm okay, Andy. Thanks for asking. I just want to move forward. One foot in front of the other, right?"

As Andy nodded, the picture of Toby burned a hole in the pocket. From her desk, Imogen cast a scrutinizing glance from my head to my toes.

"Advil?" she asked, offering me a small golden pill box with a number of unidentified medications floating around inside. "You must be as hungover as me."

I shook my head. "I rinsed my system with coffee this morning. Thanks though."

"Hmm." She capped the pill box and rolled her chair closer to mine. "How are you really? You don't have to pretend you're fine. You can tell me the truth."

I subtly rolled a few inches away from her whispered breaths and pretended to busy myself with my computer. "I'm fine, Imogen." The picture flashed in my head. "Actually, did you happen to see my notebook yesterday? I misplaced it."

"Don't you carry that thing around like a prized teddy bear?" she asked. "I didn't see you without it."

Technically, she didn't answer my exact question.

"I must have set it down somewhere," I fibbed. "So you didn't see it? Not in the dance room or Ward 13?"

"No, sorry."

Her reply didn't prove anything. If she was guilty of slipping the picture into my notebook, she sure wasn't going to admit to it. What annoyed me was that she exhibited no signs of lying. She didn't avoid eye contact or fidget in her seat. She was as sturdy as a rock.

The office phone rang, and Andy answered it.

"Hello? Mm-hmm. Yes, she's here. Sure, I'll let her know." Andy hung up the phone and swiveled around to face me. "Nat? Eli wants to see you in Ward 13. Something about a new patient being admitted."

I pulled a face. "Why would he want to see me? I don't do patient intake."

Andy shrugged. "No idea. He asked for you to head up as soon as possible. Before you start your classes for the day."

. . .

WARD 13 WAS ODDLY QUIET. Perhaps Toby's death had triggered something in the other patients. When I passed Wilson's room, he wasn't performing his usual morning workout regimen. He lay flat on the floor, his feet propped up against the wall as he stared at the gray sky through the one window that led to the outside world, as if contemplating his existence in this universe. When he noticed me watching, he mustered a slight smile that didn't reach his eyes.

"Hang in there," I mouthed through the glass. He gave me a thumbs-up.

"Natasha!" Eli barked. He stood outside Toby's old room and waved me toward him.

My feet weighed eighty pounds each as I walked over. I purposely stopped short of the room. My throat tightened. If I looked inside and saw Toby's empty bed, there was a good chance I'd lose all composure.

"I heard you have a new patient," I said.

"Luna Lamont," Eli confirmed. "She's been on the waiting list for a while. I'm happy we're finally able to treat her. Scout and Dashiell are bringing her up now."

The Belgian waffles twisted in my stomach. "Here? To Toby's room?"

"It's just a room, Natasha," he said. "It didn't belong to him."

"He died *yesterday*."

"When a room opens up, we fill the space," he replied shortly, as if explaining this concept to a five-year-old. "That's how it works here. We don't have time for emotions."

"I guess the Center doesn't kid about turnaround

times," I commented. "All that matters is the money, right?"

The hard lines around Eli's mouth softened. "I can see how you might think that. Let me assure you, my main goal—always—is to help as many people as possible. In the end, we couldn't help Toby, but we might be able to help Luna. Doesn't she deserve that chance? Don't we owe it to her to immediately give her the best care possible, regardless of what happened here yesterday?"

A stone dropped into my stomach. He had a solid point. Because of Toby's death, I'd already fostered an unwarranted bias against Luna, but that wasn't right. She had nothing to do with Toby's death, and it wasn't her fault that she'd be taking his place at the Center. Whatever my feelings, I had to work as hard for Luna as I did for Toby.

"What am I doing here?" I asked Eli. "Did you want me to help with her evaluation?"

"No, Scout and Dashiell can help me with that," he answered. "I called you up here because I think she would benefit from the same private sessions you afforded to Toby. She's sixteen, diagnosed with bipolar disorder. I want you to meet her."

"Why can't she join the group sessions?" I fiddled with the embroidered logo on my scrubs, finding comfort in the smooth threads beneath my finger. "Toby was a special case. If she's able, I want her to socialize with her peers." Boldly, I added, "I swear half the reason you don't see as much improvement as you want to is because you keep them so isolated from each other. Loneliness isn't conducive to a healthy mental status, especially for developing teenagers."

Eli's severity returned at once. "The adolescents treated here are considered dangerous to others."

"Regardless, they need to participate in more group activities."

"We lack the additional personnel to supervise such activities."

"So hire more personnel," I said dryly.

"We don't have the mon—" He cut himself off and tossed his hands in the air. "I'm not discussing this with you. We're a nationally ranked facility for a reason. Our treatments *work*. Now, can we get back to Luna—"

A maniacal laugh rent the air as Scout and Dashiell wheeled a stretcher into the ward. The laugh—high-pitched and endless—came from the throat of the teenaged girl sitting atop the stretcher. She had hair so blonde, it appeared white, and her skin was pale enough to see the veins in each arm. Like Toby, she wore restraints around her wrists and a clinical gown with a loosely tied collar. When it slipped down, the girl did not appear to notice how much of her was revealed to everyone in the hallway. She laughed and laughed, her eyes rolling wildly in her head.

As Scout and Dashiell pushed the stretcher into Toby's old room, I reached out to pull the clinical gown up to the girl's throat again. No matter her state, she deserved her modesty.

"Don't—" Scout warned.

It was too late. Faster than a dart, the girl clamped her teeth around my hand and bit down hard. I yelped but left my hand in place, lest I hurt the girl's neck by yanking away. Eli rushed forward to pry the girl's jaw open, but she let go before he could touch her. Then she went back to laughing.

I cradled my hand to my chest. She had drawn blood, but more than that, she had bitten down with such force that the skin had already begun to bruise. The muscles beneath ached.

Eli shoved me into the hallway. "Go down to the clinic and take care of that," he ordered. "Then come back up."

ACCORDING to the Center's on-duty nurse, who I was becoming very familiar with these days, my hand wasn't broken. I would have been impressed if it had been. Luna's jaw was stronger than an alligator's. The nurse irrigated the wound, wrapped it, and warned me to go easy on that hand for the next few days. It was bound to feel worse before it got better.

When I returned to Ward 13 thirty minutes later, Eli and the aides had yet to finish Luna's intake procedure and initial evaluation. As they tried to take her blood pressure, she writhed and squirmed and laughed. Always laughing. Even with the restraints, she moved too much for Eli to get a decent hold on her.

Luna's eyes found mine. They were a beautiful gray, the same color of the sky before it snowed. She blended in with the view beyond the window. At last, she stopped laughing.

"Please," she gasped, talking directly to me. "I don't belong here."

The words triggered a flood of memories. Not long ago, Toby had said those exact same words. I averted my eyes from Luna's.

171

The next laugh came out as a scream. Her face turned red then purple. She drew no breath. Eli held his hand out, and Scout put a syringe in his palm. He pushed it into Luna's arm.

I refused to look away as any sign of independence drained from Luna's eyes. Her laughs faded as she kept my gaze, her energy fading fast as the sedation rushed through her veins with every heartbeat.

"I shouldn't be here," she murmured, sinking into the pillows. "I don't belong here."

Eli swabbed the sweat from Luna's forehead with a damp towel. "You'll find your place, Luna. We're going to help you." He pushed himself to his feet and wiped his own brow on his sleeve. "You're shaking," he said to me, taking me gently by the arm. "Come with me."

ONCE WE WERE in Eli's office, I dropped into a chair, scared my trembling legs wouldn't support me for much longer.

"I'm sorry," I said. "I don't know what's gotten into me. This thing with Toby has been so hard, and Luna—"

"No need to explain." Eli settled himself in the large leather seat behind his desk and unbuttoned his shirt sleeves. "I know you haven't experienced a setting like this one before. What did you think of Luna?"

"She looks like she's being tortured," I said truthfully. "She doesn't trust you. That's obvious. She doesn't want to be here."

"None of them do," Eli murmured, more to himself than to me. "I want you to spend time with her. Get to know her like you did with Toby. Talk to her."

I swallowed the lump in my throat. "With all due respect, I'm not sure if that's a good idea. I saw Toby the most leading up to his decision to end his life. I don't think—"

"I don't believe for one second that your treatment of Toby had anything to do with his suicide," Eli said firmly. "I'm not sure what was going through his head in those last few moments, but I *am* sure that he was grateful for your influence in his life. He was intolerable and inconsolable before you arrived at the Center. You made all the difference."

"If that were true, he wouldn't have killed himself."

Eli scratched beneath his eye, perhaps to conceal the emotion in his irises. "Despite advancements, much about the brain is still misunderstood. Please don't doubt yourself. I know a talented caretaker when I see one."

I accepted his compliment with a nod. "When should I check on Luna? How long will the sedatives last?"

"Actually, I want you to take the rest of the day off," Eli said. "I should have instructed you to go home yesterday. I saw the toll Toby's death took on you, but certain priorities distracted me from caring for my employees."

"Thank you, but I can stay."

"It's not a request," he replied. "I've already informed your patients that their sessions will be rescheduled. I'd like you to use this time to recover from yesterday's shock. Please," he added in a soft voice. "I need you at your best."

"Yes, sir." I got up to leave but hesitated at the door. "Eli, how did Toby do it? I don't mean to be morbid. I just wondered how he managed, so we can prevent such instances in the future."

Eli's voice lost all emotion when he replied. "He pried out a loose nail from the floor moulding and used it to puncture several vital arteries. We've since inspected every room in the ward for similar hazards."

My stomach heaved. I rushed away without replying.

HALFWAY ACROSS THE LOBBY, I remembered Baz's research paper and made a quick about-face to approach the front desk. Cameron, as always, manned the phones with an annoyed expression.

"Sir, I can't release medical records to you," she was saying, barely concealing her exasperation. "They're confidential. No, it doesn't matter if you're the patient's friend. Uh-huh. Sorry about the misunderstanding." She hung up with a tired sigh. "What can I do for you, Natasha?"

"Does the Center have a library?" I asked. "Anywhere they keep old articles or information? I recall Eli mentioning something of the sort when I first got hired."

"Basement level," she replied. "Past the morgue and the records room. Last door on the left."

I thanked her and took the stairs down to the basement. The chilly air and the smell of sterility laid like a blanket across my shoulders. I rushed past the morgue, intentionally averting my eyes. The door was closed, but I wasn't taking any chances.

At the end of the hallway, I found the library, if you could call it a library. Ugly metal shelves were cramped end to end, stacked high with unalphabetized books, huge piles of paper, handwritten journals, and old newspaper clippings. It was not a neat and organized tactile history as I expected from a facility as fancy as the Trevino Center.

Since there was no rhyme or reason as to how information was stored in the library, I started with the closest shelf and moved on from there. I skimmed over tons of articles praising the center, outdated medical magazines that had interviewed Eli or the previous Trevinos, and copies of a recent photoshoot Lindsay and Eli had done as the "most powerful couple in healthcare." When it became obvious that I wouldn't find anything useful at the front of the room, I squeezed through the tiny spaces between the shelves until the familiar smell of old books reached my senses. I drew a stack of yellowing paper into my lap and sat on the floor to go through it.

Two hours later, I emerged from the Center's past with a ton of information for Baz's research paper. Some of it did not reflect well on the Trevinos, and it sure didn't do anything positive for my opinion of Eli's grandfather. I took pictures of the articles I'd singled out, replaced the papers on the shelf, and made my way out of the basement. Upstairs, in the hallway that led to the lobby, I stopped short when I heard Eli, Lindsay, and a pair of unfamiliar voices talking. When I peeked around the corner, I spotted Toby's mother—crying again—and Banks Billings, Toby's stepfather.

"You've put us through enough," Banks was saying, his index finger uncomfortably close to Eli's face. "If she wants to see her son, you'll goddamn well show us her son."

Lindsay stepped in since Eli's face was redder than a

firetruck. She focused on Toby's mother instead of Banks. "Mrs. Billings, I understand how you're feeling, and I wish I could bring you to your son, but I feel it would be too traumatizing for you to see him in this state."

"I just want to see my beautiful boy," Mrs. Billings sobbed. "Please let me see him."

Lindsay turned Mrs. Billings away from her husband and said in a hushed voice, "I know you do, sweetheart, but what good will it do? Think of it this way. If we allow you to see Toby, you will remember him that way forever. You'll only think of his body and the damage he did to it. Wouldn't you rather he stay happy and healthy in your memories?"

Mrs. Billings blew her nose in a handkerchief. "I can't fathom never seeing his face again."

"It won't help to see his face now," Lindsay said. "He looks different. It won't comfort you. Please, I'm only telling you this for your benefit. Don't cause yourself more suffering. It isn't necessary."

Mrs. Billings nodded tearfully.

"A closed casket ceremony would be better for your health too," Lindsay added.

"Oh!"

Mrs. Billings's tears restarted, and she ran across the lobby to get away from the Trevinos. Mr. Billings rolled his eyes and moseyed after his wife. Lindsay dropped her shoulders.

"Christ, this is a disaster," she mumbled under her breath. "If they decide to pull the money they promised us, we're screwed."

Eli's lip curled. "Is that all you can think about? The

money? Their son killed himself in *our* facility. They brought him to us to prevent such an outcome."

"They brought him to us because he was driving them crazy with his behavior," Lindsay snapped. "Or did you forget what Toby did to his stepfather before he was committed here?"

"It doesn't matter anymore, does it?" Eli rolled his shoulders and stretched his neck out. It did nothing to relieve the tension in his posture. "Toby's gone. We have to deal with the consequences."

"Yeah. *We.*" Lindsay smacked Eli's chest to emphasize the point. "I feel like I'm working alone. You're not helping me with Mrs. Billings at all."

"If she wants to see the body, let her," he said. "She needs closure."

"She's not going to get it by laying eyes on her son's dead, mutilated corpse," Lindsay retorted. "If she sees what Toby did to himself, she'll pull the donation for sure."

"Once again, all you care about is the money," Eli muttered.

"I'm trying to keep *your* family's business afloat," she hissed. "Maybe if you cared a little *more* about our finances, we wouldn't be in this kind of trouble."

Eli rubbed the back of his head, ruffling his hair. "Linds, I'm trying my best."

"Try harder."

Mr. Billings, who must have doubled back after escorting his wife to the car, stepped between Eli and Lindsay and cleared his throat. "Pardon me. I just wanted to let you know, if it wasn't already obvious, that I no longer plan on contributing to the Center. That donation was contingent on Toby's successful rehabilitation. Since he failed to thrive—since *you* failed to cure him—I see no reason to uphold my end of the agreement either."

"Mr. Billings, wait." Eli hurried after the older man. "I'm sure we can come to an understanding. Toby was well cared for."

"Tell that to my wife," Mr. Billings said. He tipped his hat to Eli. "You can expect to hear from my lawyers. I think it's only right that we sue. Good day, Mr. Trevino."

---

13

*L*ater that afternoon, I sat with Baz at the local café. We pored over the pictures I'd taken of the content in the Trevino basement. Baz buzzed with excitement.

"This is gold," she squealed, zooming in on my phone to read a fuzzy article. "God, with this kind of information out there, who the hell would ever agree to treatment at Trevino?"

"This stuff is years old," I reminded her. "The Trevino Center was established before certain advancements were made in the field."

"They were performing lobotomies," Baz countered. "I don't think picking apart the brain because the patient had behavioral issues was ever kosher. Did you see this one?" She held up the phone to show me the article. "It talks about how Trevino's early patients were all women, most likely admitted for symptoms of PMDD or learning disabilities. It's like Trevino heard about Rosemary Kennedy and decided to feed the fire."

"Yes, I read it. Send it to yourself so I can have my phone back."

She tapped expertly on the screen as she went on. "Honestly, it's crazy what men did to women back in the day. I'm totally going to write my paper on how Trevino contributed to modern-day misogyny. Elijah was a total quack. Are you sure that place is legit?"

"I've started asking myself that question every day," I muttered.

Baz finished sending herself the files, returned my phone to me, and opened her laptop to read the articles on a larger screen. "Wow, this one's about how the Center covered up a botched operation that left the patient brain dead."

"Baz, I told you. These articles are from the thirties and forties." I flagged the barista down and motioned for a refill. Maybe if I drank enough coffee, the caffeine would drive my anxious thoughts out of my head. "Medicine has changed since then."

"This article is from 2008."

"Let me see that."

I pulled Baz's laptop toward me. Sure enough, the article was dated roughly ten years ago. I remembered skimming the beginning of the article in the basement library, but I hadn't taken notice of the recent date. As I read on, Baz poked me between the eyebrows.

"You're going to get wrinkles there if you keep scrunching your face up like that," she informed me. "The article's legit, isn't it?"

I skimmed the article again, hoping I'd misread it. "I don't understand. Eli's father was a psychiatrist, not a brain surgeon. Why would he have operated on a patient?"

"Maybe that's why they tried to cover it up." Baz took her laptop back. "This is juicy. Hey, do you think if I do an exposé on this, an actual newspaper might pick it up?"

I tapped on her screen. "This *was* an exposé. Did you read the last paragraph? Trevino was found not guilty. The court decided the family of the patient was lying to get money from the Center."

Baz scoffed. "A likely story."

As Baz continued her research, taking notes on the Trevino Center's strange history, I pondered the details we'd uncovered. The Center's current reputation made it difficult to question its legitimacy. As far as the nation and thousands of medical professionals were concerned, Trevino was a trusted, reliable facility. Despite this, I couldn't reconcile the Center's dubious discrepancies with its widespread repute. Something didn't add up.

Baz's eyes went wide with astonishment. "Oh. My. God."

"What is it?"

I craned my neck to look at her screen, but Baz was staring at her phone. She showed me a picture of a familiar teenaged girl on Instagram.

"She broke up with Bryan!" Baz whisper-yelled. It was hard to tell if she was ecstatic or furious. "I can't believe this! Look. Hashtag: single life. Ugh, give me a break!"

An idea hit me out of nowhere. "Baz, could you look up someone on Instagram for me?"

"Why don't you do it yourself?"

"I don't have one," I told her.

She stared at me. "You're kidding."

"No, I'm not. You owe me," I told her. "I got you all of this information on the Center, and I'm not entirely sure the public is supposed to have access to it."

"Yeah, yeah." She pulled up the Instagram search page. "Give me a name."

"Toby Gardner."

She typed it in and clicked on the first profile that turned up in the search results. "Oh, he's kind of cute if you like the baby face. He hasn't updated in, like, a year though."

I decided not to mention that he was dead. "Can I see?"

Baz handed over her phone and went back to reading on her laptop. As I laid eyes on Toby's Instagram page, a shudder ran through me. Here, there was no evidence of Toby's struggle. A tanned, laughing Toby manned the sails of a small boat in one picture. In another, only his bright, excited eyes were visible beneath a full-face helmet as he straddled a motocross bike. In the next, he posed with a group of friends outside a miniature golf course. The teenager was a stranger to me. This version of Toby looked like he had no notion of how a mental disorder would change and ultimately end his life.

"Finished?" Baz asked. "I need to text someone."

I took one last look at the smiling Toby I never knew before letting go of the phone. On my own laptop, I searched for Banks Billings. The first several results detailed his dealings on Wall Street. Since stocks never made sense to me and I wasn't interested in his business anyway, I scrolled past this. On the third page of results, I finally found a marriage announcement. I checked the date.

"Hey, Baz? Sorry to bother you," I said. "But could you tell me the date of Toby's last Instagram post?"

"Okay, but I think it's weird you're stalking a teenager." She glanced at her phone. "September eighth of last year."

I shivered involuntarily. The Billings' marriage announcement was dated August thirty-first of the same year. Toby had stopped posting on social media shortly after his mother's wedding. My mind flashed back to that day he'd begun to tell me about his stepfather.

Baz nudged my shoulder. "What'd I tell you about scrunching your face like that?"

WHEN I RETURNED to work the next morning, the hallway outside the therapists' office was unusually quiet. On a normal day, I could hear Imogen and Ariel chatting and gossiping from a mile away. Upon my entrance, I immediately realized why everyone was so focused on their work: Eli sat at my desk. I caught Imogen's nervous eye and understood what Eli was waiting for, even before he stood up.

"Natasha," Eli said and checked his watch. "Do you always arrive so late?"

"My first session isn't until nine o'clock."

"Hmm." He put his hands in his pockets. "Walk with me. I'd like to talk with you."

"Good luck," Imogen muttered so only I could hear.

In the corridor, Eli didn't seem quite so keen to walk anywhere, only to get out of the other therapists' earshot. We stopped a few feet from the office.

"Have you gotten the chance to visit Luna yet?" he asked.

I fixed him with narrowed eyes. "No. She bit my hand, remember? And you told me I could have the rest of yesterday off. When was I supposed to go to her?"

He pressed the flat of his palm against his forehead. "Right, of course. Well, I need you to familiarize yourself with her as soon as possible. I emailed you a copy of her chart, as well as the notes from the doctor who recommended her to us. If you can go up now—"

"My first session starts at nine," I said again. "I need this time to set up the dance room. I have a break after my ten o'clock. I can see Luna then."

"You can't go now?"

"No." I studied Eli's darting eyes and tapping foot. "I have to prepare for my class. If you don't mind me asking, what's the rush?"

Eli, unaware that I'd eavesdropped on his and Lindsay's conversation yesterday, put on a smile so stiff it looked like cardboard. "Oh, I'm concerned about her well-being. That's all. I'd like to be more proactive with treatment options, and you seem to be our secret weapon. I can expect you in Ward 13 around eleven o'clock then?"

"You sure can."

Eli took his leave, and I returned to the therapists' office.

"What was that all about?" Imogen asked.

"He has a new patient for me."

Ariel popped a gum bubble, sending a waft of sickening artificial cherry across the room. "You know, he hardly ever came down to this floor before you started working here, Nat."

"So I've heard."

Suspicions bubbled in my head like a shaken can of soda ready to pop. Between Eli and Lindsay's desperation and Trevino's past scandals, I couldn't help but let conspiracy theories creep into my subconscious. My fingers found the photograph in my pocket. *Trevino kills. Find out the truth.*

I logged onto my work account and downloaded the paperwork Eli had sent me for Luna. Most of it was general information: intake papers, her chart, and details about her diagnosis of manic depressive bipolar disorder. I read everything, paying particular attention to the notes from Luna's doctor. His name, Dr. Charles Williamson, tickled my memories, though I couldn't recall where I'd heard of him before. A cursory online search revealed that he was a pediatric mental health specialist who ran a private practice in New York City.

Like every other teenager who ended up at the Center, Luna was admitted because she had been deemed an "uncontrollable hazard" to her parents, classmates, and anyone within biting distance. Her doctor's notes included a testimony from Luna's parents, who claimed she went through weeks of hyperactivity, during which she caused unending trouble at school and at home, followed by a period of intense depression, during which Luna refused to get out of bed or leave the house. Apparently, Luna's "intense, hypersexual" behavior was the final straw. When her parents discovered she had been sneaking out of the house to visit various boys, their attempt to discipline her catapulted Luna into a violent mood swing. According to Dr. Williamson's notes, Luna threw a glass sculpture at her mother's head during the incident, causing her mother a concussion and the need for twenty stitches in her hairline. Shortly after, Dr. Williamson referred Luna to the Trevino Center for treatment. Whilst on the waiting list, her parents had committed her to a hospital in the city that was ill-prepared for mental health patients. If I had to guess, her condition only worsened during her time there.

My class started in ten minutes. I made to close out Luna's details on my laptop, but something caught my eye and stayed my hand. Eli had forwarded me the emails between himself and Luna's mother, Emily Lamont, as they discussed Luna's treatment. Such conversations were supposed to be confidential between Eli and Emily. I surmised Eli had meant to sent me a file attached to the email, but he'd accidentally forwarded the whole thread instead. I told myself I should refrain from reading it, but curiosity got the better of me. I scrolled to the top.

The more I read, the tighter my lips pressed against each other, until Imogen rolled her chair over to my desk and said, "Uh, Nat? You look murderous. Is everything okay?"

I rearranged my face and clicked out of the emails. "I'm fine. Late for my first class. Do you have time to help me get ready for it?"

Imogen and I set up the dance room together, and it was a good thing she agreed to stay during the session because my head was in a different space entirely. The contents of Eli and Emily Lamont's email enraged me. It turned out Eli had a massive reason for rushing me to take care of Luna: Emily Lamont had agreed to immediately donate twenty-five thousand dollars to the Center if Eli admitted Luna ahead of the other patients on the waiting list. Furthermore, Emily had agreed to donate another twenty-five thousand if Eli could "cure" Luna by March of the following year, in time for a charity gala the Lamonts were throwing. The event was mere months away, and while Luna would likely improve in that time with the right treatment, there was really no "cure" for mental illness.

After my morning classes, I showed up in Ward 13 buzzing with adrenaline. Eli was with another patient, but when he saw me, he excused himself to meet me outside Luna's room.

"Did you read her file?" he badgered.

"Yes."

"It's important to remember she can be dangerous," Eli rambled on. "I shouldn't have to tell you that, considering what happened to your hand yesterday. Try not to hold a grudge. We need Luna to trust you."

Through the window, Luna watched as Eli yammered in my ear. When he wasn't looking, I mimed crying, as if tortured by Eli's constant yapping. The corners of Luna's lips lifted.

"Eli," I said sharply, shutting him up. "I'll handle it."

"I'll come in with you."

I blocked his path to the door. "Don't. You want her to trust me? Go find something else to do. I'll be fine."

He looked into the room, skeptical. Luna averted her eyes.

"Fine," Eli said, "but I want a full report when you're finished."

He swept away, returning to the patient he'd abandoned in favor of Luna. With a deep breath, I let myself into Luna's room. Allowing no fear to creep in, I extended my hand—the one she bit—to shake hers, which were strapped to the bed. She lifted her fingers, a gesture of consent, and I fit our palms together. As soon as we were connected, she dug her fingernails deep into my skin. Before she could do much damage, I slipped my hand out of her grasp.

"Nice try," I said, adjusting the bandage around the bite mark. "But you're going to have to be more clever than that. I grew up on the wrong side of the tracks."

"It doesn't matter where you grew up."

"You have a point there." I pulled up a chair and sat next to her bed. "You're from the right side of the tracks, and you still ended up here."

Her expression turned sour, her upper lip curling as if she'd caught a whiff of rotting garbage. "You don't know anything about me."

"I agree," I said. "I only know what your mother and your doctor have written on your charts, and sometimes I find paper to be misleading. Why don't we get to know one another?" I crossed one leg over the other and relaxed back. "My name's Natasha. I'm a dance and movement therapist. My role here at Trevino is to help people feel better through physical activity that promotes a healthy brain and body."

"You want me to dance?" she asked with a scoff. "Fat chance."

"We'll get back to the dancing in a minute," I said. "Tell me about yourself."

She sealed her lips and stared straight ahead.

"Okay, let's make a deal," I offered. "Tell me one thing about yourself, and I'll extend the range on your wrist restraints. You could at least be able to reach that water bottle on your bedside table."

Luna eyed the bottle with envy. "Fine. One thing. I hate therapists."

"Oh, yeah. I don't blame you." I leaned forward and loosened the straps on Luna's restraints so that she could move her arms away from the bed posts. Her hands flexed, as if she was getting ready to strangle me with the straps. If she was quick and audacious enough, she might be able to do it, but I had a feeling she wasn't as unpredictable as Eli thought she was. "Therapists are lame. Good thing I'm not a real one."

Luna's tense fists loosened as my statement distracted her. I moved away from her bedside, just in case she changed her mind about throttling me.

"How can you work here if you're not a real therapist?" she asked with genuine curiosity. "Don't you have to have a degree?"

"I have one," I said. "But it's, like, for dancing. Weird, right?"

It was half a lie. My degree did grant me the official title of therapist, but the focus had been on dance. Regardless, the half-lie had caught Luna's attention. As she reached for the water bottle and drank, she scanned me from head to toe.

"So you're the good cop, huh?" she asked, wiping a droplet from her chin. "They send you in to make me feel like someone here is on my side. Then you turn on me and they torture me anyway?"

"I have no intention of turning on you," I assured her. "In fact, I like to think of myself as a double agent. You see, I don't always agree with the way teenagers are treated here. Being strapped to a bed isn't good for anyone."

A tiny sparkle of trust lit Luna's eyes, but she didn't dare to voice it. She kept popping the lid on and off the water bottle, unable to keep still.

"I read you've been diagnosed with bipolar disorder," I said. "Do you think that's true?"

She lifted her eyebrows. "No one's bothered to ask me that before."

"I'm not no one."

Luna's gaze wandered off. "Sometimes, I feel like I'm on top of the world, like I can do anything. Other times, I'm so tired I can barely move. Does that make me bipolar?"

"It could."

Her sharp gray eyes captured mine. "Really? Because a lot of my friends say they've felt the same way. Does that mean we're all bipolar?"

"Probably not. Mood swings are common in teenagers due to so many hormonal changes happening."

"Then what defines me as bipolar?" she asked. "Why are my mood swings different than my friends'?"

"Is that rhetorical?"

"No, I want to know," Luna said, her mouth hardening. "Why am I here when all of my friends with 'mood swings' are still in school?"

"Because your parents decided your behavior was unacceptable," I answered her truthfully. "That's the thing when you're a minor. *You* aren't in charge of yourself. Someone else is. Any idea why your mother would put you in here?"

Luna crossed her arms and glared into the distance. "She hates me. I'm not good enough for her."

"Why do you think that?"

"Because I don't want to do her dumb society stuff," she snapped. "I don't want to wear gowns and pretend to like the sons of her boring old man friends so she can raise money for her stupid charity. Did you know she keeps most of the donations for herself? Only ten percent of the funds she collects goes to the actual cause." She harrumphed and added under her breath, "That's another reason she wants me in here, so I can't tell anyone that she's a fraud."

"Is that why you threw a glass sculpture at her head?"

"No." She remained tight-lipped until I fixed her with a withering stare. "She caught me sneaking back into the house one night and pulled my hair so hard that my scalp tore." She turned around and lifted her hair to show me a jagged pink scar on the nape of her neck. "It was a vase, not a sculpture, by the way. And I hit her with it so she'd let me go."

"Your dad didn't stop her?"

Her laugh, though not as creepy as the unending one she'd served upon her arrival, was empty of humor. "My dad's a pushover. He's afraid she'll divorce him if he says anything about the way she treats me, and if she divorces him, he'll be broke. You get the picture."

"I sure do."

If Luna's side of the story was true, I had a case of child abuse on my hands. I wanted to report it to Eli, but something told me he wouldn't be on mine or Luna's side, not with fifty thousand dollars on the line.

Luna peered at me warily. "I thought the other guy—

the one who thinks he's handsome—was the psychiatrist. Not you. Why do you want to know my life story?"

"You should tell Dr. Trevino the truth about your mom," I said, avoiding her question. "He needs to know about it."

"Like he would believe me."

I shifted uneasily in my seat. Luna noticed.

"Mm-hmm," she vocalized, the sound of it conveying more than any worded reply could. "I'm not stupid. He'll think I'm making stuff up to get out of here."

"I could vouch for you."

"And risk losing your job?"

"There's a different way," I said, scooting my chair closer to her bed. I checked over my shoulder to make sure no one was listening from the hallway. "Work with me privately. I can modify your program to include whatever kind of movement you'd like to do."

She looked doubtful. "How does that help me?"

"Number one, it gets you out of this horrible room." I disguised a shudder as I remembered the walls around us coated in Toby's blood. "Number two, you won't have to wear restraints. Number three, it gets you out of any kind of sedation, as long as you don't do anything alarming to Dr. Trevino or the aides before our assigned sessions."

Luna's permanent scowl lessened slightly. "What's the long game? Are you going to help me get out of here?"

"I might be able to do better," I promised. "Work with me and we might be able to prove you aren't bipolar. If I can get one of the doctors to sign off on the reversal of your diagnosis, you can use it to defend yourself against your mother."

"How am I supposed to do that?"

"Assuming you're of sound body and mind," I said, adding the warning to make sure we were clear on the rules of this relationship, "you could file for emancipation. Then you'd be out from under your mother's wing. No charity galas. No repercussions for sneaking out. *But* you would have to figure out how to take care of yourself."

Luna's excitement betrayed her. A grim smile crossed her face. "I'm in. Let's do it."

"Let's go over some ground rules first," I said. "Then you can decide."

14

I was well aware that my deal with Luna could go sideways for any number of reasons. It was Luna's word against her mother's. The biggest piece of evidence she had of her mother's abuse was the scar on the back of her head, but if Luna was truly deranged, she could have easily made that part of her story up too. Nevertheless, I put my trust in the teenager's story. Unlike the emails between Eli and Emily Lamont, Luna didn't give me sketchy vibes. All I saw was a helpless teenager with a rebellious streak who'd been victimized by her mother.

The ground rules I'd given Luna were pretty obvious. She agreed to them without argument. She couldn't tell anyone—not Eli, Scout, Dashiell or anyone—that we were working to overturn her diagnosis. She couldn't lash out at me or anyone else in the ward; doing so worked to the advantage of her mother. Lastly, I informed her that all of this could be for naught. Regardless of her home life, there was a chance that Luna was actually bipolar.

"If that's the case," I told her, "I can't help you get out of here in good conscience. Mental health is no joke, and I want to make sure you're healthy and in a good state of mind if I'm going to help turn you loose on the world."

Luna, with no better options, accepted my terms. Later, I caught myself wondering if I had made a mistake. If this went south, I'd lose my job, and getting fired from the Trevino Center would make it hard for me to find another position elsewhere. Not to mention, I was officially alienating Eli, the one person who'd hired me with the belief that I could make a positive change.

But then Toby's face would pop into my head, and it helped remind me why I was doing this. The Trevino Center—Eli and Lindsay—were taking advantage of their patients. They were exploiting rich parents, which wasn't ethical or okay, regardless of how much money the Center was hemorrhaging. Luna had been admitted to the Center because Eli had accepted a bribe and Toby's parents had also promised money for their son's improvement. If it happened twice, it was bound to happen again.

"Why don't you go to the police?" Lauren asked that night at dinner.

Baz had been yammering on and on about her research paper, asking me endless questions regarding the Trevino Center. After a solid hour, I finally lost my patience and spilled the beans, making sure not to mention any patient names. Confidentiality still mattered, even in situations like these.

"I don't have any actual proof," I answered. "These people are donating to the Trevino Foundation of their own free will. There's no documentation that says they're being coerced into giving the Center money."

"You don't think the emails do that?" Lauren said. "Or the conversation you overheard between Lindsay and Eli? It's obvious they're committing fraud."

"Passively, I suppose," I said. "It's not illegal for a foundation to accept donations. It's how things are done."

"But if they're making deals for the money—"

"It's not just about the money," I said shortly. "If I report the Center to the police, the Center might get shut down. Hundreds of people—good people who don't know anything about the business's fraud—will lose their jobs, and who knows what might happen to the patients?"

"Including you," Lauren added. "You might lose your job too."

"I might lose my job anyway." I sprinkled a pile of salt onto the table and drew designs in it. "If anyone finds out what I offered to Luna, I'm done for."

"Are you sure she's not crazy?" Baz chimed in. Though her gaze was glued to her tablet, she managed to participate in the conversation when she wanted to, a master of multitasking. "It would be kinda crappy if you went through all this trouble and this chick turns out to be a nut job anyway."

"My instinct says she's telling the truth," I said. "I don't know how to describe it. It's a gut feeling, you know?"

Baz rolled her eyes. "If you say so."

"Don't you have any faith in your generation?"

"Sure I do," she replied. "But I'm also aware that mental health issues are becoming more prevalent in younger generations due to increased stress."

"Yeah, and increased screen time," added Lauren, snatching the tablet from Baz.

"I'm literally doing homework," Baz protested.

Skeptically, Lauren glanced at the screen. "Oh. You *are* doing homework." She gave the tablet back. "God, education is so different these days."

I pushed my plate away. As if Marcel could sense that I hadn't finished my meal, he emerged from the kitchen. His nose twitched as he looked down at me.

"Is there something wrong with zee pasta?" he questioned.

"No, Marcel. It was wonderful."

"But you did not eat it."

"I had a few bites." I patted my stomach. "Stress makes it harder for me to eat."

He narrowed his eyes at me. "So lose zee stress."

"If only it were that easy."

Lauren shooed the chef away from the table. "Leave her alone, Marcel. She's got a lot on her mind. What did you make for dessert tonight?"

"*Mousse au chocolat.*"

"Great. We'll take three."

With a dramatic huff, he retreated to the kitchen. Baz snickered under her breath. I let out a long sigh and rested my forehead in my hands.

"Ignore him," Lauren advised me.

"Marcel's fine. It's everything else."

"What are you going to do?"

"I don't know," I said. "I guess I'm going to play it by ear."

Marcel reappeared. He set two crystal cups full of chocolate mousse on the table, one each in front of Lauren and Baz. They were topped with fresh whipped cream and tuille cigars. In front of me, he set down a spoonful of chocolate mousse on a clean coffee saucer.

"Are you kidding me?" Lauren said to him.

"Why waste it?" he demanded. "I import zee *chocolat* from Paris!"

"It's like you're asking to get fired."

I rested a hand on Lauren's arm to keep her in her seat. "Don't worry about it. Honestly, he's right. I probably can't stomach any more than a spoonful."

"*Voila!*" Marcel said, then he yelled as Jean Paul wound himself around the chef's legs. "*Chat de merde!* Stay out of my kitchen! I know you've been stealing the pancetta!"

Jean Paul, ever the troublemaker, sat at Marcel's feet and meowed.

"Pah!" Marcel threw his hands in the air, stepped daintily over my cat, and stomped off.

INSTEAD OF PUTTING TOGETHER a solid plan, I spent most of my spare time staring at the handwriting on the back of Toby's picture. I traced the handwriting, studying each turn of the pen. Had Toby written those words? Had he slipped the photo into my notebook before he decided to take his own life, determined for someone to delve in Trevino's messy history?

Late at night, in bed, I slid the picture between the pages of my notebook and tried to set it all aside, but no amount of compartmentalizing or reasoning gave me peace. I tried to convince myself that no fourteen-year-old would leave a clue, asking me to thwart an entire medical foundation, before killing himself. Then again, Baz was buried deep in her research paper, determined to expose more of the Center's mistakes. Teenagers these days had determination seeping out of their every pore.

SECRETS IN THE WOODS

Besides, I'd ruled out Imogen as a suspect, and I doubted anyone else in the office had the gall to pull a prank like this one.

Could the writing on the back of the picture be Toby's? Since I had nothing to compare it to, I wasn't sure. If I could get something of Toby's with his handwriting on it... but where? It wasn't like I could call up his mom and ask for one of his old writing assignments. Everything was done on the computer these days anyway. Toby probably hadn't written manually since he was removed from high school over a year ago.

A potential solution came to me right as I was dozing off, and my eyes sprang open. There was one surefire way to access Toby's writing. Upon arrival at the Center, every patient was asked to fill out a questionnaire to let the staff their preferences for being taken care of. It was meant to help the nurses and aides keep the patients comfortable. In some cases, like with Luna, the patient was too distraught to fill out the form right away, but I remembered Eli quoting Toby's during one of our sessions. One problem remained: the questionnaire would be filed away in the records room, which was kept locked at all times and off limits to most employees. I didn't have the key card that would open the door, but that didn't mean I couldn't try to get in.

"YOU WANT ME TO DO WHAT?" Luna asked warily. It was our first movement session together, and I'd taken the opportunity to proposition her with an idea of mine.

"Add a jump at the end of that sequence," I said, demonstrating it for her. "We're going to build up from there. Vertical movement is frequently used to encourage people with depression."

"Not the dance." Luna half-assed the move and finished off with the assigned twirl. "You want me to steal Dr. Trevino's badge?"

"No, no. *I'll* do the stealing." I showed her the next eight beats of the dance I was teaching her. "I just need you to distract him."

After watching me once, she performed the sequence perfectly, albeit with less enthusiasm than I preferred. Her silvery hair billowed around her shoulders and she spun lightly around the room. "What do you need his badge for anyway?"

"I can't tell you," I said. "It's better if you don't know, but if I can get the badge, it'll help you too."

What I couldn't tell Luna was that Eli's ID badge opened every door in the Center with a single swipe. If I could get ahold of it without Eli noticing, I could access the records room in the basement with no problem.

Without me asking her to, Luna went back to the beginning of the dance and did the whole thing, from start to finish, without messing up. She closed her eyes and leapt gracefully through the air, landed softly, and pirouetted like a professional ballerina. If I didn't know any better, she was starting to enjoy this.

"What are you writing?" she snapped when she noticed me scribbling in my notebook. Her dance came to an abrupt halt, and she crossed her arms over her chest, closing herself off.

"That you're a natural," I said, showing the paper for her to see.

Luna peered at my notes and read aloud, "*Though hesi-*

tant at first, Luna picks up the dance steps with ease. When she thinks I'm not watching, she fully commits to the movement. Her instinct suggests a background in dance." She let her arms fall to her sides. "You're right. My mom forced me to do ballet classes when I was in preschool, and I had to dance at all her gala events. It wasn't fun."

"Do you want to stop?"

She gnawed on the inside of her cheek. "No, it's okay."

I set aside my notebook and gave her all of my attention. "Do you resent your mom for making you dance?"

Luna unsteadily rose to her toes, but without the proper shoes, she couldn't sustain the stance for long. "I hate her for everything she made me do." Bracing herself against the wall with one hand, she turned her hips and feet outward to take up the first position of ballet. "I liked ballet at first, but she was determined for me to become a professional. I didn't have the discipline, and I was also too tall. Still, she forced me to keep going with it, to audition for a dance school that I didn't want to go to…"

"What happened?"

"I didn't get in," she answered. "I intentionally flubbed the audition. My mother didn't speak to me for weeks afterward. I'd embarrassed her."

"I'm sure that's not true."

"Oh, it's true," she scoffed. "You've never met my mother. All she does is seek everyone else's praise. If I do something right, she says it's because of how she raised me. Because she gave so much to me. But if I fail—" She rolled her eyes. "She can't stand failure, especially mine."

I watched as she went through the dance moves I'd assigned her again. This time, she perfected each step and added her own personal flair to it. Mentally, I took note of the changes she made, intending to use them for other patients in the future.

"You know, just because your mother made you do something doesn't mean you have to keep hating it," I told her. "If you like to dance, you should keep doing it. You obviously have a natural talent for it."

She sat heavily on the floor. "I refuse to do anything that might make her happy."

"Look at this way," I said. "No matter what you choose to do, your mother is going to try to take credit for your accomplishments, so you might as well do the things you like."

"That's not fair."

"There are other ways to deal with parents like yours," I promised her. "But you have to make it out of this damned place to do it. Get back up. We still have fifteen minutes left of our session."

She didn't object, getting to her feet and readying herself for my next instruction. "I'll do it," she said.

"Do what?"

"I'll help you get Dr. Trevino's badge."

THE PLAN WAS SIMPLE ENOUGH. Luna would distract Eli while I snatched his badge from where it was clipped onto his belt. We decided to pull it off the next day, right before Luna's session with me. Like Toby, Eli had required Dashiell to assist me in getting Luna to and from the dance room, so he was right behind me.

Luna, as agreed, lay listless against the pillows, eyes closed. She didn't move or acknowledge us as we came in.

"Luna?" I said, hoping my nervousness sounded

sincere. "It's time for our session together. Do you want to get changed out of your pajamas?"

She didn't reply. I admired her commitment. From where I was standing, I couldn't even see her chest rise and fall with her breathing.

Dashiell approached the bed, took Luna's wrist, and felt for her pulse. "It's normal," he said, comparing Luna's heart rate to the seconds on his watch. "A little slow, but nothing worrying."

I stepped closer to Luna's bed and leaned over her. "Luna? Are you feeling okay?"

She raised one lazy eyelid and stared at me with a deadened expression. If we hadn't planned this ahead of time, I would have been legitimately worried.

"Can you get Eli?" I asked Dashiell. "Something's not right."

"Isn't she bipolar? It's probably a depressive episode."

"Exactly." I sharpened my tone as I glared at him. "She's bipolar, and Eli is her doctor, so if she's having an episode, I'd like him to have a look at her. Go get him."

As a therapist, I outranked Dashiell, but I didn't make a habit of ordering him around. Expressionless, he swept out of the room and slammed the door.

"Ooh, he's mad," Luna whispered conspiratorially.

"You're doing great," I muttered back. "Keep it up."

She winked and resumed her dead-eyed state. A minute later, Dashiell returned with Eli in tow.

"What is it?" Eli asked, rushing to Luna's bedside. He pulled open her eyelids and shone a flashlight into her pupils.

"She's not responding," I said, doing my best to infuse my tone with worry. I spotted Eli's badge, clipped to his

belt on the back, right side of his waist, as always. I
clenched my teeth. Eli's focus was completely on Luna,
but with Dashiell looming behind me, I couldn't make the
grab. "Dashiell, get her some water and a snack. Maybe
she has low blood sugar."

Clearly annoyed that I'd once again ordered instead of
asked politely, Dashiell left the room. Relief flowed
through me. One obstacle down.

Eli used the opposite end of his flashlight to draw a
line across the bottom of Luna's bare foot. She didn't
flinch or move at all. Hell, she deserved an Oscar for
the act.

"She's catatonic," Eli muttered. He wiped his brow and
planted his hands on his waist, mere inches from his
badge. If I went for it now, he would definitely notice. I
was running out of time before Dashiell returned. Eli
rubbed his forehead. "It can happen with bipolar disorder,
but I didn't think she was at this point. I'll have to
medicate her—"

Desperation took over. If Eli used this as an excuse to
give Luna more prescriptions, she would never
forgive me.

"She just moved her head!" I said loudly.

Eli looked back at Luna. He leaned closer to her.
"Luna, can you hear me?"

Luna, bless her acting abilities, waited until Eli was
mere inches from her. Then she flipped over, opened her
eyes, and laughed right in Eli's face. "Oh, Dr. Trevino. You
sure know how to suck the fun out of everything."

Over Eli's shoulder, she made eye contact with me. I
shook my head and waved my hand to let her know I
needed a few more seconds to get what I wanted.

"You were faking?" Eli said incredulously.

"You act like your wife's never done that before," Luna said. She plucked the flashlight out of Eli's hand and directed it towards his eyes. "How's it feel when someone's shining this thing into your eyeballs, huh?"

Eli blocked the light and scrambled to take the flashlight from Luna. This was my chance. I darted in, snagged the ID badge off his belt, and tucked it into my pocket.

"Hey!"

My heart jumped into my throat at the sound of Dashiell's voice behind me. Had he seen me take the badge?

But he strolled right past me and over to Luna and Eli. He set down the cup of water and pudding cup I'd requested before wrestling the flashlight out of Luna's grasp.

"That's enough," Dashiell grunted.

Luna pretended to look innocent. "I was bored. Sorry for needing a little drama."

Eli's face reddened as he accepted the flashlight from Dashiell and put it back in his shirt pocket. "I don't think it's appropriate for you to attend your private session with Natasha today. Not after a show like that."

Luna's face fell. I stepped forward.

"Shouldn't that be my decision?" I asked. "Luna's already shown improvement since yesterday. At least she's talking instead of laughing."

Eli considered this. I could almost see the wheels turning in his head. He didn't want to do anything to hinder Luna's treatment, lest her mother withdraw her generous offer to the Center.

"Fine," he said shortly. "But if something like this happens again, we'll have to devise a way to deal with it."

Minutes later, when Luna and I were alone in the dance room, we squealed with glee and high-fived. Luna was light on her feet for the entire session.

I KNEW it wouldn't be long before Eli noticed his missing badge, so I decided to make my move at lunchtime. When no one was paying attention, I ducked out of the therapists' office and made my way down to the basement. More than once, I hid behind a corner to let someone pass before I proceeded along my route. The less people who saw me somewhere I wasn't supposed to be, the better it was for me.

When I reached the records room, I took Eli's badge out and swiped it through the card reader. The LED light flashed red. The door remained locked.

"That can't be right," I muttered.

I tried again, running the badge through slowly this time. The reader flashed red again. With a frustrated growl, I reached forward to run the badge once more time. Then a door slammed down the hallway.

"Crap!"

Instinctively, I ran into the first unlocked room I could find and hid until the footsteps in the hallway faded into the distance. I let out the breath I was holding and turned around to see where I'd ended up.

I was in a storage room of some sort. There were rows and rows of organized boxes, each one labeled with a patient's name. I suddenly knew where I was. When someone was admitted to the Trevino Center, their personal belongings were confiscated and stored, much like prison, and would be returned to the patient upon their release. I'd happened upon those items.

I checked the hallway to make sure no one was coming then made a beeline for the boxes in the row labeled G. I was surprised to find that Toby's box was still here. After a patient's death, the items were usually returned to the family or donated. I pulled the box off the shelf and set it on the floor to go through it.

The box contained mostly normal things: Toby's ugly school uniform complete with gray plaid pants and a horrendous red tie, a handful of dollar bills and change, a pocket version of the Bible with whole passages crossed out and rewritten, and Toby's dead smartphone. I pocketed his phone. Then I checked the pockets of his pants and drew out a piece of paper that had been folded into a tiny triangle, the type you'd play table football with. Ink bled through part of the paper. I unfolded it and flattened it out.

It was a letter addressed to someone named Emma Brown, a generic message from one teenager to another. I skimmed through it, and though the written words didn't expressly say it, it was obvious that the letter writer had a huge crush on this Emma girl. My eyes floated down to the signature down at the bottom. It was signed Toby Gardner.

Heart pumping, I pulled out Toby's photograph, flipped it over, and compared the writing on the back of it to the letter.

It matched.

15

"What are you doing in here?" a voice demanded.

I swiftly pocketed Toby's letter to Emma and swiveled around. Scout stood in the doorway, feet spread and shoulders squared. She carried a crow bar in one hand, as if she'd heard noises in the basement and planned to bludgeon the trespasser.

"Sorry." I contorted my face and let my bottom lip wobble. "I couldn't help myself. I tried not to let this thing with Toby get to me, but I had to see if his stuff was still here. Why did you keep it instead of giving it back to his parents?"

"The investigation into his death is ongoing," Scout replied stiffly. "The items won't be returned until his suicide is confirmed."

"The police don't think he killed himself?"

"They do," she said. "But this is common procedure after we have an unexpected death here. They want to make sure the patients aren't in danger." She stood aside and waved me out of the room. "Put that stuff back. We're not supposed to touch it."

I slid Toby's uniform back into the box and replaced the box on the shelf. Both the letter and his phone weighed the pocket of my scrubs down, but I hoped Scout wouldn't notice.

"Have you seen a name badge around?" Scout asked without warning.

My heart dropped into my stomach and splashed acid into my throat. "No, I haven't. Why?"

"Someone with high-level security clearance lost theirs," she answered. "Security had to put a temporary lock on all the card swipers. I can't get into my materials room."

That explained why Eli's badge hadn't opened the records room. He had already reported it missing to security. The piece of plastic burned a hole in my pocket. I never considered how I was going to get it back to Eli once I was finished sneaking around.

"That's a bummer," I said to Scout, letting her usher me out of the basement. "I'm sure the badge will turn up soon."

With Scout tailing me all the way back to the inpatient therapy ward, I had nowhere to drop Eli's badge. It stayed in my pocket with the other items I'd stolen all through the afternoon. I dared not commit to the more furious dance moves I'd assigned to some of my patients for fear of the incriminating items falling out for everyone to see. I moved like a series of rubber bands were connected to my arms and legs, rooting me to the floor. My patients noticed.

"Is everything okay?" Bonnie asked as I escorted her back to the room. "You seemed a little stiff today."

I wished I could tell her everything: that I was a thief who had broken almost every rule in the Center's book within the past two days. That a two-sentence note written on the back of an old photograph had both broken my heart and made me livid. That the Center was taking advantage of its patients.

Instead, I said, "Just a rough couple of days, Bonnie. I'll get over it."

IT WAS a good thing Baz was so obsessed with Jean Paul because I needed a bargaining chip. I wrestled Jean Paul out from his hiding spot beneath the velvet bench in the lobby and carried him into the library, where Baz was staring with such intensity at her laptop screen that I thought her eyeballs might pop out of her skull and roll underneath the couch to get a break from her.

I held Jean Paul up like Rafiki held Simba over Pride Rock. Unlike Simba, Jean Paul kicked his hind paws against my arms and gnawed on my knuckles.

"I present to you this token," I announced to Baz, who had yet to look up, "in exchange for your Instagram knowledge."

Baz set aside her laptop to rescue Jean Paul from my grasp. She placed him on the cushion next to her. He purred happily and made biscuits against her thigh. "Again? What do you want me to do? Stalk another teenager?"

"Actually, yes." I sat on Baz's other side. "Do you mind? It's important."

"If you're going to keep being a creep, it might be easier for you to download the app yourself. That being said, I'm starting to wonder if I should report you to the police."

Baz's sense of humor and joke delivery was so dry that I wasn't sure if she was kidding or not. "I promise I'm not a creep. It's about the stuff that's going on at Trevino. Can you help me or not?"

She pressed her phone to her chest. "Only if we can make a deal."

"I gave you a cat."

She rolled her eyes. "Not that kind of deal. Besides, everyone knows you're Jean Paul's one true love. He only likes me because I give him pancetta from the kitchen."

"That was you? You let Marcel yell at me!"

She shrugged. "It was funny."

"Fine," I grumbled. "What do you want?"

"The down low on the situation at Trevino," she bargained. "If I help you get this information, you have to tell me everything that's happening there."

"Have you ever heard of a thing called a confidentiality agreement? Yeah, I signed one. I means I can't tell you about any of my patients by name."

"Then don't tell me their names." She opened Instagram and waved her phone just out of my reach. "Use code names. But I want to know what's going on."

I fixed her with what I hoped was a piercing look. "I could get arrested."

"First of all, stop trying to look serious," Baz said. "You're getting that wrinkle between your brows again. Secondly, if I've been hearing you correctly, you've already done a bunch of illegal crap already. What makes this any different?"

"You're a kid," I reminded her. "What makes you think I can trust you with information like this?"

"You trust Luna," she shot back, "and you don't even know if she's crazy or not."

I wagged my finger in her face. "Bipolar people are not crazy. If you're going to write a big paper on mental health, you need to debunk the stigma. These people deserve to be treated with respect, just like patients with physical illnesses that present in more obvious ways."

"I get that," Baz said, nodding. She held up two fingers and put her other hand to her heart. "I promise to alter my views on mental health *and* advocate for the people who suffer from these diseases."

"Thank you."

"You need allies," she said. "People who aren't connected to the Trevino Center. Technically, you can't trust anyone there. They could all be in on it. If you let *me* do the research, you could have another line of defense for your case."

"There is no case yet," I replied. "But I do get where you're coming from. I can't promise to tell you everything. If it puts you in danger, I won't do it. Your mom would kill me."

"That's fair. Mom is pretty scary when I get hurt. You should have seen her when I tripped on the playground and had to get stitches on my face. I think the doctor almost peed himself."

Jean Paul, displeased with the lack of attention he was receiving, meowed loudly and jumped off the cushion. I scooted closer to Baz.

"Your mom aside," I said, "can you look up someone named Emma Brown?"

"You promise to involve me?"

"As much as possible."

Satisfied, Baz finally allowed me to see her phone screen. She searched for Emma Brown's name, but several girls popped up in the results. She clicked on the first profile. This Emma Brown looked to be in her twenties.

"Too old," I said. "We're looking for a teenager."

Baz went back and selected a different Emma Brown. This one looked younger, but she wore USC colors in every picture, and some of the photos were tagged in California.

"Probably not," I said. "Our Emma Brown most likely goes to school in New York City."

"Here you go." Baz pulled up a picture of a girl with pink cheeks, strawberry blonde hair, and a friendly smile. "Emma Brown at Washington Square Park. Do you think that could be her?"

I squinted at the picture. "Does she look fourteen or fifteen to you?"

Baz rapidly scrolled through the other photos on Emma Brown's page. "I guess so. This uniform makes her look twelve though. Hazards of private school, I guess."

"Private school?" I leaned over Baz's shoulder. "Which one?"

She zoomed in on the embroidery on Emma Brown's gray sweater, but I didn't need to see the crest before I recognized the ugly plaid print of Emma's skirt.

"Saint Luke's Preparatory," I said at the same time as Baz. "That's her. Can I see that?"

Baz handed her phone over and went back to

researching on her laptop. I scrolled through Emma's photos one at a time, reading all of the comments from her friends and peers. Unlike Toby, Emma kept her Instagram up to date. She posted at least one picture a day. In a city like New York, there were plenty of Instagrammable spots. She posed in front of cafes, famous sculptures, monuments, graffitied alleyways, and the occasional brick wall.

"Is this what kids are doing with their time these days?" I asked Baz.

"Don't ask me," Baz replied. "I'm too lazy to take so many pictures of myself. I mostly use it to follow famous Internet cats."

"Of course you do."

"If you knew who Lil Bub was, you'd understand."

I took Toby's letter out of my pocket and unfolded it. Reading it felt like a violation of his privacy, but I needed more information.

Dearly detested, the letter read. An interesting start. *It is with great pain I must announce the magnetic effect you have on my body and soul. Your enchanting visage has bewitched me and rendered me inert. I am no longer a man but a parasite, and your affection sustains me. Though I am unworthy of your ardor, please do me the courtesy of allowing my worship of you. To be detached from your presence would certainly result in my death. Your significant bother, Toby Gardner.*

I shoved the letter into Baz's lap. "Read this."

Her face wrinkled as she looked over the letter. "Who the hell wrote this, Mr. Darcy?"

"It's weird, right? Teenagers don't write crap like this, do they?"

Baz folded up the letter and gave it back to me. "That's

a mystery to me. Looks like you need to rustle up some more clues, Nancy Drew."

I went back to Emma's Instagram feed, hoping to find something in her pictures to explain the note from Toby. After several minutes, during which my eyes began to water from all the mindless scrolling, I passed right by a picture of Emma and Toby. Heart pounding, I scrolled back up.

In the picture, Emma and Toby stood on the front steps of Saint Luke's in their matching uniforms. Emma had her arm around Toby's neck, pretending to choke him. Toby wore a dramatically breathless look as he faked trying to get out of Emma's hold. I read Emma's caption:

Last day at school with this knucklehead! I can't believe you're leaving me for some fancy schmancy magnet school on the West side. I guess we can't always play in the sandbox together. Good luck, Toby! Love your stupid face. #bestfriends-forlife

I checked the date on Emma's picture. It was right before Toby had been committed to the Trevino Center. From the joy on his face in this photo, he had no idea what was about to happen to him. He certainly didn't go to a magnet school on the West side, as Emma believed.

"I'll be right back," I said to Baz. "I have to make a call."

On my own phone, I found the number for the front office of Saint Luke's Preparatory School and dialed it.

"You've reached Saint Luke's Preparatory School," a pre-recorded voice answered. *"The school is currently closed. Please call back between the hours of nine o'clock am and five o'clock pm between Monday and Friday or leave a message after the tone."*

The tone buzzed in my ear. I panicked and blurted out the first thing I could think of.

"Hello, my name is Natasha Bell," I said then immediately smacked myself on the forehead for using my real name. "I'm a therapist at the Trevino Center. A former student of Saint Luke's, Toby Gardner, was one of my patients. You may not be aware of this, but Toby recently passed away—"

Baz showed up in the archway of the library and mouthed, *What are you doing?*

I waved her off and turned around so her expression wouldn't make me feel like an idiot. "The Center wants to hold a memorial for Toby, but we don't have any contact information for his friends. If it's possible, would someone be able to contact me with a list of Toby's classmates and a way to reach them? It would be a shame if his friends weren't able to say goodbye to him."

I left my number and hung up. Baz stared at me open-mouthed.

"What?" I demanded.

"You really think that's going to work?" she asked. "School security is nuts these days. One time, my aunt was visiting and tried to pick me up early, but my mom forgot to tell the front desk about it. They almost arrested my aunt."

"I need Emma's contact information," I said. "How else was I supposed to get it?"

"You could have DM'd her on Instagram?"

"I could have what?"

She pivoted back toward the library. "Never mind. You're hopeless. Let me know how that works out for you."

· · ·

THOUGH BAZ'S comment filled me with doubt, the school called me back the next day while I was filling in some notes in the therapists' office. Stupidly, I answered without checking the number first.

"Hello, this is Barbara Forest from the front office at Saint Luke's Preparatory. Is this Natasha Bell?"

I tripped over my chair in my haste to get up, drawing Imogen and Ariel's attention. Waving them off, I left the room and found a supply closet to take the call in.

"Hi, yes. This is she," I said.

"Hi, Natasha," Barbara said. "We got your message. I am so sorry to hear about Toby. None of us were aware that he had been sent to the Trevino Center."

I dug into the actual pain I felt for Toby and let it water down my voice. "Yes, everyone here is devastated. I worked with Toby closely. He was such a great kid. So dedicated to getting better. It's kids like Toby that made me want to work in healthcare."

Barbara sniffled. "I understand why you would want to hold a memorial for him, but I'm afraid we can't give out student information."

I clenched my teeth. Baz was going to be insufferable when I told her she was right.

"But," Barbara went on, "I think we can make an exception in this case. I just need some personal information from you first."

I pumped my fist and accidentally knocked over a bottle of cleaning product. It careened into an empty mop bucket with a loud bang.

"Miss Bell?" Barbara said. "Are you okay?"

"I'm fine. What do you need from me?"

After sending Barbara a picture of my driver's license and my Trevino Center identification badge to verify that I actually worked there, Barbara forwarded me an email that contained the numbers on file for each of the students in Toby's class. My only hope was that this wouldn't come back to bite me in the butt if Eli or anyone else found out what I was doing.

"Thanks, Barbara," I said over the phone. "I really appreciate this—"

A custodian swung open the closet door, dousing me in fluorescent light. As my pupils adjusted, the custodian let out a yelp of surprise.

"Goodness, is everything okay?" Barbara said.

"Yup. Thanks, gotta go!" I slid out of the supply closet and past the startled custodian. "Sorry about that. Had to make a private call. Have a great day!"

SINCE THE NUMBER on file for Emma Brown was listed as her emergency contact, I decided not to call it in case her mother, father, or other guardian answered. Instead, I sent a message to her student email, which Barbara had helpfully included. I treaded carefully with my wording. It seemed cruel to let Emma know her best friend was dead over an email, so I left that part out. However, I did identify myself and my relationship to Toby, keeping it as vague as possible.

I half-expected that she wouldn't get back to me. Fifteen-year-olds weren't known as the most punctual human beings. But hours after I sent the email, I received a text from a number I didn't recognize: *Hi, Natasha. This is Emma Brown. Can we FaceTime?*

I texted back a yes, and my phone rang a minute later. When I answered, I found myself face to face with Emma Brown. She looked far less put together than she did in her Instagram photos. Then again, it was eight o'clock on a Wednesday night. It made sense she was wearing pajamas and no makeup.

"Hi, Emma," I said. "It's nice to meet you."

"You too," she replied. "But I'm confused as to why we're meeting. Your email didn't make much sense."

"You were friends with Toby Gardner, right?"

"I *am* friends with him," she corrected me. "Even though he hasn't talked to me in, like, a year. I'm gonna kick his butt when he comes home."

My heart sank. "That's why I'm calling, Emma. I'm afraid Toby won't be coming home."

Her breath hitched. "What are you talking about?"

"Toby never went to a new school," I told her. "His mother and stepfather committed him to the Trevino Center of Health and Wellness because he was diagnosed with narcissistic personality disorder. His parents were concerned that his violent behavior would eventually harm someone."

"That's impossible!" Emma said, her voice shaking. "I've known Toby since we were four years old. There's nothing wrong with him! Let me talk to him. Please. He probably needs a friend."

My heart, already in my stomach, might as well have exited my body and broken into a thousand pieces. "Emma, I have to tell you something terrible. Toby passed away. He took his own life a few days ago."

She was silent and still for so long that I thought the video feed had frozen.

"Emma?"

"I don't believe you," she murmured, hugging her knees up to her chest. "Toby wouldn't do that."

"He's gone, Emma. I'm so sorry—"

She furiously shook her head. "No, it's not him. He wouldn't do that. He would *never* do that. He wasn't even sick! You're wrong!"

"Actually, that's why I'm calling you," I said. "I have reason to believe that Toby was misdiagnosed. I was hoping you could tell me about your relationship with him."

Emma wiped the tears spilling over her eyelashes. "What do you need to know?"

I unfolded the letter from Toby to Emma. "He had this in the pocket of his pants when he was committed to Trevino. Were the two of you dating?"

Emma squinted at the paper and, to my surprise, laughed. "No, we weren't, but all of our friends made fun of us because we were so close. It became an inside joke. That letter was a homework assignment. We read Pride and Prejudice, and we had to write a letter to a friend in a similar writing style. Toby never turned his in. I guess now I know why."

"So you were just best friends?"

She nodded. "Since preschool."

"Did Toby make trouble at school?" I asked. "Did he get detention often?"

"No," she answered. "The teachers loved him. He was super smart. Straight As every semester."

I scribbled her replies in my notebook. "Did he ever

seem full of himself? Or seek attention, admiration, or acknowledgement when he didn't deserve it?"

"That doesn't sound like Toby at all," Emma said. "He is—was the nicest person I knew. He didn't brag about himself or anything like that. Actually, he was pretty humble. He won an award for perfect attendance last year and gave it to a kid who *would* have gotten the award if he hadn't caught mono."

"So you never witnessed Toby behaving poorly?" I pressed. "He never got angry or yelled or seemed distant with you?"

Emma hesitated, glancing away from the phone camera. "Well, he sort of changed when his mom started dating an old guy."

"Banks Billings? His stepfather?"

"Yeah," Emma said. "Toby hated him."

"What changes did you see in Toby?"

"He got quiet," she replied. "He wasn't as talkative and happy-go-lucky as he usually was. He cut all his hair off, which was weird. He's had long hair forever. He told me his stepdad made him do it" —she put on a deep voice to imitate Billings— *"because it made him look like a hobo.* He also wasn't allowed to hang out after school anymore. I barely got to see him."

"Anything else?"

Emma chewed on her lip. "I think his stepdad did something to him."

An uneasy feeling stirred in the pit of my stomach. "Like what?"

"I don't know," she said. "He came into school one day looking sick. Like pale green. And he had a bruised eye. He didn't want to go home that afternoon. He called his mom and told her he was staying at his friend Jacob's house, but he came over to mine instead."

"He didn't tell you what happened?"

"Not a word."

I was beginning to dislike Banks Billings more and more, though I'd technically never met the guy. "Thanks, Emma. This was helpful. I'm sorry to have called you with such bad news."

"I don't want Toby to be remembered the wrong way," she said tearily. "If you need to know anything else, text me at this number. I'll help with whatever you need."

"I'll keep that in mind."

"Natasha? Can you send me Toby's letter? It's the last thing he ever wrote to me."

"Yes, Emma. Right away."

BY THE TIME I'd hung up with Emma, the inn's kitchen was closed. I'd missed dinner, and Marcel was too fed up with me to gift me with leftovers. I bundled up and headed into the snowy streets. Yet another few inches had fallen, covering Lone Elm in fresh powder.

I ordered takeout at the Shadows Restaurant and sat in the lobby to wait for it. While I went over my conversation with Emma in my head, a man in a long black coat came in and stomped the snow out of his boots on the rubber mat. He approached the hostess's stand.

"Hi, table for two?"

The hostess checked her seating chart. "It'll be a few minutes. Everyone's here for the hump day special."

"No problem."

The man sat across from me and stretched his long

legs out in front of him. I peeked over my phone at him. He wore his long dark hair tied in a neat bun at the top of his head. His matching beard was smooth and well-kept. Beneath his coat—which looked designer and expensive— he wore a workman's thermal shirt. Definitely not designer.

"You remind me of someone," I said to him. "Do people ever compare you to celebrities?"

The man smiled. "Not that I can recall."

"Oh. Never mind then."

"You work at the Trevino Center?"

I forgot that I'd never taken off my scrubs that day. They peeked through the collar of my coat. "Yes, I do."

"Is it true a boy died there recently?"

I swallowed the lump in my throat. "Unfortunately, yes."

The man's lips turned downward. "That's a shame."

"Sir?" The hostess waved a menu at the stranger. "Your table is ready."

The man stood up and nodded to me. "Have a good night."

"You too."

Later, as I walked back to the inn with my food, I couldn't stop wondering where I'd seen the man's face before.

16

*T*he next day, all hell broke loose, but not for the reasons I expected. When I arrived to work, every person I passed stared at me with wide eyes. Cameron sank below the front desk as I entered the building then craned her neck to watch me pass. The custodian who'd found me in the supply closet yesterday leapt out of my path and ran away, leaving the marble floor half-mopped in the lobby. Dashiell, who was working with a patient near the therapists' office, gave me a hard look as I walked by.

"Didn't think you had that in you," he commented.

Confused, I didn't respond. I was relieved to finally enter the therapists' office. "Do I have something on my face? Everyone's treating me like I have the biggest chunk of spinach between my teeth. Or a booger. Oh, God, is it a booger?"

No one answered. Jewel, trembling, excused herself from the room. Imogen and Ariel scooted their chairs closer together and clasped hands. Andy's attention remained affixed to his computer, though I could see his eyes darting off to the side to catch a glimpse of me.

I threw my hands up in frustration. "What is going on?"

Imogen reached over and shook my computer mouse to wake up the screen. It showed the home page of the Lone Elm Gazette, the local newspaper. The bold headline might as well have punched me in the teeth: *Trevino Hired a Killer!*

"Oh no."

I collapsed in my office chair and read the article:

An anonymous tip from inside the Trevino Center has brought a terrifying fact to light: Natasha Bell, 30, the Center's newly hired movement therapist, is guilty of murder. Bell, a product of the foster care system, reportedly killed another girl at knifepoint when she was a teenager. "I always thought something was up with her," the insider told the Lone Elm Gazette. "She seemed off from the first day she got here." With the recent supposed suicide of a high-profile patient, one has to wonder: has Bell resumed her violent ways?

A sharp pain went through my jaw. I'd been clenching my teeth with so much force that the muscles in my face protested.

"Is it true?" Imogen asked, arms crossed. "Did you kill someone?"

"You don't understand," I said. "This isn't the whole story. I'm not a murderer."

"You didn't deny it," Ariel pointed out.

"Is this why Jewel ran out?" I asked in a quavering voice. "She's scared of me?"

Andy cleared his throat. "We're all a little scared, to be honest, Nat. Is the article true?"

I clicked out of the Gazette's website to get the heinous headline off of my screen. "You don't know the whole story. I was thirteen. The other girl stabbed me first."

Imogen covered her mouth. "You actually killed someone?"

"It was an accident," I insisted. "And it was out of self-defense. If I hadn't reacted, she would have killed me first."

"Oh my God," said Ariel. "I think I'm going to be sick."

"I was a minor," I continued. "When I turned eighteen, the incident was cleaned off my record. I'm not—"

"You shouldn't be allowed to work here," Imogen hissed. "With children! God, it's like you're not even human. You've been lying to us the entire time."

"I don't usually bring it up in conversation!" I said hotly. "What did you want me to say? Hey, everyone! Thanks for the job, can't wait to get started. Oh, by the way, I accidentally killed someone when I was a teenager."

"That would have been better than hiding it!" Imogen shot back.

My hands trembled. I curled them into fists to stop them from shaking. "I don't talk about it. It's in the past, and I refused to let it affect my future. I'm no different than the rest of you."

"Yeah, right," Imogen scoffed. "None of us have killed anyone." She looked at Andy and Ariel. "Right?"

Andy and Ariel quickly nodded.

"Did you ever have to fight someone for lunch money?" I asked Imogen. "Were you ever threatened at school because you didn't have parents to stand up for you? Did your guardians exploit you for money from the government?"

Imogen's cheeks turned pink. "No, but—"

"I wasn't so lucky as you," I said. "I had to make my own way in the world, and a lot of times, that meant defending myself from people who wanted to hurt me. This incident was expunged from my permanent record. I was not charged for murder, and whoever tipped off the Gazette obviously has no idea what actually happened that day. If this was printed, I would have used it to line my cat's litter box."

No one dared make eye contact with me or contradict my statement. I took a deep breath and squared my shoulders.

"I can't expect you all to look at me the same way you did yesterday," I told them, "but I hope you realize that what happened to me in the past doesn't mean I'm a bad therapist. I care deeply for my patients, and this under-handed accusation that I might have killed Toby—" My voice hitched unexpectedly, cutting off the sentence. I forced my vocal chords to function. "It's not fair. Shame on you all for feeding into the gossip before asking me about it. I expected more out of you."

Rather than cry in front of them, I stepped out of the office and ran down the hallway to let loose. I freely sobbed in the farthest corner of the inpatient care area, letting every emotion from the last few days pour out of me. I'd had enough. Toby's death was a bear to deal with on its own, let alone my personal investigation into the Center's mysterious dealings. Adding the outing of my past transgressions on top of everything pushed me over the edge.

I'd never told anyone at the Center about what happened when I was thirteen. Except for Toby. That day in the dance room was the first time I'd talked about the incident since the hours I'd spent in therapy as a minor. The only reason I'd told Toby in the first place was because he needed to hear about it.

Had someone been eavesdropping on us? According to the Gazette, an "inside source" had tipped off the paper. That meant someone I worked with had overheard me and ratted me out. It was the only explanation. Though articles about the incident were published years ago, my name had been withheld from the papers because I was a minor. If someone searched my name on the Internet, they would find my LinkedIn account and maybe a few old Facebook photos, but they would never come across my childhood trauma.

"Honey?" a gentle voice echoed from the closest room. "Natasha, is that you?"

I wiped my face and peeked inside. "Hi, Bonnie. How are you doing?"

"I think we ought to turn that question around," Bonnie said, offering me a comforting smile. She sat in the armchair by the window rather than lying in her usual place beneath the bed covers. "What's with the waterworks?"

"Did you get to that chair all by yourself?"

"Don't change the subject, you hooligan."

My laugh got caught in the back of my throat. Another tear ran down my cheek. I caught it on the sleeve of my sweater. "I guess you haven't seen the front page of the Lone Elm Gazette."

Bonnie made a face. "Lord, no. I couldn't possibly read

that trash. I tried once, but it's no better than a super-market tabloid. Where I come from, reporters actually have integrity. Although, not much news happens in Lone Elm, so I can see why their journalists grasp at straws so often. What garbage did the Gazette print now?"

"Something that's half true about me," I said, sinking onto Bonnie's empty bed. "And now everyone here thinks I'm dangerous and crazy."

"It can't be that bad."

"If I told you, you'd think the same."

"Try me."

Blissfully, Bonnie understood. Her sister fostered children and understood the unique challenges that kids in the system faced.

"My sister's one of the good ones," Bonnie said. "She does it out of the kindness of her heart, not for the money. She tries to show those kids as much love as possible, but some of them won't trust anymore. Not after what's happened to them." When she patted my cheek, I almost started crying again. "Don't let the gossip mongers get you down, kiddo. You're a good one too."

"Natasha?" Lindsay stood in the hallway, wearing a stern look. She beckoned me over with one finger. "I need to see you in Eli's office. Immediately."

"I have to teach a class in five minutes—"

"Now," Lindsay said.

I was naive to wish this impromptu meeting wasn't about the article in the Gazette, but I did anyway. As I followed Lindsay to Eli's office, I repeated a single thought in my head. *Please don't fire me. Please don't fire me.*

Lindsay ushered me into the office and closed the door. She remained standing, and I noticed that she had maneuvered me into the far corner of the room. She kept close to the only exit. Like Jewel, she was scared of me, though she didn't let her fear get in the way of her anger.

"What the hell is this?" she demanded, slamming a paper copy of the Gazette onto Eli's desk.

"Oh, wow," I said flatly. "The headline is even bigger in print."

"So you've read it?"

"The other therapists were eager to show it to me this morning."

Lindsay flailed her hands. "*And?*"

"And what?" I asked. "It's gossip. There's hardly any real information in that article."

Lindsay ran her fingers through her mane of blonde hair. She looked on the verge of tearing it out. "I don't understand. We run thorough background checks on all of our employees. How could something like this not come up?"

"My record was expunged when I turned eighteen." In a way, it was lucky the therapists had confronted me about this before Lindsay did. It was like practice for the real thing, and this time, I had better luck containing my emotions. "As far as the law is concerned, I was never guilty of anything."

Lindsay glared at me. "As far as *I'm* concerned, you're guilty until the Gazette prints a retraction."

"Would you like to know what happened? I already explained it to the other people downstairs who believed I was a killer."

"I don't care what happened," Lindsay snapped. "What

I care about is the reputation of this facility. We're already in hot water because of what happened to the Gardner kid. If the national news gets ahold of *this*" —she waved her arm at me like I was a Wheel of Fortune prize — "the Center will lose more of its footing. I can't afford that."

"What would you like me to do about it?"

"Keep quiet," she answered through clenched teeth. "If anyone asks you about it, tell them it's not true."

I fidgeted, unwilling to lie. These days, it felt like all I did was lie.

"I want you to go home for the day," Lindsay ordered, tossing the Gazette into the garbage. "Let this die down. A lot of our patients read the local paper, and they don't need to worry that a killer is treating them."

"With all due respect," I began, "I think that's the opposite way we need to deal with this. If I go home, it will look like an admission of guilt. Besides, my patients are relying on me, and I've already missed sessions with them in the past few days. I don't want to mess up our schedule any more."

I'd never seen anyone roll their tongue in a condescending manner, but Lindsay pulled it off with pure perfection. Before she could answer, Eli came in.

"Oh," he said, eyebrows lifting in surprise when he saw that his office was already occupied. "What are you two doing in here?"

"I was sending Natasha home for the day," Lindsay said, as if gauging Eli's opinion on the matter.

"What?" Eli looked at me in shock. "Why? Are you sick?"

I reached into the wastebasket and fished out the

Gazette for Eli to read. His brow furrowed as he skimmed over the article.

"Is this true?" he asked.

"Does it matter?" I replied dryly.

He threw the Gazette back into the trash can and dusted his hands off. "Well, we can't worry about that now. I need you at work, Natasha. I've decided to hire an assistant for the dance therapy department, and I need you to screen the applications."

Lindsay stepped between me and her husband. "We didn't agree to any new hires, Eli."

"No, we didn't," he said firmly. "I decided to do this on my own."

"Why?" she asked.

Eli sidestepped his wife and sat behind his desk. "Because more patients have requested to be involved with Natasha's dance program, but she doesn't have the time to treat everyone."

"We can't afford to hire another therapist," Lindsay argued.

"Which is why I'm hiring an *assistant*." Eli organized a stack of patient information papers on his desk. "Natasha, I'm going to forward you the applications I've already received. I'd like you to go through them. Check out the applicants' credentials. You have a better idea of who might be a good fit. Choose people you think you'd want to work with."

I glanced at Lindsay. Her face was pink. She was so frustrated with her husband that she looked ready to explode.

"I'll get right on that," I said and hurried out of the office.

Though the door shut behind me, I could still hear Lindsay and Eli arguing. I lingered around the corner to listen.

"What were you thinking?" Lindsay bellowed. "How are we supposed to pay another employee? We're up to our eyeballs in debt."

"We're fine," Eli replied dismissively. "As long as Natasha stays on pace with Luna Lamont, we'll be out of the woods in a few months. Why do you think I'm trying to keep her happy?"

"Did you read what's in that article?" Lindsay asked. "She killed someone. She's a murderer, Eli!"

"You know as well as I do that the Gazette will print anything for the sake of a story," Eli said. "It's more important to keep Natasha than get rid of her. Speaking of which, what makes you think you have the authority to send my employees away from their jobs? Last time I checked, I'm the boss here."

"Last time I checked, you'd checked *out*," Lindsay growled. "Or did you forget that I'm the one who kept this place up and running after your father died?"

"That's a low blow, Linds."

"We're supposed to be a team," she said in a softer tone. "But I feel like I'm doing all the work, Eli."

"We're on the same side," he reminded her. "Have a little faith in me."

THE GAZETTE ARTICLE followed me around like a pesky mosquito for the rest of the day, biting me on the neck whenever I thought it had finally flown away. Every patient who read the local paper looked at me like I was about to pull out a knife in the middle of dance class and perform a ritualistic sacrifice with bongo drums and a full moon. After three hours of this, I started making an announcement at the start of my sessions:

"For those of you who read the front page of the Lone Elm Gazette this morning," I said wearily to a class of outpatient dancers, "the accusations against me are not true. Dr. Trevino fully believes my side of the story and trusts me to be here with you. And a-five, six, seven, eight."

Halfway through the day, I learned the best way to keep the patients from gossiping about me was to keep them busy. I increased the intensity of the dance moves, within reason, until they were too out of breath to talk about me. Still, they watched me with nervous, darting eyes, and many of them were scared to let me pass behind them.

They weren't the only ones. As word spread, the other Center employees began avoiding me like the plague. They darted out of sight when we crossed path in the corridors. The nurses and aides who usually helped me set things up or break them down were nowhere to be seen. I cleaned the dance equipment by myself after each session. The extra time put me a full half hour behind schedule.

The only time I caught a break was in Ward 13. The psych patients weren't allowed to read the news, lest the stories about global warming and collusion trigger their paranoia or anxiety. Wilson, Luna, and the other teenagers treated me normally. I was so grateful that I thanked them profusely at the end of our sessions.

"You're being weird," Luna informed me as I babbled about her positive behavior. "It's weirding me out."

On another bright note, Luna had been doing extraordinarily well. Without her mother around to provoke her, she exhibited almost no signs of bipolar disorder. It strengthened my suspicious that she, and possibly Toby, had been misdiagnosed and sent to the Center for no reason other than teenaged rebellion. Thankfully, Eli had already made note of this. He lowered Luna's medication dosages to almost nothing, but he refused to discharge her.

"If a patient is admitted due to a psychiatric hold, they're required to stay for a minimum of five days," he told me later when I asked about Luna's state. "Furthermore, Luna's doctor suggested she stay at the Center for at least ninety days. We need to study her patterns. She could flip in the other direction just as quickly."

Both Luna and I knew Eli was full of crap. He wanted to keep Luna at the Center longer to ensure her mother would donate the extra twenty-five thousand dollars.

By the end of the day, all I wanted to do was go home and fall into bed, but I still had to go through the applications for assistants that Eli had sent me. Instead of staying at the office, I brought my work laptop with me and headed to the local café.

As soon as I left the Center, it became clear that almost everyone in Lone Elm had read the Gazette. People stared into the windshield of my car as I drove down the main street. They stared as I parked on the curb and got out. They stared as I walked into the café and up to the counter to order.

"Can I get a chicken pesto panini and a black coffee?"

The cashier looked up from the receipts she'd been organizing, recognized me, and gave a little yelp under her breath. She stepped away from the counter.

"Don't worry," I said, annoyed. "I'm not armed. I just want coffee."

"Mm-hmm, of course. Whatever you want." She typed my order into the tablet as quickly as possible. "One pesto panini and a black coffee."

"And a chocolate croissant," I added.

"Whoops. Okay, gotta go back to the first page." She was so flustered that she rang up the wrong order and had to start over. "That'll be fifteen dollars and twenty-seven cents."

I reached into the pocket of my coat for my wallet and came out empty-handed. I let out a groan. "I left my wallet at work."

The cashier looked nervously around. "You don't have cash on hand?"

"No, I don't carry it. Damn it!"

From behind me, a long arm in a black coat handed the cashier a credit card. "Put her order on my tab," said a familiar voice. "Can I also get a Monte Cristo sandwich and a matcha latte?"

As the cashier hastened to complete the order, I looked up to find the man from the Shadows Restaurant yesterday. He smiled down at me, his dark eyes twinkling.

"Bad luck about your wallet, eh?" he asked in a subtle Midwestern accent. "I attach mine to my keys so I don't make the same mistake. See?" He lifted a small cardholder with a keyring. "Genius, right?"

"That's smart," I agreed. "Maybe I should get one for myself. Thanks, by the way. You didn't have to do that."

"Don't worry about it."

He began to walk away, but I called after him. "You want to share a table?"

WE ENDED up at a tiny round table in the far corner of the café. The man hung his jacket over the back of his chair. Today, he wore a dark green sweater with pilling all over it. It brought out the flecks of color in his dark eyes.

"I'm Duke," he said, lowering his long frame into the tiny café chair. "You're Natasha, right?"

"How'd you know?"

He jerked his chin at the other customers who were all staring at me. "Just a guess. I read the Gazette this morning."

I flushed bright red. "I suppose you want to know who I killed too?"

"Well, I am a journalist," he replied. "But it's not you I'm interested in. Anyway, I can spot a poorly-researched story when I see one. I'd guess you're no more of a killer than that cashier you scared to death."

The tension leaked from my body. Duke's voice had a humorous lilt to it; it automatically put me at ease. Maybe it was because I felt like I already knew him.

"Besides, I know what you're going through. I've been on the wrong side of the gossip factory myself," Duke said. "I lost everything because of it."

"Oh?"

"Yes, but I've rebuilt," he went on. "Of course, some things you can never get back. However, you *can* fight for justice, which is exactly why I'm so happy to have run into you."

A different café employee dropped off our drinks. As I poured a packet of stevia into my coffee and stirred it, I asked Duke, "What do you mean?"

"As I said before, I'm a reporter." He sipped his latte. "And I've come to Lone Elm to take down Eli Trevino."

17

"I hope you don't feel like I've targeted you specifically," Duke said, regarding my stumped expression. "The rumors triggered my interest in you, and I have reason to believe you're not as brainwashed by the Trevino family as the other employees at the Center may be."

"What reason is that?" I asked sharply.

"You worked closely with Toby Gardner, correct?"

"Yes."

"Do you or do you not believe that he committed suicide?"

The question took me by surprise. Until this very moment, I had not considered any other options. "He's gone. I saw the blood."

"But not the body?"

"No, but—" I leaned forward. "Are you suggesting someone at Trevino killed Toby?"

Duke's face remained impassive. "It wouldn't be the first time."

"Okay, I don't know what you're getting at here," I said. "Do you think the Trevinos hired me to kill their patients? What kind of absurd notion is that?"

With practiced nonchalance, Duke cut his Monte Cristo sandwich across the diagonal. Cheese oozed out from between the bread slices. "You're misunderstanding me, Miss Bell. I wish to work *with* you on this matter. I need someone on the inside. With your help, we could put a stop to Eli Trevino's unethical and fraudulent practices."

I studied him for a long minute. He didn't come off as the type of guy determined enough to take down a business as well-known as the Trevino Center, at least not for the sake of journalism.

"What happened?" I asked him.

"I beg your pardon?"

"You're personally invested in this," I said. "I can tell from how hard you're trying to hide it. Who did you lose at the Center?"

Duke stared into his lap, unable to lift his sandwich to his lips for another bite. "That might be a story for another time, if I decide to trust you." He cleared his throat and shook off the memories that were clearly gnawing at him. "Are you interested in helping me or not?"

"Yes," my mouth replied before my brain had time to think about it. "What do you need me to do?"

"Behave normally," he instructed. "That's the most important thing. Other than that, keep your eyes and ears open. If you see or hear about anything weird, do your best to record it somehow. At the very least, let me know about it as soon as possible. Now eat your panini. It's getting cold."

. . .

IT WAS ALSO GETTING cold outside. The intensity of the snow had steadily been building over the last several days. When Duke and I left the café, a vicious gust of wind nearly swept me off my feet. Duke grabbed the sleeve of my coat to keep me upright. The snow blew sideways, whirling in every direction. The visibility on the road was horrible.

"Blizzard's coming," Duke commented, buttoning up his trademark black coat. "It's going to be freezing tonight."

"I think I'll walk back to the inn." I squinted up the street. The inn was only two blocks up the road, but I couldn't see its turrets from here. "I'd rather not risk the drive. Where are you staying?"

"In my van."

I whirled to look at him. "In your van? You'll freeze!"

"Well, it's a camper van," he said. "I've got blankets and a mini heater, but it tends to run out of gas halfway through the night.'

"You're no use to me dead." I linked my arm through his, for my own balance as well as to guide him up the street. "Come on."

LAUREN, Baz, and Jean Paul were relaxing in the living room of the inn, nursing hot chocolates, when Duke and I arrived home. A comfortable fire burned in the hearth, bathing me in blissful warmth as I walked in. Cinnamon and clove wafted from the kitchen. If my nose was correct, Marcel had made apple crumble for dessert.

My hair and shoulders were covered in snow. Duke's beard looked made of snowflakes. As I stomped my boots on the welcome mat, Jean Paul—who'd been pawing marshmallows out of Baz's mug—noticed my arrival. He hopped off Baz's lap to rub around my legs, then meowed with disgruntlement when a dollop of snow landed on his head.

"Sorry, dude," I said, stooping to pet him.

"Thank goodness you're home," Lauren said, rising from her cozy spot on the couch. "I was starting to worry." She noticed Duke, who hadn't taken his coat off yet, and brought out her dazzling smile. "Oh, who's this?"

I made quick introductions, leaving out Duke's reason for visiting Lone Elm. "Do you have a room for him, Lauren?" I asked. "He was planning to sleep in his van."

"We can't have that!" Lauren beckoned Duke over to the front desk. "I just need some ID and a credit card."

After giving Lauren his information, Duke thanked her profusely. "It's a beautiful place," he said with a charming smile. "I appreciate you accommodating me on such short notice."

Lauren beamed. "It's no problem at all."

He folded his long coat over his arm. "If you don't mind, I'm going to head upstairs for a hot shower. Melt some of this snow off, you know?"

"Enjoy," Lauren said.

As Duke made his way up the stairs, Lauren came over to me and let out a low whistle, her eyes following Duke until he disappeared around the corner.

"Whew!" she said, pretending to wipe sweat off her brow. "Where did you find him, the camping aisle at the sporting goods store?"

"The café actually."

"You don't know each other?" Lauren asked.

"No, we just met," I said. "He and I share a similar passion though."

Her gaze lost focus, as if her mind had drifted to a different scene entirely. "Oh, he looks passionate."

"I'm right here!" Baz said from the other room.

"Can it, kid," Lauren replied. She turned back to me. "All good for the night, Natasha? Do you need anything?"

"I wouldn't mind a hot bath either," I said. "I'm soaked through. But can you send up a hot chocolate and some apple crumble?"

"You got it."

I bid everyone good night except for Jean Paul, who braided himself through my legs as I went upstairs. Wearily, I stumbled into my dark room, stripped off my cold, soaked socks, and fell into bed. Jean Paul curled up on my chest. For once, I was happy to share his warmth despite his fat butt crushing my lungs.

A floorboard creaked. I looked across the room and screamed.

"Shh! Natasha, it's me!" whispered a familiar voice. "Sorry, it's me!"

A figure stepped out of the shadows. Small, pale, and thin. Matted hair curling around his chin. A baggy sweatshirt swamped his frame, while the pants he wore were too short to cover his ankles. He shivered with cold or fear, though it was hard to tell which one.

My heart had forgotten how to pump blood through my veins. Adrenaline washed over me, making my skin tingle.

"Toby?"

He took another tentative step forward, nervously twisting the extra length of his sleeves into tight whips. He waved sheepishly and said, "Hi."

"Oh my God!"

Without thinking, I vaulted off the bed and threw myself across the room to wrap Toby in the tightest hug I'd ever given to someone. He let out a short grunt, as if I'd squeezed all the air out of his lungs. I pressed his face between my cheeks and stared at him, trying to make sure that he was real.

"You're here!" I said. "You're alive!"

"Not for long if you keep squeezing my face like that."

"Oh, sorry." I let him go. "How is this possible?"

Toby rubbed his cheeks. "I came through the back door and found the room with the cat. It was pretty easy. You're not mad, are you?"

"No, I'm not mad," I said. "But I also didn't mean how you got in here. I meant how are you alive?"

"Why wouldn't I be?"

The scene from that morning, the day Toby had gone missing, flashed in my head again: the blood splashed all over the walls, the herd of emergency vehicles outside, Toby's mother sobbing into Lindsay's shoulder.

"Toby." I sat him on the cushioned window seat. "Everyone thinks you committed suicide."

His face fell. "Why the heck would they think that?"

"Because there was blood all over the room," I explained. "The police showed up. Your mom—" I hesitated. "Your mom was really upset."

Toby's lip trembled. "My mom thinks I'm dead?"

I sat next to him and massaged my aching forehead. "I

don't understand. If you're alive, what actually happened that night? You ran away?"

"Are you mad?" he asked again.

"Toby, are you kidding?" I hugged him again. "I'm just glad you're not dead." He shivered underneath my grasp. "Are you cold? Where did you get these clothes?"

"I stole them out of one of those containers where people drop off donations," he said. "I know you're not supposed to do that kind of stuff, but all I had to wear was that clinical gown, and I've mostly been outside this entire time. I was freezing—hey, do you know what frostbite looks like?" He held up his thumb. "Does this look weird?"

I grabbed his thumb and examined it under the desk lamp. "Toby, that's dirt."

"Whew. That's a relief."

"Go take a shower," I told him. "I'll find you some clothes and something to eat. Once we're both comfortable, I want you to tell me the whole story."

He balanced on one foot, chewing on the inside of his mouth. "You're not going to tell anyone I'm here, are you? Like the police? Or Dr. Trevino."

I took him by the shoulders. "Look at me. You're safe here. You can stay for as long as you need, okay? I'm not going to tell anyone, especially Dr. Trevino. I don't trust him anymore."

Toby's eyes widened. "Did you figure it out?"

"Your message?" I took the photo—worn at the edges —out of my back pocket, where it lived as a reminder to keep moving forward. "Trevino kills. Find out the truth. Is this about you and the other kids in Ward 13?"

He nodded. "People talk there. The nurses and the aides. Kids have died in there, and their families donate a

ALEXANDRIA CLARKE

bunch of money to the Center for trying to help. Or to make their kid a legacy. It's Dr. Trevino, Nat. He's killing us. That's why I had to leave."

He trembled from head to toe. I ushered him toward the bathroom. "Let's talk about it after. Get in there, kid. You smell."

SINCE MARCEL WAS GONE for the day, I managed to get in and out of the kitchen without incident, securing Toby a double portion of artisanal macaroni and cheese, some roasted broccoli, and two servings of apple crumble. One of those, however, was for me. On my way back up to my room, I knocked on Duke's door. He answered, freshly showered, his long hair around his shoulders.

"Sorry to bother you," I said, "but I have a weird situation in my room. Would you happen to have any clothes I could borrow? Pants and a shirt?"

To Duke's credit, he didn't question my request. I returned to my room with a pair of insulated sweatpants and a long-sleeved thermal. Both items were too big for Toby, but he needed something clean to wear. Tomorrow, I could go out and buy him clothes that fit.

A few minutes later, Toby—clean and warm—devoured his meal on the bed I'd made up for him on the long window seat. I'd lined the glass with extra blankets to keep him from the cold. After a shower for myself, it was time to get the truth.

"Start from the beginning," I told Toby as I warmed up our apple crumble in the microwave. "I want to know everything."

"Everything?" Toby blew his wet hair out of his face.

He had cheese on his chin. "I guess that means I have to tell you about Banks."

"He hurt you, didn't he?" I asked softly. "I talked to your friend Emma."

"He tried to—" His voice wavered and broke off. Squaring his shoulders, he began again. "He tried to touch me. When my mom wasn't home."

Utter disgust hit me like a brick. I tried to keep it off my face. "Did you report it?"

"No," Toby said. "Because I hit him to make it stop, and he threatened to tell the police I assaulted him. He's friends with the NYPD chief."

"Yeah, but the chief doesn't know he tried to molest you," I pointed out. "That might affect their friendship. Did he try again?"

Toby rubbed his eyes, obviously exhausted. "Only once. I took a cricket bat to his head."

The details clicked into place. "That's why you got sent to the Center?"

"Yup." He stabbed a piece of apple but didn't bring it to his mouth. "Banks told my mom there was something wrong with me. That I was violent and unpredictable. She believed him. So they took me to a doctor, and the doctor said I had that stupid disorder, and I ended up at the Center. Once I was there, I thought maybe I did have some disorder. I was mad at everyone. I hated them. That's why I always lashed out. Then you came along and proved you weren't one of them."

"I'm so sorry all of that happened to you," I said.

"It's okay," he said. "But I can't go back to the Center and I can't go home. At least, not until someone proves that Dr. Trevino is killing kids."

A chill came over me. I pulled the comforter off the bed and wrapped it around my shoulders. "Do you have proof?"

Toby looked down. "No."

"We need it," I told him. "There's definitely a lot of illegal stuff going on at the Center, but that's for the adults to figure out. Your job is stay safe, which for now means staying out of sight. Fess up. How'd you get out of the Center without anyone seeing?"

"The night nurse helped me," he answered. "Misty. The one who brought me dinner and checked on me at night. She left my door unlocked that night."

"Why would she do that?"

"Because I asked her to."

I remembered Misty, crying on the curb the morning of Toby's supposed disappearance. She was a damn good actor.

"Where were Scout and Dashiell?" I asked.

Toby shrugged. "No idea. They usually stand at either end of the ward, but neither one of them was there that night. I made sure before I snuck out."

"So you just walked out? What about the cameras?"

"I tried to avoid them," he said. "Stuck to the dark corners, and I left through the first door I could find. Still, I figured security would have seen me on the footage. Why would they say I died?"

"To cover their own asses," I muttered. "The Center only cares about their reputation. They'd rather say you committed suicide than admit you got away from them."

Toby pondered this while taking his first bite of apple crumble. He groaned happily. "This is so good. I haven't eaten real food in days." He caught me looking at him. "What are we going to do now?"

"You're not going to do anything except hide," I said. "I'm going to get to the bottom of this. Believe me, Toby. I won't let anyone else hurt you."

I CONFIDED in one person about Toby's presence at the inn, and that was Baz. She agreed to keep the maids out of my room and bring food up to Toby for breakfast, lunch, and dinner.

"It's the kid you stalked," she said to me after meeting him. "Are you sure this still isn't weird?"

"It is weird," I agreed. "But you can't tell anyone he's here. It's for his own safety."

"What about my mom?"

"That's fine. I trust your mom."

Work was exhausting. On top of running my movement sessions and reviewing more applications for the assistant therapist position, I also had to pretend that Toby hadn't shown up out of the blue, alive and well. It proved harder than I thought. With every passing minute, my desperation to expose the Center's seedy underbelly grew. I worried for every patient in Ward 13, wondering if Eli and Lindsay had devious plans for them.

Toby's accusation weighed heavily on me. Were the rumors about the kids in Ward 13 true? Was Eli over-medicating them to the point of death, just for money? It didn't make any sense. These parents were paying the Center to *cure* their children. How would murdering them benefit the Center?

I told one person at the Center about Toby, and that was Misty the nurse.

"Oh, thank goodness," she breathed. "I was so worried about him."

"You let him out," I said. "You believed he wasn't crazy. Why?"

"I've seen so many kids come and go through this ward," Misty replied. "When they leave, all the light has gone from their eyes. Sometimes, they don't make it out. Toby deserved the chance to get out. I don't regret it, and if you report me to the police—"

I shook my head. "I'm not going to do that. Keep doing what you're doing, Misty. The patients here need you. Don't give up on them."

AFTER MY SESSION WITH LUNA, I found Scout in the corridor of Ward 13. I approached her from behind as she folded clean sheets and arranged them in the linen closet. I put on my best sad face, trying to get my bottom lip to tremble.

"Hey, Scout?" I said in a wavering voice. "Can I talk to you about something?"

Scout didn't bother to turn around. "I'm kinda busy. You need something for a patient?"

"No, I—" I faked a sniffle and pinched my arm to get my eyes to water. "Actually, I was hoping to ask you about Toby?"

She stiffened, and the sheet she was folding came undone. "What's there to talk about?"

"I just can't get closure," I said. "He had such a huge

impact on me, and I keep feeling like it's my fault he died. Like I couldn't keep him from killing himself."

Scout stacked the last sheet on the pile and turned around. "It's not your fault. It's no one's fault. Toby didn't want to be here anymore. He made that decision on his own."

"You were here the morning after, right?" I asked, fishing for details. "You leave last at night and you get here first?"

"The Center is short on aides," she said. "I work overtime because I need the money. So does Dash."

"Does that mean you were the one to find him?"

Scout pushed the linen bin back toward the laundry room. Though she hadn't exactly given me permission to follow her, I did so anyway.

"Yeah, I found him," she said. "It wasn't pretty. He did a number on himself."

"How did he do it?"

"He stole a pair of scissors from one of the nurses and stabbed himself with it."

"I thought he pried a loose nail out of the wall?"

Scout looked over her shoulder. "Is that what happened? I just heard rumors. Why are you asking if you already knew?"

"Oh, I heard rumors too," I said hurriedly. "Wondering if they were true."

She rolled the bin into the laundry room then began transferring wet towels from the enormous industrial washing machine to the dryer. "No offense, but how is this going to bring you closure? I don't like talking about it. I can't close my eyes without seeing his blood everywhere."

"Neither can I," I said. "I guess I just needed to connect with someone."

When Scout faced me, she had tears in her eyes. "I get that, but I can't be that person. You don't understand what it's like. Every time we lose a patient, I'm the first one to see what happened. I'm the one who has to call 911 because someone else has committed suicide. I've worked in Ward 13 for almost ten years. Do you know how many dead bodies I've seen?"

"I'm sorry," I stuttered, taken aback by her sudden burst of emotion. "I didn't mean to make you relive that."

She blinked away the tears. "I don't want to talk about this anymore. Have a good night, Natasha."

ON THE DRIVE HOME, I pondered Scout's reaction. It wasn't what I was expecting. She had never warmed up to me, so I figured she treated the patients the same way. I had to remind myself that Scout was the only aide who had the power to calm patients in Ward 13. Then again, she always had a helpful syringe up her sleeve.

As soon as I entered the inn, Baz practically assaulted me with her laptop.

"Look at this!" she hissed, shoving the screen in front of my nose. "I've been working on this all day with Duke. We didn't find anything about Trevino killing kids—I didn't think we would because that's just nuts—*but* we did figure out something else! Come here!"

She dragged me into the living room, where Lauren and Duke were snacking on spinach and artichoke dip before dinner. Baz sat next to Duke as if she'd known him her whole life. I shot a questioning look at Lauren.

"Don't look at me," Lauren said. "I don't know what's going on either."

"Duke's an investigative journalist," Baz announced. "He's been helping me put some puzzle pieces together. Mom, this is about Grandma, so you should listen."

Lauren sobered, the smile vanishing from her face. "What are you talking about?"

"I've been looking into the Trevino Center," Baz said, "and I found out that a *lot* of elderly people die there. Totally sad. But what's weird is that the Center isn't for end of life care, you know? It's a rehab facility. These old folks are supposed to go home after they get better. *But*" —she paused for dramatic effect— "they didn't."

Lauren and I stared blankly at Baz. Duke crossed one leg over the other and fished another hunk of artichoke out of the dip.

Baz huffed at our lack of reaction. "Almost every one of the older patients who died at Trevino donated all of their assets to the Center."

"Like Lenny," I said. "He passed away during my first month."

"Yeah, he didn't have any family to take him home."

"How did you know that?"

She turned her laptop to face me. On the screen was a list of names, phone numbers, and dollar amounts. "Because that's the pattern here. I spent today calling the living relatives of the deceased people who donated to the Center. They all told me the same story. Take Lenny for instance. I spoke to his granddaughter today. She told me that shortly after Lenny was sent to the Center, he stopped calling home. When she tried to visit him, the Center told her that he didn't want to see her."

"That doesn't sound like Lenny," I said. "He was a good-humored guy. He would want his granddaughter to visit."

"Exactly." Baz said. She looked at her mother. "Remember Grandma? You and her never had a good relationship, but *we* did. I tried to visit her a couple times in the Center. I got in the first time. After that, the staff always made up some excuse so I couldn't see her. When she died, you were so pissed that she didn't leave you anything—"

"She left it to the Center," Lauren said, wide-eyed. "But how?"

"They make the patients sign these stupid consent forms." Once more, Baz turned to her computer. She pulled up a pdf. "I managed to find a copy online. Basically, it says that the patient will turn over their assets to the Center as a donation if no contact with the family is made. The Center alienates these patients from their family, feeds each party a different side of the story to make it seem like there's some feud, then takes the patients' money because no one else is there to claim it."

Lauren covered her mouth and sank into the sofa. She looked at Duke. "Did you know about this?"

"I had an inkling," Duke replied. "But Baz did all the work. I think she's discovered something very important about the Trevino Center."

"What's that?" I asked.

"They're running two scams," he said dryly. "Not just one."

18

_E_ven with Baz's discovery, we had a lack of evidence to turn the Trevino Center in. By getting their patients to sign a legal document, the Center could avoid a lawsuit, and there was no way to prove that anyone had intentionally separated the patients from their families. It was similar to what they'd been doing with the teenagers in Ward 13, asking for "donations" in exchange for the child's welfare.

"Why don't you go after Williamson?" Toby asked after I explained our sticky situation to him. "Don't you think it's fishy that he's sending kids to Trevino with diagnoses that don't make any sense?"

Once I explained the connection between Dr. Williamson and the Trevino Center to Duke, he immediately agreed it was something we needed to look into. We hatched a crazy plan, and the next day, I called out of work to go on an adventure with Duke.

"Okay, so I'm Martha D'Angelis," I said, riding shotgun in Duke's camper van. "I'm a rich, Upper East Side wife with a twelve-year-old daughter named Elizabeth. I'm scared that Elizabeth has borderline personality disorder, as she's been exhibiting signs of manipulation and violence."

"Right, but don't say it like it's rehearsed," Duke advised.

"Do yours then."

Duke cleared his throat and put on a nasally voice. "Dr. Williamson, thank you so much for putting us on your schedule so last minute. I'm Paul D'Angelis. This is my wife, Martha. We're so grateful to you."

He sounded exactly like a worried father. Perhaps he'd gone undercover more than once during the course of his career as an investigative journalist.

"Fine, you do the talking," I said. "Don't forget, you'll need to get Dr. Williamson out of his office so I can check his computer."

"And if it's locked?"

"Then we're probably screwed," I replied.

Duke chuckled, steering with his knees as he tied his long hair into his signature bun. "I'm glad to have found you, Nat. Not many people would do this sort of thing with a random guy they've just met."

"You showed me your credentials," I reminded him. Duke had let me read his past articles and scrutinize his driver's license to make sure he was legitimate. Besides that, there was something about him that seemed trustworthy. Though I couldn't place his familiar face, I felt like I already knew him. "If we can find proof, we're going to blow this thing wide open."

. . .

IN THE FEW months since I'd moved to Lone Elm, I'd all but forgotten what it was like in the city. New York was a mess of impatient locals, excited tourists, and traffic. Tons and tons of traffic. Duke, on the bright side, weaved in and out of the other cars with practiced ease, and he did it without cursing up a storm at the other drivers. I admired his control and temperament.

"Here we are," he said, expertly parallel parking outside Dr. Williamson's private practice. "Are you ready for this?"

I smoothed the wrinkles from the blazer and slacks I'd borrowed from Lauren to look the part. "Let's do it."

As we entered the lobby, I did my best to look like a forlorn parent. In my head, I imagined how I would feel if something terrible happened to Jean Paul and used it to perfect my act.

Dr. Williamson's office was as stuffy as I expected it to be. The walls were painted a sad shade of gray. A plug-in air freshener pumped out an artificial lemon scent that made my throat close up. One other pair of parents waited for Dr. Williamson's attention. The woman wore a ridiculous hat fit for a royal wedding, and the man sported an expensive suit. Both Duke and I looked under-dressed.

"May I help you?" the woman at the front desk droned.

"Yes," Duke said, taking the reins. "We have an appointment with Dr. Williamson. Paul and Martha D'Angelis?"

"Have a seat," the woman replied.

After twenty minutes, the other couple was called to the back. Half an hour later, they reappeared with white faces and couldn't stop bickering as they left the office.

Another thirty minutes passed, and no one addressed us. Duke finally approached the desk again.

"It's forty-five minutes past our appointment time," he said. "Is Dr. Williamson going to be ready for us soon?"

The secretary stared Duke down. "It won't be much longer."

After a final fifteen minutes, a woman in a green dress collected us from the waiting room. "I'm Shay, Dr. Williamson's assistant," she said, checking paperwork on her clipboard. "I see this is your first time meeting with Dr. Williamson, so I'll give you a little rundown on what might happen. First, Dr. Williamson will ask you about your child and your lifestyle. If he chooses to treat your child, another appointment will be made to assess the child's behavior. Clear so far?"

Duke and I nodded. I began to worry that we hadn't practiced enough for this kind of scam. I had no idea what I was supposed to say about our fake kid.

"Here we are."

Shay led us to an office near the back of the practice. Three tall windows looked out onto the busy New York street. A massive oak desk took up a third of the space, but all that occupied its surface was a single computer, a leather notebook, and an expensive fountain pen. The rest of the room was lined with bookshelves, filled with titles like *The Essential Guide to Diagnosing Mental Illnesses in Children* and *What Having a Bipolar Child Could Mean for Your Family.*

"Take a seat," Shay said, indicating two ugly chairs covered in green felt across from Dr. Williamson's desk. His own chair was much taller and throne-like. "Dr.

Williamson will be with you in a moment. Can I get you anything? Water or tea?"

"We're fine," Duke said before I could ask for something to quench the dryness in my throat. "Thank you, Shay."

Once she was gone, I let out a sigh of relief. "This is more nerve-wracking than I thought it would be. Do you think we have time to check his computer before he comes in? That way, we don't have to—"

Duke rested his warm heavy hand on my forearm. "Stick to the plan. We want him to log into his computer first. Then I'll draw him away."

I took a deep breath and reminded myself this wasn't Duke's first rodeo. All I had to do was play along.

"Good morning!" a deep voice boomed from behind us.

Dr. Williamson had made a nearly silent entrance. He was a short man with a round face and a robust belly. Though he shaved as close to his skin as possible, the white stubble on his cheeks didn't match the suspiciously copious amount of silky brown hair on his head. He wore an Oxford shirt the same color as the green chairs buttoned to the very top. His chin poured over the collar as if in an attempt to escape from the rest of his body.

Duke stood up and offered Dr. Williamson his hand. "Morning, Doctor. I'm Paul—"

"Yes, I know who you are," Williamson said, taking Duke's hand and shaking it a beat longer than was socially necessary. He moved behind his desk, yanked his pant legs up to better suit his short legs, and sat down. "Paul and Martha D'Angelis. You suspect your daughter Elizabeth has borderline personality disorder. A tricky disease, that one. I do hope you're wrong about it."

He scooted his chair forward and woke his computer. As he typed in a short password, I tapped Duke's knee excitedly. Duke wrapped his hand around my fingers but kept them on his knee, a little show of husbandly affection.

"Let me get a file started for you two," Williamson murmured, clicking around. "There we go. Okay, let's get started. Tell me about life in your home. What do the two of you do? Are you happily married? Do you have designated family time with Elizabeth? That sort of thing. Martha?"

Duke elbowed me to remind me of my codename.

"Oh, right." I chuckled nervously. "Um, well, I'm a stay-at-home mom. I run a book club with my friends and host a lot of parties. Between Paul's job and my inheritance, I don't need to work anymore."

I let out a shrill laugh. Duke winced and squeezed my fingers. My act was a little heavy-handed.

"I work a lot," Duke said in a much calmer tone. "I run an architecture firm, so I travel most of the time. I'll admit I don't get to see Elizabeth often."

Duke was annoyingly better at this than I was. Williamson sat up straighter in his chair and fixed his attention on "Paul."

"Which architecture firm?" Williamson asked. "Perhaps I know it."

"Blackwell Incorporated," Duke replied easily. I wondered if he'd anticipated the question or pulled the answer out of thin air. "But you probably haven't heard of us. The firm is small, and we work mostly overseas?"

"Ah, where at?"

Duke could have been having coffee with a friend. That's how casual he acted opposite Dr. Williamson. "London's a big market for us, but we've completed projects in Dublin, Paris, and a few other cities. I quite like Ireland. Lots of stout and whiskey."

Williamson pursed his lips. "Do you drink, Mr. D'Angelis?"

Duke's eyebrows lifted. Williamson had actually thrown him off. "Not liberally, I don't think. I enjoy a good nightcap every once in a while."

Williamson typed something on his computer. "What about you, Martha? Do you drink? Take drugs?"

"No," I replied quickly. "Well, I have wine with dinner on occasion, but I don't take any drugs."

"Nothing?" Williamson pried. "No anti-anxiety meds? Painkillers? Decongestants?"

"I suppose if I was congested—"

"I'm only asking to determine what behavior Elizabeth might be emulating," he cut in. "If she sees her parents' coping mechanisms include drinking and pill-taking, she might find her way into your liquor or medicine cabinets. Do either of you know anything about borderline personality disorder? I presume you diagnosed her via the Internet."

"We haven't diagnosed her," Duke said coldly. "That's *your* job. We'll be glad to take our money elsewhere if you'd prefer to continue your condescension with another client."

Williamson put on a bright smile that showed off all of his strikingly white teeth. "Forgive me, Mr. D'Angelis. I get a lot of parents who believe only what they read on the Internet. I'm afraid I like to weed those clients out, as they won't usually allow me to help their children with the methods I see fit. I now understand you are not like them."

Duke settled in his seat, his lips untwisting from their scowl. "I'm glad we agree. As for Elizabeth, both my wife and I have noticed her exhibiting worrying behaviors. Her mood flips from ecstatic to traumatic in the blink of an eye, and she often attempts to manipulate us into getting what she wants."

"Manipulation is a key symptom of BPD," Williamson said. "Many people with the disorder have an intense fear of being abandoned. It generally stems from past trauma. Has Elizabeth experienced anything traumatic in her life?"

Duke and I shook our heads.

"Nothing you can think of?" Williamson pressed.

"Can you give us an example?" I asked.

The doctor folded his hands together. "It is common that people who suffer from borderline personality disorder were abused as children, often sexually, by a family member. I am in no way accusing either of you, but I implore you to take a long hard look at anyone who's ever been with Elizabeth alone. Sometimes, you don't realize it's happening."

As a fake mother, this seemed like an appropriate time to burst into tears. In fact, it was the moment we'd been waiting for. Little did Dr. Williamson know, we'd read everything we possibly could about borderline personality disorder so we would come off as convincing as possible. This terrible fact was the perfect segue for our next order of business.

"Oh, goodness." Mr. Williamson fished a fresh packet of tissues from the drawer of his desk as if he had stock down there for all of the crying wives who broke down in his office. "There, there, Martha. It's shocking, I know, but we can get to the bottom of this."

"Forgive my wife," Duke said, calmly rubbing my back as I heaved for breath and let a fresh wave of crocodile tears flow down my cheeks. "She's sensitive. If this is the case, if Elizabeth has been—you know—what can be done about it? I fear she's endangering herself and others, me and my wife included."

Williamson twiddled his thumbs. "She's violent?"

"Yes. She's prone to lashing out."

"Hmm." Williamson pondered Duke's stalwart dignity and my teary collapse. "Well, I need to see the child first, but in cases like these, I often recommend intensive therapy. That may or may not include sending Elizabeth to a rehabilitation facility. First, Elizabeth will attend sessions with me. If I don't see her progress in a given amount of time, we'll look into facilities."

"We only want the best of the best," Duke insisted. "I won't send her to some mental prison to be treated like a dog."

"Of course not," Williamson said. "Personally, I would recommend you to the Trevino Center in Lone Elm. Dr. Eli Trevino and his wife are close friends of mine. They take excellent care of my patients."

"And she would be able to attend immediately if necessary?" I squeaked through a handful of tissues.

Williamson clicked his tongue. "Unfortunately, the Trevino Center has a long waiting list. However," he added with a sly wink, "I happen to know that if you make a sizable donation to the Trevino Foundation, you can move your child to the top of that list."

Bingo.

"Whatever it takes," Duke said. In a lower voice, he went on, "Is it possible to talk to you alone, Doctor? I'd like to explore some treatment options for Elizabeth, but I don't want to upset my wife."

I feigned deafness, pretending to be absorbed in the many book titles on the shelves, as Williamson looked me over.

"Of course," he answered Duke. He rose from his chair. "Mrs. D'Angelis, you won't mind if I show your husband something in another room? I have an old painting of a mysterious building, and I was wondering if he might be able to place the setting."

"No, no," I said, waving them off. "I'll be along in a few minutes. I need to get myself together."

Duke winked as he followed Williamson out. As soon as the door closed behind them, I checked the office for cameras. Then I tossed aside my used tissues and got behind Williamson's desk. His computer remained on and unlocked. I opened the browser, clicked on the favorites tab, and navigated to his email inbox.

Unsure of what I was looking for, I scrolled through advertisements from pharmacies begging Williamson to prescribe their new drugs, confidential exchanges between Williamson and his various patients, and various invitations to play golf. Along the sidebar, I noticed a folder labeled "Private."

"Private, my ass," I muttered, clicking on it.

The first several emails were direct links to porno-graphic websites. I almost gagged and clicked out of the

SECRETS IN THE WOODS

folder, but something told me to keep scrolling. There, beneath all the inappropriate garbage, was a series of messages between Williamson and LindsTrevino@thetrevinofoundation.org. I opened the first one:

Lindsay, Williamson wrote. *I have a thirteen-year-old boy who might be of interest of you. His parents have dubbed him out of control, and they are too dim to apply disciplinary action to prevent his outbursts. This, of course, is of use to you and me. I have decided to diagnose the child with schizophrenia. We haven't done that in a while, eh? The parents are desperate for change and they are willing to pay for it. They offered fifty thousand dollars to the foundation up front and promised to give more after the child is treated at the Center. Let me know if you agree to these terms, and I'll send along the paperwork for him. I hope you're well. Best, Chuck.*

Rage and triumph warred within me. Though I'd known it for a while, it was different to see proof of Lindsay's crimes in writing. The triumph came from finally getting what I needed to stop the Trevinos from abusing children ever again. Every email in the folder—other than the porn, which was a clever way to distract nosy people like me from the real crime—contained information about a child that Williamson intended to misdiagnose and send to the Center. He didn't bother if the parents weren't loaded enough to donate thousands of dollars to the Trevino Foundation. For every inquiry, Lindsay replied in turn, either accepting the offer or asking Williamson to pry more money from the parents.

I slipped a USB drive into the computer, downloaded the entire folder, and exited out of the browser, leaving the computer looking the same as it did before I snooped around. Then I pinched my cheeks to make them look red from crying, gathered the counterfeit Louis Vuitton purse I'd borrowed from Lauren, and began to leave the room, but a silver shine on the bookshelf caught my eye.

It was a framed black-and-white newspaper clipping. The photo featured Williamson when he was a teenager—maybe seventeen years old—and a younger girl, both wearing high school track uniforms and holding first place medals. The article was titled *Williamson Siblings Take All at Local Track Meet.*

The younger girl in the photo was Lindsay.

"YES!" Duke boomed, shaking the roof of his van when I showed him the emails I'd pulled off Williamson's laptop. His reaction was so enthusiastic that we skidded toward a crowd of startled pedestrians crossing the street. The locals banged on his hood as he righted his path, but he didn't let it phase him. "Yes! That's exactly what we needed."

"That's not all," I said. "I figured out why Williamson is working with Lindsay in the first place. They're siblings."

"Send that to the NYPD and the Lone Elm Police Department." Duke took something out of his pocket and tossed it in my lap. "Along with the audio off of that."

It was a small recording device. "You recorded our interview with him?"

Duke grinned and navigated the van away from the busy city streets. "He basically confessed to accepting bribes for treatment. Between the recording and those emails, the Trevinos are toast." He held up his hand. "High five me!"

I laughed and slapped my palm against his. "Is this

what it always feels like when you get to the bottom of something rotten?"

"Not always," Duke said. "Sometimes, it sucks to find out the terrible things that people are doing. This, on the other hand, feels pretty good. Those kids at Trevino will be evaluated again. Maybe their parents will think twice before automatically assuming their teenagers are losing their minds."

Toby, Luna, Wilson, and the other kids of Ward 13 came to the front of my mind. "One can only hope."

A COUPLE HOURS LATER, we arrived home in Lone Elm. By that time, I'd sent all of the collective evidence to every relevant police department in the state. Still, it was a shock to see how quickly things took a turn. In the middle of Main Street, red and blue lights flashed from a police cruiser as a group of cops pulled a struggling blonde woman from the back seat.

"Is that—?" Duke muttered, peering through the window as we drove by.

"It's Lindsay." I watched as she yanked her cuffed hands out of a policewoman's grasp, yelling at her captors. "They already arrested her."

"Should we let her know why?" Duke asked wryly.

The cops led Lindsay up the steps to the police station and practically carried her inside.

"No," I answered. "I need to find Eli. Take me to the Center."

19

*T*he Center was closed for the day. As Duke pulled the van around to the back parking lot, the other employees were on their way out. Imogen and Ariel walked side-by-side to their shared car. Andy and Jewel bid each other goodbye and went separate ways. I instructed Duke to park in the far corner of the lot to wait out the traffic, then I scanned the cars still here.

Lindsay's fancy sedan was gone. She must have left the Center early and gotten pulled over by the cops somewhere. Eli's Cadillac SUV, however, was parked closest to the building. He must be inside somewhere.

Once everyone was gone, I climbed out of the van. "Get back to town," I told Duke. "I want to know everything that's going on with Lindsay."

"What about you?" he asked.

"I'll be fine. I'll get a ride with someone."

He nodded. "Good luck in there."

Gravel spun beneath the van's tires as Duke left to chase his story. Inside, Cameron had left the front desk for the day. Since the Center was closed for visitors, no one waited to greet me in the lobby. I headed up the marble stairs, straight to Eli's office. The door was cracked two inches or so. I peeked in.

Eli was throwing various items into a designer suitcase. The suitcase was already full of unfolded clothes, bathroom supplies, and random bits and bobs from Eli's life. His office was a wreck. Books and paperwork were strewn across the floor, the file cabinets had been opened and dumped out, and a shelf of various awards granted to the Trevino doctors throughout history was overturned. I stepped inside.

"What the hell are you doing?" I demanded.

"What does it look like?" Eli said, throwing a framed certificate into the suitcase and zipping the mess shut. "I'm getting the hell out of here. I suppose you heard the news already. They dragged Lindsay down to the police station. I knew she was imbalanced, but the extent of this —" He went to the computer and began mass-deleting emails. "Christ, look at all this stuff she's got on here! Did she expect to never get caught?"

I stood between Eli and his suitcase. "You're running away?"

"No," he replied. "No, no, no." His head-shaking turned to nodding. "Yes. Yes, I am. I've got a cabin in Washington that no one knows about. It's not even listed under my name. I'll be damned if Lindsay pulls me down with her."

"You're responsible too!" I said angrily. "You knew she was doing deals with Williamson. You knew the kids in Ward 13 were being treated for disorders they never had! What is wrong with you? You can't run away!"

"I sure can," he insisted. "All of this was Lindsay's idea.

She started it without me. I didn't know half those kids weren't actually sick. If I did—"

"You would have turned Lindsay in?"

"Of course not. She's my wife." He glanced at my furious expression. "Natasha, you don't understand. I didn't expect my father to die so soon. It completely ruined me. I practically ran the Center into the ground because I hadn't bothered to learn the business side of things as I was expected to. If it weren't for Lindsay, this place would have closed down a long time ago. I owe her, even if she employed some illegalities on the way."

"She committed fraud," I said. "Over and over again. What's the point of running a rehabilitation facility if you're not helping anyone?"

Eli puffed out his chest. "It was a matter of pride, and as I said, I didn't know—hang on." He deflated slightly. "How did *you* know about all of this? About Williamson and Ward 13?"

"I spent hours with those kids," I reminded him. "After a while, it became pretty obvious most of them weren't supposed to be there. They *told* you over and over they didn't belong there. They begged you! But you drugged them and belittled them, all because you wanted their parents' money. You think I wouldn't *notice?*"

Eli, stunned, took a step away from me. "This is your fault, isn't it? I can see it all over your face. You turned Lindsay in!"

"To be honest, I'm shocked they didn't arrest you too," I said. "You're implicit in all of this. Toby was right. You're a quack."

His lip curled. "Too bad he's dead. Are you sure he was

misdiagnosed? A normal kid wouldn't slit his own arteries."

I let out a scoff. "Are you playing stupid again? Toby isn't dead. You faked his death!"

Eli smiled at me, amused by the accusation. "That is downright preposterous. Where on earth did you get that idea?"

"Because Toby is sitting in my room at the inn," I spat in his face. "Very much alive."

His face drained of color. "How is that possible? I saw the blood!"

"But never the body," I said. "He ran away. Lindsay must have realized he was gone and come up with a cover story to protect the Center's reputation."

Eli shook his head. "No, she was devastated by his death. All she could talk about was what the parents were going to do. If Toby was alive, she would have dragged him back to the Center and convinced his parents he needed more treatment."

"Then someone else made it look like Toby killed himself," I said. "Who would have done something like that?"

"I have no idea—"

I slammed my fist against his desk.

"Really, I don't know!" he said, cowering in the corner. "If I knew, I would tell you."

"You're a coward," I hissed. "A coward and a liar. I hope you rot in a jail cell. I'm calling the police."

"No!" He darted across the room and smacked the phone out of my hand. The screen shattered as it hit the floor and went dark. "I can't let you do that." Eli grabbed his suitcase and pushed past me. "You're a good therapist,

Natasha. If things had turned out differently, I imagine you would have been quite the asset to the Trevino Center. Take care. I hope things work out for you."

He was gone in seconds, his heavy luggage thumping down the marble steps to the lobby. My phone was beyond repair, and Trevino's phones didn't make outside calls. There was no way to contact the cops.

Rather than chasing after Eli, I raided his office. Somewhere in all the torn, mussed paperwork, there had to be an explanation for the blood in Toby's room. *Someone* had covered up his escape for a reason, and I needed to find out who. Even with Lindsay locked up and Eli on the run, Toby could still be in trouble.

I found the answer among a pile of forms. The first listed the in and out times of the night aides and nurses. The second detailed each time the medical locker was opened and by which employee. The medical locker contained everything from medications, extra equipment, and bags of fresh blood in case of an emergency. A third form sported a spreadsheet that detailed every time an employee swiped their badge to get in or out of Ward 13.

One name popped up in the correct time window on the night of Toby's supposed suicide on all three forms.

"Scout."

As usual, she prowled the corridors of Ward 13. I caught her at the window to Luna's room, watching as Luna stretched her long legs. Luna faced the opposite wall, gazing at the pink sunset beyond her room. She had no idea that Scout was spying on her.

"Natasha," Scout said. "Isn't it a bit late for you to be creeping around Ward 13?"

"I could ask you the same thing," I replied, crossing my arms. I jerked my chin toward Luna. "Thinking of killing her too?"

To Scout's credit, she did a wonderful job of hiding any guilt. Her brow crumpled in consternation. "I'm sorry? I don't understand what you're talking about."

"Don't play stupid," I said. "I finally figured out what happened that night. Toby escaped. He slipped right out because neither you nor Dashiell were at your regular posts."

Scout's shoulders began to rise toward her ears. "I don't know what you mean."

"I saw the paperwork," I told her. "You and Dashiell swiped your badges and exited the ward at one o'clock in the morning, even though your night shifts didn't end until three. Where'd the two of you go?"

The veins in her neck strained as if she had forgotten to breathe. "What business is it of yours?"

"You returned at five AM," I went on, ignoring Scout's question. "*After* your shift had already ended, I might add. By that time, Toby had already left the Center. I assume you checked his room and realized a patient had gotten away on your watch. Rather than admit to your mistake, you attempted to cover it up. So you went into the medical locker, checked out a few bags of blood, and splattered them all over the walls of Toby's room. How did you fool the paramedics when they got here? How did you explain the lack of a body to them?"

"You have no proof," Scout snarled through clenched teeth.

"Oh, I have plenty of proof." I pointed to the badge hanging from her belt. "That thing has a chip in it. It records every little thing you do, including where you swipe it and at what time. So you wanna tell me what you were really doing while Toby got out of here? It's got to be pretty mad if you had to fake someone's death to cover it up."

Scout wasn't going to confess that easily. She took careful steps around me, one hand hidden behind her back. "How did you figure out Toby wasn't dead? He disappeared. We combed every inch of this town for him and couldn't find him."

"Good thing he was smart enough to avoid you."

"He came to you, didn't he?" she asked. As she moved, so did I, keeping the same amount of distance between us. "He wouldn't have survived in the cold on his own. Not for more than a few days. Where is he? Your motel?"

"He's gone," I said. "No idea where he went."

Scout's lips spread in an eerie smile. "You're an excellent therapist, Natasha, but you're a terrible liar."

"While we're on the subject of lying," I went on, "let's get something out in the open. It was you, wasn't it? The one who told everyone about my past? Dashiell was outside the therapy room that day. He was the only one who would have heard me tell Toby the truth."

She shrugged. "I thought everyone here should know they were working with a murderer."

"At least I followed through," I joked humorlessly.

"Don't worry," Scout said. "This time, I intend to."

She lunged, bringing her hand out behind her back as she did so. Expectedly, she held a full syringe. I threw myself out of the way as she brought it down toward my arm. While she was off balance, I seized a nearby cart full of supplies and slammed it into her. Wrapped needles showered down as she somersaulted away, bruised but not incapacitated. We faced each other again.

"The last time someone attacked me, it didn't end well for my opponent," I reminded Scout. "And she was armed with a knife."

Scout charged at me again. I seized the clipboard hanging on Luna's door, the one that had all of her medication information on it, and swung with all my might. It connected with Scout's skull, and the edge opened a big gash under her ear. With a thud, she fell to the floor, blood staining her collar. She remained motionless.

"No, no, no." I tossed the clipboard aside and knelt next to Scout. "Not again. Please, not this again. Scout?" I turned her over to see her eyes. Her pupils weren't dilated. That was a good sign. I gently tapped her cheek. "Scout, can you hear me?"

Her arm swung up and over. I felt a pinprick on the top of my left thigh. The hallway turned into waves of white paint, like the whole place was melting. I looked down. The syringe was sticking out of my leg, all the drugs depressed into my bloodstream.

"Last time," Scout hissed, getting to her feet. "Your opponent didn't know which tranquilizer worked the fastest to knock someone out. Have fun waking up, Natasha. With the amount of drugs in there, you might never get the chance."

My head thunked against the floor, my body no longer able to hold myself up. I tried to call out, but my throat had stopped working. Helpless, I watched Scout press gauze to the wound behind her ear and swipe her badge to get out of the ward. Then everything went black.

"Natasha. Natasha!"

Someone was banging on my door. Obnoxious. Relentless.

"Natasha, please! Wake up!"

No, not a door. A window.

I groggily opened my eyes. They felt as if they had been glued shut. Above me, Luna's pale, scared face pressed against the window between her room and the rest of Ward 13. With a groan, I pushed myself up from the floor. Every muscle in my body felt like it was made out of lead. With a lot of effort, I unlocked Luna's door.

She threw her arms around me. "Are you okay? I saw what happened. I couldn't stop her."

"I'm fine." I gave Luna my ID badge. "Take this. Use it to put the ward on lockdown. The instructions are by the door. Don't let anyone in or out after I leave, okay?"

Her lip trembled. "You trust me?"

"Of course I trust you." Without thinking, I kissed her forehead. "Keep the others safe. I have to make sure Toby's okay."

I DRAGGED myself out to the parking lot, shaking my head to clear the fog the drugs had left in my body. Everything seemed to be moving in slow motion. My first problem was that Scout was no doubt on her way to the Shadows Inn to track down Toby. Considering how long I'd been unconscious, she was already there.

My second problem was that I had no car to get to town.

This, thankfully, was easily solved. Eli's Cadillac was parked in the exact same place it was before with the driver door open and the key in the ignition. Haphazard boot prints from at least two different pairs of shoes were stamped into the snow. Thick, treaded tire tracks led from Eli's car to the road into Lone Elm. Looked like the police had caught up with Eli before he'd had the chance to flee.

I brushed the snow off the car door's interior, hopped into the driver's seat, and turned the key. The engine turned over and a blast of cold air came through the vents. I didn't wait for the car to warm up, pulling out of the spot and steering onto the road.

In my condition, I should not have been driving. It was worse than taking one too many tequila shots and making the mistake of thinking I could operate a vehicle. As the road wound back and forth, my stomach threatened to empty itself on Eli's fancy leather seats. I swallowed bile as I carefully navigated down the mountain and into town.

Eli's SUV bounced over the curb as I tried to park in front of the inn. I lost my balance as I got out and stumbled into a snow bank. Soaked to the bone, I staggered inside.

"Natasha?" Baz ran over to me and held me upright as soon as she saw me. "Oh my God, what happened to you?"

"Toby," I gasped, forcing Baz to help me to the stairs. "Where's Toby?"

"In your room," she said. "What's the matter? Natasha!"

I'd left her to climb the stairs. As her footsteps hurried

away, I made it to the second floor and down the hall to my room. When I looked inside, relief washed some of the drowsiness out of my system. Toby was sitting in the shadows, gazing out of the window.

"Toby, thank goodness you're okay—"

He whirled around. His mouth was gagged. His hands were tied. As I stepped further in, he shook his head in warning, eyes widening at something behind me.

A blow landed on the back of my skull. I fell to my knees, so stunned that the pain didn't register. A thick boot pushed me the rest of the way over. My head swam as an enormous figure loomed over me.

"Dashiell," I breathed. "She told you."

"You should've stayed at the Center," he said. "It would have been a lot safer for you."

"Why?" I gasped. "What have you done?"

"We've been running drugs," Dashiell admitted easily. "It was simple. It was Scout's job to log the incoming shipments. All she had to do was write down the wrong amount on the company log so we could take the excess and sell it. That was my end of the job. Addicts are less likely to start something stupid with someone as large as me."

Everything clicked into place. No wonder Scout and Dashiell didn't want anyone to know Toby had escaped. It would make people question their whereabouts that night, and they had most likely been out selling their materials.

"You won't get away with this," I said. "Someone will find out."

"No one's going to find out, darling," Dashiell said, leaning over me. "Because no one who knows the truth will be in any position to tell it. If only you'd kept your nose out of our business. As they say, ignorance is bliss."

Toby yelled through his gag as Dashiell's meaty fist connected with the side of my head. Lights burst like fireworks behind my eyelids, but Dashiell wasn't done. He landed another punch to the opposite cheek, and I felt one of my teeth pop out. Blood and mucus dribbled out of my mouth as I rolled feebly to one side, hoping to avoid another blow.

"Oh no you don't."

Dashiell rolled me back toward him and straddled me. He put his fingers around my neck and pushed against my windpipe. I struggled to breathe and found no oxygen. Everything hurt.

"No!" Toby screamed in a muffled voice. The chair he was tied to scooted across the floor, but he couldn't get up. "Get away from her!"

Dashiell paid Toby no mind. My vision began to blur at the edges as he pushed harder against my throat. I half-wished I'd lost that fight when I was thirteen. Then this all would have ended much sooner. When a sense of relaxation washed over me, I knew it was the end. It was the same sensation I'd felt bleeding out in an alleyway before the paramedics found me. It was time to let go.

The door to the room swung open, and Duke stepped in, his face contorted with rage. He seized the desk chair and slammed it over Dashiell's head. I saw the light go out of the massive man's dark eyes. As he fell unconscious, his grip loosened from my throat, and I pulled in a painful, ratty gasp of air.

"Natasha!" Duke shouldered Dashiell off of me and checked my pulse. He snagged a pillow from the bed and carefully braced my head with it. My eyes were so swollen I could barely see him as he shone a light across my face. "Hey, can you hear me? Baz came to get me when she thought you were in trouble. Lauren called the cops. They should be here any minute. Hang in there."

A muffled squeak echoed from the corner of the room, and Duke looked up to see Toby. His lip trembled as he separated himself from me and stood up.

"Toby?" he asked softly. He gently pulled the gag, a pair of my socks, out of Toby's mouth.

Toby's eyes filled with tears. "Dad?"

"Oh my God."

Duke wrapped Toby in a hug. Tears ran freely down both their faces. Through my injury, the enormity of the situation still registered. I cried too, finally realizing why Duke looked familiar. It was his face I'd been staring at in the picture of Toby and his father all along.

20

ONE YEAR LATER

he first snow of the year was a beautiful one. It blanketed Lone Elm in a glimmering coat of white, coating the trees and the rooftops. A natural hush fell over the town. Everything seemed quieter and more peaceful when it snowed.

That morning, Jean Paul draped his fat self across my nose and mouth. I woke up, shoved him off, and gulped fresh hair. Jean Paul purred and nudged my face with his own.

"Maybe I shouldn't let Baz feed you anymore," I muttered, giving in to his cuteness and scratching his ears. "You weigh twice as much as you did when we moved here."

Despite my decision to stay in Lone Elm permanently, I hadn't moved out of the inn. Six months ago, when I'd voiced the option of getting my own apartment, Baz had thrown a temper tantrum. She didn't speak to me for three days, until I finally told her that Lauren would allow me to rent my room indefinitely. Ever since then, we hadn't revisited the topic. I liked my room at the inn and Marcel's food. Lauren and Baz had become my family. Not to mention, Jean Paul would riot if I dared move him elsewhere.

Downstairs, the beautiful smell of coffee wafted through the dining and living rooms. I followed my nose to the fresh pot, poured myself a cup, and sat at one of the tables to wait for breakfast. Not long after, Baz stumbled down the stairs in her pajamas and sat across from me.

"Coffee," she groaned, rubbing her eyes.

I got her a mug. "What are you doing up so early?"

"Are you kidding? It's opening day. *You're* the one who said you wanted me at the ribbon cutting ceremony."

"Which doesn't start until noon."

She stared blankly at me, slumped over her coffee. "You could have told me that before."

"I did. Twice."

As Baz's glare poked me like the point of a dagger, Lauren pranced into the dining room. Unlike her sleepy daughter, she was bright-eyed and bushy-tailed.

"Morning, everyone!"

Baz winced. "Keep it down, Mom. What's gotten into your Cheerios? Ecstasy?"

"A natural sort," Lauren replied slyly. She joined our table.

Duke came down the steps a moment later, buttoning his thermal shirt. His new haircut—shaved on the sides but longer on top—was uncharacteristically messy. Even more suspicious, he didn't have a room here.

Baz looked from her mom to Duke and back again. "Ugh, really? You couldn't have given a girl a heads up?"

Lauren blushed and lifted a newspaper to hide her

face. Duke grinned sheepishly and took the last chair at our table.

"Sorry, Baz," he said, using his fingers to fix his hair. "I thought Toby would have told you. With how often you guys text, I wouldn't be surprised if you were dating too."

Baz wrinkled her nose. "Gross. Toby's like my little brother. Besides, he's totally obsessed with Emma. You should check on that. That amount of clinginess seems unhealthy."

"He's happy," Duke said. "That's all I can ask for."

Marcel emerged from the kitchen, shot everyone a dirty look, and put a basket of hot buttermilk biscuits on the table. "I'll be back with ze clotted cream and jam."

"How is Toby anyway?" I asked Duke, reaching for a biscuit. "He's still coming today, right?"

"He's coming," Duke assured me. "I wrote a letter to the school to excuse him. He's doing great. He's already caught up on his work, and he'll be able to graduate with the rest of his class."

"And you're okay?" I asked in a lowered voice. "That he's staying with his mom in the city?"

He dunked a biscuit into his coffee and bit off a large chunk. "I'm fine. I wish I got to see him more often, but he promised he'll be here for the summer."

"And they haven't heard from Billings?"

Duke's face darkened, his mouth setting in a hard, straight line. "Not since the divorce."

After Duke's story broke about the Trevino Center, a lot of things changed. First, every patient was evaluated again. Eighty percent of the teenagers in Ward 13 were released, their diagnoses overturned. The Trevino Foundation was discredited, and most of the donations were returned to the donors. Dr. Williamson was arrested and his private practice was shut down.

Scout and Dashiell were arrested and charged shortly after Dashiell tried to kill me. They were both in jail. I hadn't escaped our incident unscathed. Dashiell had pummeled the side of my head so hard that I was partially deaf in my left ear. Ironically, I attended therapy to adjust.

Eli and Lindsay were also serving long sentences at government institutions. With no danger left to Toby except that of his stepfather, he was able to come out of hiding. With me and Duke on his either side, he returned to his mother. After her shock at his survival wore off, he told her what Banks Billings had done to him. His mother immediately called the police and had Billings arrested. Unfortunately, there wasn't enough evidence to put Billings away, but Toby's mother got her revenge through different methods. She sued him for divorce and took most of his savings, leaving him nearly destitute.

I also learned the mystery of Toby's last name. Gardner was his mother's maiden name before she married Billings. She and Duke had never been married, so Toby didn't inherit his father's surname. Duke and Toby's mother were a poorly matched couple, and the pregnancy was a surprise for both of them. Due to multiple miscommunications, Duke had never been able to reconnect with Toby. For their son's sake, he and Toby's mother decided to leave the past in the past.

"A toast," Lauren said, lifting her coffee mug. "To Natasha. We'll do a real one later with champagne," she added to me. "But I want the four of us to celebrate together first. Congratulations, Nat! You made it to opening day!"

I blushed and grinned as everyone clinked their cups together. "I couldn't have done it without you all."

THE LONE ELM Health and Rehabilitation Center had been a group effort. When I first proposed the idea to the other employees a year ago, they'd all looked at me like I was insane. The Trevino Center was no more, but it seemed a shame to let the hardworking, dedicated staff and beautiful setting go to waste. Those of us who remained were dedicated to helping others, and we were determined to right Eli and Lindsay's mistakes.

For a month, Imogen and I had traveled to every investor in New York City. For a therapist, she had wonderful business sense and a sly charm that could convince any hedge fund manager to invest in our cause. We eventually garnered enough attention and money to break ground on the new and improved rehabilitation center we had proposed.

Lauren helped me find the right contractor for the job. It was the same man she'd hired to renovate the Shadows Inn when she had first bought it. The contractor and his team completely reworked the old Trevino Center building. We knocked down walls and opened more of the place up to the surrounding nature. We got rid of the cell-like rooms in Ward 13 and turned the entire floor into a recreational space for future patients. We installed basketball courts, a swimming pool (which wouldn't open until summer for obvious reasons), and a walkway that took hikers all the way down to the lake and back.

When construction was almost done, we hired back the entire staff, including Ariel, Jewel, Andy, Misty,

Hilary, and Cameron. Trevino's displaced patients would return to the newly-minted Lone Elm Health and Rehabilitation Center if they still required treatment. We also expected several new patients to arrive.

Duke published articles online about the new Center, posting photographs of the construction progress throughout the year and informing readers about the services we would soon be offering. When we announced the date of the grand opening, Duke's website crashed because so many people had clicked on the link to read the article.

THE FOUR OF us rode up to the Center together. Photographers and reporters already swarmed the front lawn, along with employees, locals who had come to support us, and potential patients who wanted to explore the facilities. When I got out of the car, camera lenses and microphones swirled around me.

"Natasha, did you ever think something so great would come out of Eli Trevino's madness?"

"Natasha, how do you plan to avoid a scandal like the one that hit the Trevino Center last year?"

"Miss Bell, do you have a employee screening program in place to ensure your staff doesn't boast criminal backgrounds?"

"I'm deaf!" I shouted at the crowd, very much milking it. "I can't hear any of you!"

One thoughtful person signed a greeting and their next question. The rest badgered on in louder voices.

"Back off!" Duke barked across the crowd, using his

muscled arm to separate me from the swarm of reporters and photographers. "Let us through!"

The crowd parted to let us through. We made our way to the front of the Center. All the ugly marble and gray cobblestones was gone. I'd replaced it with beautiful red brick that stood out richly against the white snow. Come spring, I had plans to plant new trees in the front area to make the Center as colorful as possible.

I'd also had the contractor add a massive wraparound porch to the entire building. It made it look more homey and welcoming, a place patients didn't have to be scared to come to. Today, the porch was dressed for the opening day ceremonies. A huge banner was strung above the door, and an equally long red ribbon stretched from one side of the steps to the other. I ducked under it.

"Natasha!"

Toby launched himself up the steps like a rocket when he saw me. He'd grown a foot over the last year, closer to Duke's height than mine. My chin tilted up as he hugged me.

"Easy, kid," I said, patting his back. "You'll break my neck."

"Sorry." He drew back and bounced on his toes. "I want you to be meet someone." He drew a familiar teenaged girl out of the crowd by the hand. "This is Emma. Emma, this is Natasha, the one I've been telling you about."

"We've met," Emma said, smiling. She shook my hand. "Nice to meet you in real life, Natasha. I've heard a lot about you."

"Same." I nodded at Toby and Emma's intertwined fingers. "Are you two finally dating?"

They let go.

"We're focusing on school," Emma said.

"Yes," Toby added cheekily. "Academics are very important to me."

Duke dug his fist into Toby's hair. "They better be. What's wrong with you? Don't you say hello to your dad anymore?"

As Duke and Toby bantered, I noticed another familiar face in the crowd and waved them toward me. Luna weaved her way through the throng and gave me a hug too.

"You came!" I said gleefully. "I wasn't sure you'd be able to."

"I couldn't miss this," she replied. "It's beautiful, Nat. If it had looked like this when my parents dropped me off, maybe I would have stayed."

I chuckled. "Don't be silly. You're a free woman. How's emancipation treating you?"

"It's great. Tough," she added. "Thankfully, my dance school gives me a stipend each semester. Otherwise, I'd be out of luck."

"And your parents?"

"Haven't seen them," she said. "Don't care to. Thank you, by the way. I never would have been able to get out of that situation if it weren't for you."

I hugged her again. "You don't have to thank me, and my job offer still stands. I'll hire you to dance in the hallways if I have to."

"You're very kind," Luna replied. "But I've got enough on my plate with all the performances and classes coming up. I might take you up on it later though."

"Anytime."

Imogen came up behind me. "Hey, Nat? Sorry to interrupt, but it's noon. Everyone's expecting you at the podium."

I HAD NEVER ENVISIONED myself standing in front of a crowd this large with a microphone at my lips. Nevertheless, here I was, shaking from nerves and excitement.

"Good afternoon, everyone!" I said into the mic. "I hope you're all keeping warm. Doesn't this place look great in the snow?"

A cheer went up from the crowd. I smiled.

"I want to thank everyone who had a hand in bringing this dream of mine to life." I gestured to everyone behind me. I'd had the employees line up on the porch with Imogen at the front, for recognition. "Without these people, we never would have been able to overcome the travesties of last year. These beautiful souls, like me, believe that everyone deserves the chance to be treated with kindness, patience, and intelligence. At this new facility, we intend to do just that."

Another round of applause echoed through the crowd. Toby, Luna, Baz, and Emma cupped their hands around their mouths and howled like dogs. I settled them with a wave of my hand.

"I'm sure you're all excited to get inside and have a look around," I said, "so without further ado, I present to you the Lone Elm Health and Rehabilitation Center!"

As the roar of the crowd reached a breaking point, I cut through the red ribbon. The Lone Elm Health and Rehabilitation Center was officially open for business.

Made in the USA
San Bernardino, CA
31 May 2020

72537365R00164